HOLD TO NATURE

SURVIVING
THE WRECK

SURVIVING THE WRECK

SUSAN OSBORN

A JOHN MACRAE BOOK

HENRY HOLT AND COMPANY   NEW YORK

Copyright © 1991 by Susan Osborn
Published by Henry Holt and Company, Inc.,
115 West 18th Street, New York, New York 10011.
Published in Canada by Fitzhenry & Whiteside Limited,
195 Allstate Parkway, Markham, Ontario L3R 4T8.

Library of Congress Cataloging-in-Publication Data
Osborn, Susan.
Surviving the wreck / Susan Osborn.—1st ed.
p.   cm.
"A John Macrae book."
I. Title.
PS3565.S387S87   1991
,813'.54—dc20   91-594
                                            CIP
ISBN 0-8050-1586-8

Henry Holt books are available at special discounts
for bulk purchases for sales promotions, premiums,
fund-raising, or educational use. Special editions
or book excerpts can also be created to specification.
For details contact: Special Sales Director,
Henry Holt and Company, Inc., 115 West 18th Street
New York, New York 10011

First Edition—1992

Book designed by Claire N. Vaccaro
Printed in the United States of America
Recognizing the importance of preserving
the written word, Henry Holt and Company, Inc.,
by policy, prints all of its first editions
on acid-free paper. ∞
1   3   5   7   9   10   8   6   4   2

For P, who kept me up splendidly,
and Alana Tem, my second lucky lief.

It was my good fortune to meet and receive the critical guidance of Jack Macrae and Amy Robbins. Their insight into the complications of this story enabled the final revision. I also thank the New Jersey State Council on the Arts for providing me with a timely and generous grant.

SURVIVING
THE WRECK

PART ONE

I am running toward my mother. She is standing at the door of our cottage in Connemara. I can see her even though we are still a hundred miles apart. A horse appears, white, gallant, and keen, and I jump on its back and we race across the Moorish cliffs and down the ferny glens, leaping across the gullies as if my horse were Pegasus. We are riding dangerously fast now; the wind, tearing at my skin, pulls at my clothes. We look like a great white blur, my horse and I; as we get closer to my mother, thistles and thorns scratch at my face, but they do not hurt, there is no blood. I am riding too fast, yet as long as I keep her in my sight, I feel utterly, absolutely protected.

And I do see her, there, dressed in lavender and white gingham, at the doorway of our thatch-roofed cottage on the edge of the sea. In one hand, she holds a horn; in the other, the moon. I am so close I can smell her perfume, like lilacs almost beyond their prime, all the way from where I am. We are surrounded by hills, hills so green and so soft they look like giant velvet cushions. As I get closer, I can smell the musky, earthy smell of a peat fire and there is smoke coming out of the chimney. My mother has baked bread for me.

She holds me, she actually holds me; then she caresses my hair with her hand. We move inside, just the two of us. After we eat, we undress and she lets me feel her stomach—it's just like the unkneaded bread we will bake together tomorrow to replace the loaf we ate

3

tonight. I think this—my mother's stomach—is the most potent, the most luxurious stuff in the world. We look outside, see that a light mist has begun to fall, and then we go to sleep.

But—of course—that never really happened. My mother's not Irish, she's German, and we don't have a house in Connemara, never even spoke of one. And yet, I write this and I feel as if I'm becoming her again, that little girl with those dreams. It doesn't matter how I tell myself that I'm different, an adult, that it was all a dream, she's still there—that wishful little girl.

My mother, however, is not there. It's Monday or Tuesday or Wednesday or Thursday and she's gone to a Weight Watchers meeting or an Al-Anon meeting or a Board of Education meeting or a Women for Peace meeting—any meeting as long as it keeps her out of the house. An hour before she goes, she prepares a quick meal: hamburgers, boiled potatoes, and green beans. Then, launching my brother Kyle before her as if he were a frigate escorting her to safety, she heaves through the back door. When my father comes home, careening around the newel post and bumping into the hall table, I serve the meal my mother has made and we eat dinner, he and I, just the two of us. I am there and I am listening intensely, as intensely as I can, as if such intensity could protect him from my hatred, the murderous rage I am as yet not even aware of. I see us at the kitchen table, a reproduction of George and Martha Washington's, my hands holding the edge, his missing his mouth.

When I see this scene this time, I am lucky. This time, I see that my father has passed out at the table. That means I can go upstairs to my room by myself—after, that is, I have cleared the table and washed the dishes and put away the leftovers and scoured the sink and mopped the floor. My mother likes things clean—"hygienic" is the word she likes to use—she only gets angry at me on the nights when I do it better than she. Then she says, hitting the *t*'s hard, "It looks to me as if you and your father don't need me at all."

My parents were atheists (although now, since the divorce, my mother's substituted Episcopalianism for my father's alcoholism), but I imagined that if I got down on my knees by the side of the bed and pressed my palms together the way other kids did, things might be different. I didn't know what I was doing, but whatever it was, it caused the miraculous ride to take place.

It's very hard for me—nearly impossible—to remember what happened on the other nights, the nights when my father didn't pass out and Connemara remained a vague dream on the other side of an ocean.

It is 1960, July, four months before the big election. I am seven and we are sitting around the kitchen table. The electric fan is working to distribute the New Jersey humidity. A pitcher of instant iced tea and three partially filled glasses sweat, forming amorphous pools on the table.

We have just come home from a Kennedy campaign rally. My older brother, the eight-and-a-half-year-old politico, the young moralist, the future philosophy professor, is still there with neighbors, converting the heathen to the Democratic cause. I, however—too young, my mother tells me, to understand the importance of such things—have had to come home with my parents. The tension in the air is so keen it's like a noxious odor that makes you choke every time you breathe.

I am practicing holding my breath. My parents are arguing about the candidates; it is a squabble my mother foolishly began in the car. They turn to me only when they need to gain time.

"But why won't you see? Jack Kennedy will get this country moving again. He's promised us a New Frontier."

"Country seems to be moving along just fine, my dear." Then, after a delicate throat-clearing, he adds, winking and smiling at me, "I've got everything I want."

"If you would just be reasonable for one minute, you'd see that the country is far from fine."

Hearing this, one of her favorite if somewhat shopworn accusations, my father levers his chair back on its two rear legs until the back is touching the sill, then gazes at my mother over the top of his bifocals; he smiles, his eyebrows rising to mid-forehead as if he were watching a gussied-up dog at a circus and were expecting his full nickel's worth. Ignoring or failing to perceive his gaze, she plows forward.

"But what about the Negroes? Kennedy has the power to change things; he's pulled together all the right people: the labor people, the liberals, the Negroes, the farmers," and, she adds, not exactly sure what she means, "the old city machines. He's got the power to really do something."

That makes my father laugh. I don't know whether it's the thought of him being reasonable or of Jack Kennedy being able to change things that makes him laugh so much, but he acts as if this is all very funny; he acts as if my mother—all this—is so ridiculous that he can do nothing but humor her until she has run out of steam.

Unable to find an effective strategy to combat his dismissal, she marches forward: "But don't you understand? He can restore us to what we were before; he has that certain something." Gaining momentum, she adds, "He says he'll support the right of every American to stand up for his rights even if on occasion he must sit down for them."

It's a line she got from the Op Ed page and my father knows it. He can't resist: he turns to me, pulling me in with his eyes as securely as if he had thrown a net over my head. I puff out my cheeks and begin to blow the air out as my father, laughing, says, "But but but; Mommy's pretending to be a motor boat."

This, his teasing, only exasperates her further; he knows she's nearly at wit's end when she begins to swear.

"That Nixon's just an insouciant son of a bitch!"

"*Insouciant*, my dear?" My father's tone lets me know that he's on to something; he draws the word out, gives it a French twist. "Did you say 'insouciant'?"

"Yes, damn it, insouciant!"

"Meaning?" He is leading her on, setting the trap that will close around her neck as soon as she says another word.

"You know damn well what I mean: cruel, unkind, unsympathetic."

"Is that what 'insouciant' means?"

"Megan! Go get the dictionary!"

Which I did, always, still holding my breath.

When I returned, the block of pages held tightly against my chest, my father always had my mother look up the disputed word. Then we watched as her cheeks turned red and her ears got hot, watched as the fist hit the table and the chair shot back to the wall. After we heard her slam the door to her bedroom, he would come over and stroke my hair; he'd rub his finger along the edge of my ear and laugh until it seemed his sides would split.

Twenty years later, my mother tells me that had she known, had she known what was going on those nights, she would have killed the bastard. "It's a good thing I didn't know," she tells me, "because if I had, I wouldn't have been able to control myself; I would have had to kill the son of a bitch."

It's a Saturday, cold, early morning. My father and I are outside. I don't know where my mother and brother are; they are not in the picture. I am wrapped around a brushed-aluminum signpost that has our name and house number on it. My legs are crossed around the stem of the pole. My father supports me, one hand on my three-year-old buttocks, the other around my waist. The little girl looks beyond the photographer; her smile detached, oblivious. I cannot see—I do not imagine—what my father looks like.

I blink, I shake my head, but the image sticks in my mind like jelly. I shake my head, but the image won't be erased.

It is 1983 and I am an adult now, thirty years old, living in an apartment in a converted brothel on West Fifty-seventh Street in Manhattan, trying to sort things out, to arrange them so they make some kind of sense. I am looking at photographs, real pictures this time, of my father as a child and his family; his aunt in Florida has just bequeathed them to me. In one, the family is positioned on the steps of a massive, mansard-roofed Victorian villa. (When I was young, my father and I passed this monstrous and dilapidated construction many times during our "drives"; it was, however, only after I asked about the structure that he identified it as a family landmark.) The house is ornamented with an intricate array of fish scales and broken dentils and window boxes and pinnacles, and yet, despite the sheer number of windows and other decorative apertures, it is impossible to see inside. By some trick of the light, all is hidden, covered by darkness. When I first received these photographs, I borrowed a friend's magnifying glass, but even enlarged, I couldn't see anything—there is not a single photograph in which the interior of that house becomes at all visible.

But, of course, there is always the family sitting on the porch in post-Victorian disarray. There's Ali, the addict, and Rip and Rory, the carpenter drunkards, and Polonius, who died of mustard gas poisoning, and Old Weird Edith, the only one who preferred schizophrenia to drugs, and Tootie, who had the misfortune to fall in love with Rip, and James III, the mad-as-a-hatter builder who slipped, one afternoon, from a girder. And there is my father, his father gone after the dogs (flight, my father once insinuated with a wink and a coy toss of the head, was perhaps his father's most distinguished attribute), his mother is not in the picture. His coat, twice too long for him, is draped carelessly around him, and someone has hung a driver's cap, many times too big for his three-year-old head, from the edge of his ear. A thick ribbon, perhaps made of crepe, is wrapped around his neck and tied in a bow at the chin. There are circles under his eyes, circles far too deep for a child his age. None of his relatives looks too sober; all of them look positively deranged.

I study these pictures to try to work up some sympathy for him. I do this to try to find a way of saying that we have all had it bad, that my situation isn't so special, that what happened really wasn't that awful. After all, bad things happen to everyone. Besides, I tell myself, there is a reason for what happened, a real reason—his family's craziness—that explains it all.

Yet, even when I think it's over and done with, I still find myself looking through photographs, searching for a way to forgive him, for a way to excuse what he did.

During the 1950s and '60s, we lived on Country Club Drive. It was an exciting street to live on, bordered on one end by the dump, that enchanted sanctuary that held so much fascination for my father and me, and by Passaic Avenue on the other, that glamorous and racy drag which businessmen used as a conveyor belt during the day to get them to and from their shiny chrome and glass offices and which teenagers used by night to test their cars and sexual mettle.

The houses on our street, like those in every other suburban community for miles around, were so seemingly decorous, with shirred, opaque curtains pulled discreetly across bay windows, name-plates and knockers of polished brass, and rows of cheerful blue and pink hydrangeas bordering weed-free lawns and meticulously cared-for shrubs, that they made any failure to recognize their gracious authority seem downright heinous. Every pinewood fence, of which there were many, stood in defiance of anarchy; every mechanically edged lawn proclaimed a respect for order; every happy border of impatiens and begonias affirmed that nothing unruly, nothing pernicious could ever happen here. This world was governed by order. One had no choice but to trust that order; attesting to anything out of place here would certainly be found more indecorous, more unseemly than would the cause of the allegation itself.

This night, my father is coming home, as he did on occasion, sober. It is 1957, a short time before the real trouble began, before my mother began staying out. There is no explanation for this sobriety. He called, and my mother told my brother that she could tell by his tone, by the way he said hello, that he is actually coming home tonight, that it's not a trick.

I am delirious with excitement. Even though I am only four, my mother has said that I can walk to the corner of Country Club and Passaic by myself to wait for my father. I will do this many more times in the next few years, will do it every opportunity I have; I will do it without thinking, without having an inkling of the consequences, will do it simply because I love, I adore, my father.

I walk by other houses like ours, three-bedroom bungalows filled with children and the smell of meat fat, walk by houses where I can hear forks tinkling and glasses being filled with milk or iced tea and chairs scraping across linoleum floors and I think how special I am to be out at that hour, to be walking by myself, to be allowed to go up to the corner to meet my father, who I'm sure our neighbors don't realize is the best, the biggest, the most wonderful man in the world.

To control my excitement at the corner, I grab onto the stop sign as if it were an anchor that could keep me from hurtling my small body in front of the cars speeding by in the twilight. I know he will be driving from the north, but just in case, I check every car that passes from the north or the south, or from the other end, the dead-end part

of Country Club Drive. I am afraid somehow that he will miss me. I
feel myself growing anxious, fearful that something has gone wrong,
that my mother got it backwards, that he must have said he's not
coming home tonight.

But then I see it, off in the distance, coming in from the north,
the black and yellow Chrysler New Yorker. He hasn't forgotten me. I
am twirling around the stop sign, skipping as if it were May Day; I am
hardly conscious of my actions when my god, my world, turns the
corner and stops at the other side of our street.

He is smiling, laughing at my antics, and then he hollers, "Who
let you up here, little nutmeg, ginger spice, my cinnamon buns?"

"Mommy said I could come!"

He laughs again, only this time he looks a little like the Cheshire
Cat in *Alice's Adventures in Wonderland*. Later, I would recognize this
smile as a warning, but I had no way of understanding it then.

Still laughing, he asks me if I want to drive, if I would be willing
to drive him the rest of the way home. I'm not sure I've heard him
correctly when, catching me with his eyes, he adds, "We won't tell
Mommy."

I am so excited—I can't believe this is really happening—I feel as
if I am about to burst. He swings open the door to the brand-new
Chrysler New Yorker, the car he won't even let my mother, let alone
my brother, go near, and then he pats his thighs. "Here, little
nutmeg; sit on my lap."

He slowly pulls the door shut—I can still hear the sound of the
click—and there we are, just the two of us, enclosed in his big
machine, isolated from the rest of the world where no one can find us,
no one can see us. There is something that feels very dangerous about
this closing off and also something very exciting. He fits me onto his
lap the way he wants me—my legs straddling his right thigh—and
then he says, "You take the wheel and I'll work the pedals."

And I do put my hands on the wheel as he encircles me with his
arms, strapping me in like a seat belt so that I won't fall out and

nothing will hurt me. He then says, "Ready?" and we begin moving. We are gliding down the gentle slope of Country Club Drive, just he and I, my hands on the wheel, his leg pumping up and down between the thighs that straddle his, and it is glorious, the movement so slow and assured, enveloped as we are in this big expansive space with the windows rolled up and the air conditioner moving cool air over our faces. Sitting up in my father's lap, I am so high that I can see in people's windows; I see that they are eating their pork chops and potatoes while I am driving my father's car, while we—he and I—are sinking down into a dark, elaborate space, a maze of beauty and protectiveness, a place I've never been before, a place that feels so boundless it feels at once like the scariest place I've ever been and also the most irresistible. We are gliding down now, my father's thigh pumping up and down, and there is something sticking up like a spring from the seat, but I don't let it get in the way, I don't let it interfere with my pleasure, the pleasure of being alone with my father, enclosed in his spanking new Chrysler New Yorker with the windows that open when you push a small button and the antenna that hides in the trunk.

At the bottom of the hill, we turn into our driveway. He lifts my hair and gives me a kiss on the back of my neck, he rubs his nose along the edge of my collar, and then he says, "Now we won't tell Mommy, little midget." Joining us with his eyes, he says, "We won't tell Mommy and we won't tell Kyle; we don't want them to know." And that puts me over the line into heaven. I am in heaven and it is our secret and no one can know.

I have a secret with my father.

I have this dream. I am five years old or fifteen years old or twenty-five years old and I am sliding down something. Sometimes it is stairs, bumpy circular stairs, sometimes it is a slippery, muddy hill, outback somewhere, and sometimes it is just something black, some downhill space that I am sliding down at a furious pace; there is nothing to hold on to or to break my fall; I am sliding down so fast that my heart hurts, threatens to break out of my chest. It is thrilling, but it isn't pleasurable, it isn't fun, it is too fast and I want to stop but I can't because always behind me is a fingernail beckoning me, coming to get me, to stick me and poke around my insides till it hurts. I look behind me, but all I can see is this black fingernail, six or seven inches long, filed to a neat point at the tip. It isn't disembodied, but I can never see the rest of the man; I know it is a man, but I can never identify him. I am frightened—terrified—imagining what that point could do to me, to my insides. I am frightened and I am exhausted, I want to stop, to sit down, to rest my legs, which ache from sliding so fast, from the effort of trying to brace myself, to stay myself against the nothing, the no walls, the sliding down.

When the man gets too close, when the fingernail is so near that I can feel it graze the back of my neck, I pull myself out of this dream. I always pull myself out, wrench myself from this scene, before I see the end of the picture, before I can find out what happened when, or if, the nail caught up to the girl.

Many years after those car rides, in 1979, my mother and brother are at the kitchen table in the condominium my mother bought with her settlement money, discussing the allegations surrounding what later became known as the "scandal," the scandal, that is, that we could talk about, the only one we had words for. They are charging after the truth as if it were some small animal—a fox or a rabbit perhaps— something one could outwit and gun down. The hunt will continue for hours as they debate the multiple stories, examining the permutations of each one; they will look for the gaps, the flaws in each story, for threads that might run together, as they search for the clue that will put everything together and allow them to say that one is true and the others are false. And finally, they will wonder if what my father did warrants a sentence in Allenwood and, if it does, how long that sentence might be.

My mother, however, is losing patience. It is only six months since the story broke, only a few weeks since her divorce came through. She has called my brother in from the West Coast; she wants to know, needs my brother's help in determining the extent of her own involvement—of her own "unwitting" complicity—and the legal ramifications of having made her "mistake" thirty-five years ago of consenting to be our father's wife. She is desperate to defuse the tension inside her; lifting her hand to examine her pretty pink nails she seems to want to pretend that it never really happened; she asks, suddenly, if it wasn't just what every other adman does every other day of his professional career.

But my brother won't help, not this time. This time, he refuses to ease her out of her jam. It is a refusal that can be attributed, only partially, to what has seemed, since the days of Mrs. Karpaty's nursery school, his professorial nature. More, it seems based on his desire to compel her somehow to squirm, to be tortured as he has been for the last twenty-seven-and-a-half years with the moral ramifications of being related to my father, of being in his case, my father's first and only son.

And so he toys with her, with the "subject," enjoying her growing exasperation as well as his nebulous consciousness of his own brutality; he pushes himself—he wouldn't be able to tell you why—to test her seemingly boundless faith in him, her good-natured, greedy trust, which has, over the years, nearly crushed him.

"But, Mother, don't you see? It doesn't matter, it doesn't matter if everyone else did it or does it; that's hardly the point." He is lecturing at her, talking down to her as if she were an annoying student, a student who, my brother would say, is refusing out of pure obstinacy, to understand what he considers patently evident. "It's more complex than that, don't you see? There are other things at stake here, things that are more important."

He pauses for a moment, my brother the thinker, the moralist, the philosopher who has sought futilely after the Truth from the day he was born, and then he reaches for the bourbon and pours himself a second shot.

Sitting across the table from him, I can see his eyes, the formerly brilliant green-brown orbs now shrunk, diminished over the years to nearly black points someplace three hundred miles behind his glasses. He stares out into the night, looking straight ahead of him without really focusing. I don't know if he has left us entirely when suddenly he says, "This is exactly what I've been writing about, situations like these that disrupt, dislocate our whole notion of truth."

He pauses here, perhaps for emphasis, perhaps simply to allow my mother time to absorb what he's said, or perhaps the vision has been too quick for him and has passed, some fleeting moment of insight, before his cavernous eyes.

But my mother is beyond patience now, beyond infatuation with her number one son; she could give a damn about dislocations, disruptions. There is real terror in her eyes, terror and exasperation with my brother, her god, her hope who refuses to absolve her of her sins. She raises her hands, now balled into tight fists, above her head and demands, "Tell me, damn you, tell me whether or not I'm going to have to go to jail too."

But my brother doesn't say anything. He stares right back at her, stares right up at her fists, the fury of two and a half decades of coping with her denial, her blindness, her deliberate myopia hardening his eyes. He pins her with his gaze, she lowers her fists, and then, without releasing her, he says, "I don't know, Mother. I simply don't know." Then, tagging on the phrase she used throughout our childhood, he adds, "Only time will tell."

When my mother was a child, her father, an Illinois surgeon, did very well, even during the Depression. Well enough, that is, to have night and day uniforms for the staff, a woman twice a week to wash the girls' hair, and finger bowls brought in between courses. Even at his death, my grandmother refused to call him anything but the Doctor; after that, she refused to call him anything at all.

The Doctor rose precisely at 5:55 A.M., at which time he rang a bell attached via a Rube Goldberg–type contraption to the kitchen, signaling the "help" that they had precisely nineteen minutes to prepare the Doctor's boiled egg, dry toast, and black tea. When he arrived at table, he flicked the starched pink napkin open, smoothed it over his lap, and, in ten neat strokes, finished his egg, his toast, his tea. Then he walked precisely sixty-five steps around the corner of Pine Street and halfway up Main to his office, where he stayed until precisely 5:55 P.M.

My mother tells me that when he arrived back home at 6:00, dinner was to be on the table, *"Achtung!"* They lay in wait for him— she, her sister, and her mother—trembling in their patent leather shoes, their scrubbed hands pleating the edges of their starched dinner napkins under the table, out of sight of the great Teutonic warrior coming to give them grace.

Not once, my mother says, did they ever talk about the baby

who, after eight months of splenetic life, had died of rheumatic fever.

At night, the Doctor never stayed with them, but instead walked half a mile to his club, where he read the papers, smoked a cigar, and assured his confreres that his stringent authority was for his family's own benefit. As a surgeon, he felt obliged to remove any indication of unwanted trouble within and, after a drop or two of brandy, not infrequently compared his daughters and wife to the anesthetized flesh that had submitted absolutely, almost docilely, to his knife. A strong hand was, after all, the only sure way to eliminate trouble.

Renowned as a man of decision, there was no doubt in the Doctor's mind that when, at age thirteen, Evelyn contracted polio, her things should be burned at once, for her own good. That night, my mother stood alone, in the dull halo of light reflected upward from the garden into the hollow of her room, watching, her palms pressed against the cold windowpane, as the Doctor, his figure barely discernible in the moonlight, scurried back and forth, in and out of the house; like a phantasm, some satanic hobgoblin from a fairy tale or wild dream, he piled up books and school papers, stuffed animals and sweaters, photos of the family, and awards for scholastic achievement. With her nose flattened against the pane, my mother wrestled, she's told me, with some kind of unmanageable feeling gnawing at her stomach, making her feel as if she didn't know whether she would choke or scream, while the Doctor, like a priest in some kind of bizarre ritual, drizzled gasoline over the pile of her things, and then dropped a match, torching her life, cremating the heap of herself, once and for all. It took only a few minutes, not more than ten, for every tangible reminder of her first thirteen years to go up in smoke, which then dissipated languidly into the cool night air.

During her recovery, my mother taught herself to play piano, and she would play, moving her irrevocably bent body in and out of the rhythm, sometimes six or even seven hours a day. But when, one morning, the Doctor returned unexpectedly and witnessed her passion—nearly an enthrallment, he said—he slammed the cover down on the keys, silencing her, he said, for her own good.

And so my mother lived a disinfected and unsullied existence, sterilized of all unclean habits that might challenge the Doctor's authority, free of the necessity of self-affirmation since everything was affirmed for her well before she had time to think that she might have something to affirm.

Years after the divorce, when, still in awe of her father's Teutonic rigor, my mother felt a rare need to justify her behavior, she said, "You can't imagine what a fright it was, a woman of my background going from my father's home, to his!"

"You can't imagine how frightening this all would be if I thought it was true, if I had to believe it."

My brother is not facing me. He is standing next to me, but he, I can already tell, will not look at me. It is 1980 and he has just emerged from the study of his summer house on the Oregon coast, where he has been reading an article I asked him to have a look at, entitled "Secrecy and Denial: A Family Pattern." His wife is in the kitchen preparing tabouli; their single child, Aaron, is making a fort with the couch cushions. My brother adjusts his glasses. Now he takes them off, holds them up to the light, squints for a second through the lenses, then lowers them to his shirttail, where he circles the glass with the edge of the cloth.

Deborah, hearing his voice, appears from the kitchen. "What is it?" she asks, her ever-ready smile strung like small pearls across her face. She wipes her hands on the edge of her apron; it is a gesture meant to look casual, part of her new air of polished nonchalance. Deborah has just returned from a two-day rebirthing intensive, during which she claims to have released a lifetime of accumulated "negativity" and "cleansed her soul." With her heart now more open, more able to give and to receive love, she stands with her hands on her hips, while my brother remains silently bending the ends of his wire-framed glasses over the rims of his ears. Seeing him lost somewhere behind the glass, disconnected from her and the simple happy world she has filled with regular schedules, nutritious food, and clean sheets, she suddenly becomes enraged and struggles, it seems, with her temptation to throw over her newly expanded awareness and return to her pre-rebirthing self. Exasperated with me, with my family, she drops her smile and bangs her fist against the wall, hoping, I suppose, that that bang could banish me right back to the East Coast where I belong.

My brother adjusts his glasses once more, then places them on the table. Despite his long-held democratic ideals, since childhood he has been an authoritarian when it comes to pain and will do anything to keep it reined in. Although he would not call it a foreign element, he considers pain a fearsome enemy that would present, were he to allow it to roam free, too great a challenge to his peaceful if tyrannical rule.

He picks up the article, which he had tossed on the dining table, and rolls it in his hand. Like a man leveling an accusation, he points the rolled paper at me, and then, as if the pages were suddenly too hot, he drops them back to the table. His lips part, but then, like a suitcase secured for a potentially rough ride, they as quickly snap shut, sealing everything in. After a pause, he charges, "If I had to believe this, if I was forced to believe this, I'd never be able to look at my father again."

He turns, walks into the kitchen, and returns with a handful of flatware and napkins. We eat dinner in silence.

I am a grown-up now, a few years older than I was on that visit to the Oregon coast, living in my own apartment in the heart of Manhattan, and yet, if I shut my eyes, I can see that house on Country Club Drive as if I were still living there: the great big bay window extending out from the living room, the wisteria that climbed up from the driveway and over the garage door, forming a lavender and white archway enticing you into the mouth of the house. Above the garage are my three bedroom windows, the panes of which trembled just slightly whenever my father's car pulled in. Once inside, I head first for the hallway, the green and brown hallway that connects the stairs to the bedrooms with the downstairs bathroom. I see myself standing there, about five years old, at the door of the bathroom, the one my father and I used to shower in before anyone else got up. I am looking up the stairs, then I turn and look across the hall into the bathroom. I look again, first upstairs, then along the green and brown paper squares toward the bathroom. It's as if I'm expecting someone to arrive, something to happen, but I can't tell if I'm waiting for someone to come downstairs or for someone to come out of the bathroom. And I can't really tell what I'm feeling, just that I'm standing and waiting and watching. I don't know if I hope something happens or if I hope nothing will happen.

Con-ne-ma-ra. Con-ne-ma-ra. Con-ne-ma-ra.

It was the same green and brown hallway that my mother littered with Kennedy pictures and campaign paraphernalia two months before the big election. Part of her motivation was to get back at my father, this compulsively derisive and misanthropic man who refused to share her desire for world harmony, but more, it seemed inspired by her real admiration for this charismatic, charming New Englander who would make everything all right, this man who would give everybody a good-paying job, provide care for the elderly, and who would, even if it killed him, preserve peace in the world.

Most important, John Kennedy was, for her, the man who, simply by virtue of his example, would restore happy families. My mother idolized and idealized that family, that WASPy tribe led by that rich and handsome patriarch with the smile lines, and she longed to be as poised and svelte as Jackie, to have a son as precocious as John-John and a daughter who would fit as neatly into her petticoats as Caroline did. My mother adored everything about them: the way Jack drew out his vowels, the way Jackie's dresses always matched her hats, the way John-John's bowl-cut hair always fell into place, the way sun-freckled Caroline always looked precious in her shiny new Mary Janes. The "women's" magazines—*Good Housekeeping, Ladies' Home Journal,* and *McCall's*—provided my mother with most of her information about the family, who, it was said, lived in Camelot; because of my father's job as an ad executive for Premier Products, a food packaging firm, we got them all for free, and we heard regular reports about the family's trials and the spirit with which they accepted or overcame their limitations. She could tell you all about Jack's back pain, relating it as if the knowledge she possessed of his fortitude somehow reflected her own inner strength. She was especially reassured by the pictures of domestic felicity on the shores of Hyannis Port, the way the whole family really did seem to care about their old mother, the way each of them really seemed to want to share with the others.

But it was Jack's picture that she would hold up to my father, just that one picture of him standing behind the podium, his face bathed in sunshine. "This," she would say to my father, brandishing the photo as if it were a cross before the devil, "this is the man who can save us all."

It was that year, 1960, that my mother began reserving cottages for us at Cape Cod; we couldn't go near Hyannis Port, but we took our saltines and peanut butter down to the pond at South Dennis and sat in our swimsuits as my mother regaled us with the latest news of John-John's progress in school or Caroline's fairy-tale existence. "They say she leads the life of a princess," my mother said with a sigh while we, my brother and father and I, worked to construct a moat keeping the sea from our castle. "They're trying to keep her from being spoiled," she added. Then, looking up from her own deformity, the knotted and club-shaped foot that, since her polio almost thirty years earlier, had grown into a Gothic geegaw at the end of her leg, she would say, "Jack's back is going to get better." Rubbing her foot in the sand, she'd say, "I know Jack's going to be all right." They too, it seemed, had their crosses to bear.

It was especially important for her to engage Kyle in these reports, hoping that he would be, for her, the man to restore our unhappy family. Her goal, from his birth, was to transform him into someone who could, by excelling in the masculine world of "knowledge," "conscience," and especially "truth," relieve her vague sense of her own unfitness.

And Kyle did respond, becoming her great moral crusader, the successful political philosophy professor at a prestigious western university, the boy who, from age five, learned to capture and hold his mother's attention with reports about his good citizenship, or his participation in the student government association or the town history committee or the civil rights rally or the anti-war moratorium. It was my brother who organized the prison reform committee, my brother who, twenty-four hours after Kent State, organized a general strike against the schools, my brother who distributed black armbands as the toll in Vietnam rose, my brother who edited the underground newspaper, and my brother who, with Richard Castille, braved the depths of Harlem one night to interview the now dead Panther leader, Randall Hughes Jackson. Whatever it was he did, though, he managed to bring together disparate individuals as if they were a family, a family of moral crusaders, great white knights my mother could feel, by proxy, a part of.

Even now, my mother holds on to Kyle's words as she once held on to Kennedy's, holding on to a dream of a life she had desired so intensely that it almost feels like the memory of something lost, rather than something she never had. She has now, as always, endless attention for his analyses; like a little girl listening to a fairy tale, she sinks into his biographical accounts, his interpretations, his reason-

ing by analogy, his deductions and his hunches, his statistical calculations, which she hopes can secure for her—precisely—the way it
really happened, and the way it's really going to be. When he
compares Aristotle's statements on the body politic to, say, Reagan's
moral dilemma in regard to the Middle East, my mother nearly
swoons, feeling herself to be, at least vicariously, part of an enormous
struggle for righteousness, an enormous history of good families. The
thought of my brother making sense of all this, his ability to trace the
lineage of good people all the way up from Aristotle to the present
day, imbues her with such love for him and inspires such overwhelm-
ing pride, that for a minute she thinks she can forget all the rest, and
sink into her admiration for this boy who was elected, by an over-
whelming majority, to be class president two years in a row, this man
who became chair of his department not three years after being hired,
this member of the intellectual elite who, she'd put money on it, will
be a high-ranking foreign affairs adviser, the only dove in the president's cabinet, by the time he is forty.

My mother admires my brother, my strange, small, unsmiling
brother from across the sand. We have finished our moat and he is
now playing with a truck, running it up and down a sand hill that
topples with every three rides. When it does, he rebuilds the hill, a
pensive Sisyphus, then plows the truck back up to the top. Content
with this scene, my mother retrieves a magazine from the stack piled
next to her and, flipping the pages, announces, "John-John's going to
Eton!"

I am driving my father to the dumps. En route, my father, my god,
describes marketing strategies, the challenge in packaged goods, how
you position your product, how you figure out what's new or unique,
and then how you create a name and a market for it. His speech is
peppered with acronyms: Y&R, BBD&O, SSC&B, N.W. Ayer. If
not this morning, another morning he'll tell me that he'd rather be

involved with something non-packaged, something with a little more "emotional texture"—health insurance companies or telephone lines—but for the time being, he says, "the old man" will stick with packaged goods.

The way he speaks, the way he tosses sums and acronyms in the air, makes him appear, to my seven-year-old eyes, very agile, very capable; a few deft strokes and we're there: a million-dollar deal, two spots for the price of one, or a guarantee of unlimited time in the future. I see him in an office that stretches over six floors of some glittering skyscraper in Manhattan, there is an antechamber and a secretary-cum-security-guard to shoo away intruders. He is sitting behind a mile-wide oak desk with champagne-colored phones attached to each ear. There is inch-thick beige carpeting on the floor and, scattered among tropical plants and trees, four Mies van der Rohe armchairs. Three enormous color TVs sit opposite his desk and, on the desk, three remote controls.

My father's foot switches beneath me from the accelerator to the brake as he helps me make the turn from Country Club onto the gravel spit at the end of Springfield Avenue. He drops me, his "little shrimp," his "little morsel," his "little delectable one," to the other side of the chain fence, and after a short walk, we are in this treasure land of junk and debris where "the old man" and I can be together, alone, as we sort through bits of barbed wire, broken glass, and rusted metal. The sheer amount of stuff makes us giddy, and we begin to fill our pockets without restraint, stuffing them full of casters and window locks, TV knobs and door hinges, switch plates and fly nuts and wire springs. We set aside velvet paintings and cracked glass pitchers, hammer heads and old string, we make piles of broken coat hangers and radio tubes, sort through plastic flower pots and copper wire; as if time were running out, we take anything that's there—it doesn't matter if it's valuable. What matters is that these things come to my father somewhat illicitly, that they were not his originally, that he feels he has no right to them, and that he has, therefore, to gain them by stealth. Something here, there is something in these piles of debris that my father wants very badly, something he cannot name, but something he feels, somehow, is his due, his share of the pie that lies still beyond his reach; he feels almost as if he were stealing.

I watch him raise a cracked carburetor from a rusting heap of automobile parts and hold it up to the sun. He admires its shape, contemplates its sides and its fissures as if it were some sort of sacred object that could, if he understood it, explain everything to him, something that would, most importantly, restore to him what he feels is missing.

Only later was I able to attach meaning to the way he gazed at me that moment; at the time, I had no way of understanding. All I knew was that he was looking at me across our pile of junk, looking at me and smiling, wrinkling his mouth in kind of a funny way, teasing me with his eyes, and then he again raised the carburetor up to the sun.

As if confirming an agreement, a tacit pact between us, I stared hard back at him, smiled and winked, and then I raised a rusted air filter to the sky.

Once home, we unload our treasures onto the kitchen table; we display them for all the world to see, as if, during the past hour, we had made off with the king's ransom, and had made my father the king.

When I was young, my father was sometimes called Shep, sometimes Al, sometimes we called him Arty. Perhaps in deference to the distant relative he insisted had escaped cannibals after being shipwrecked in the South Seas (he would show you the three-horned mahogany club that was supposedly thrown after the fleeing sailor if you doubted the story), he most frequently referred to himself as "the Old Kipper: split, salted, and, for your delectation, smoke-cured." His real first name, as far as any of us has been able to find out, is Shepherd; none of us has been able to uncover the origin of the two apparently unrelated nicknames.

Because we didn't know his real surname either, it was just as frustrating trying to determine his paternal lineage. When we were kids, he used to tell Kyle and me, peeling back his black and gold "diamond" socks to expose his long second toes, that he was related to Charlemagne; we, of course, have no way of confirming this. When his father, an orphan, came of age, he pilfered the surname Arbuthnot, finding its aristocratic trisyllables more resonant than Smithers, the name of his adoptive family. My father retained his father's chosen name, perhaps because he found it suited him, perhaps because it saved him the bother of having to find a replacement.

To this day, my father is still a slight, delicately proportioned man (although as he's aged, his belly has expanded some few inches to "show off his wealth"); in his bare feet, he stands no more than five feet nine. As if he were a starveling, bones protrude from his narrow shoulders and thin chest, forming an artful array of caverns and gullies when he stands naked against the light. He disguises his thinness with an expansive and versatile wardrobe, one that allows him to play a variety of roles. I remember brown loafers and smoking jackets when he, a nonsmoker, was playing the man of leisure; dark shades and high-collared Burberrys when he wanted to appear enigmatic and daring; beat-up, ten-year-old jeans when he wanted merchants to think him poorer than he was; and loud colors, funny hats, and pinkie rings when he fancied himself a man among men, a pimp perhaps, a trafficker in illicit goods. The one thing he loathed were monograms, perhaps fearing that they stamped him somewhat too indelibly into a single identity.

My father used his elaborate wardrobe not only to disguise, but also to locate himself in some group—he was indiscriminate about which one: it could be "high-class" or "society" people, "poor" people or "down-and-outers"—it didn't matter as long as whatever he wore provided him with enough sense of place so that he, an irretrievably lost man, always knew where he was.

Despite his penchant for flamboyant clothes, my father was not a man to call attention to himself when he walked. Rather, you could say that he skulked from here to there, soundlessly, as if on tiptoe, not so much because he was trying to get away with anything (although that was part of it too), but more to provide himself with the advantage of arriving unseen. We never knew from where or when he would next appear. Once, when we thought it was really all over, Kyle, after a couple shots of bourbon, suggested that we might have hung a bell around his neck, but it was too late by then to seriously contemplate such maneuvers.

Beneath Shep's jaunty and ever-changing exterior, he let it be known, to me at least, that he considered himself a member of a rare and fragile species, not unlike the gross-necked moa, he'd say, always erudite and somewhat obscure, or the flightless dodo; and from the time I could speak, I agreed that his delicate build, his soft skin, his rheumatic heart, and his erratic digestive system were all signs that he was too sensitive to handle the rough world we both inhabited. I was taught early to soothe and console, to massage and make nice, to scratch and apply salves, all with the intention of preserving this exquisite if fundamentally helpless creature; regardless of what my mother said, we agreed that he must be coddled and looked after were we to keep him from extinction.

I admired his slender fingers and believed that their thinness made him, in some strange way, unique. Yet despite their attenuation, they were able to support a variety of gaudy and glittering adornments, which he rotated, when he began to disintegrate, sometimes three times a day. Shep was unconcerned about the value of his rings and would just as soon wear a piece of colored glass in a gray band from a gumball machine as he would a star sapphire surrounded by sterling and diamonds, and he sometimes liked to wear them together, the ten-cent one and the ten-thousand-dollar one, testing passersby and admirers to see if anyone would notice the forgery, suffering, as they gazed open-mouthed, the exquisite tension of one about to be found out.

I was especially fond of one star sapphire; it was a lovely, dusty lavender color with a milky white center and light-colored, opaque threads that radiated outward, and when, at age seven or perhaps eight, I admired it out loud, I was told, "Not till the Old Kipper kicks the bucket, you don't."

Some years after it was all over, my mother, her face dry and cracked like a great desert through which a river once ran, said, "If I thought killing somebody would have helped, I might have done it. I might have seriously hurt somebody, almost murdered, if I thought it would have helped to hold things together."

Shep and I have sought shelter from the rain this Saturday in the basement, where we have just finished painting bookshelves we built for Kyle. In honor of the occasion, he has donned his muslin smock and black leather beret and asks that I call him Pierre, and I try to, although sometimes I forget. I am about eight; that puts Shep around thirty-eight or maybe thirty-nine.

We have chosen loud, flamboyant colors: patches of gold with purple and white thrown in; there are splashes of coral and orange and waterfalls of green and blue; we used anything, any color left over from other painting jobs. Pierre and I think it looks right nice; we won't guess what Mommy will think.

Having covered my hands with Goop, Pierre begins to work the paint off with a towel. How our discussion came about, I can't remember; we had been reading *Travels with Charley* and tales from Romania together at night, and perhaps they were, in some way, the inspiration.

"Why don't we live in a tent, Daddy?"

He seemed amused, provoked by something in my question. "Just the two of us? Just you and your cher amour, Pierre?"

I considered for a moment. "Yes, just the two of us."

"And what about your dear mother?"

Pierre had a point. Mommy and Daddy go together—always— just like shoes and socks and peanut butter and jelly. But I quickly found a way out of our jam.

"But this is America, Pierre, and in America you can do whatever you want."

"You can?"

"Yes; that's what my teacher says."

"Well, that's the way it is then."

"You do whatever you want, don't you Daddy?"

"I'm an American, aren't I?"

"Yes."

"So that means I do whatever I want, right?"

"Can I do whatever I want?"

"You're an American, aren't you?"

I thought for a second. "Anything I want?"

He baited me with his eyes. "Whatever your little heart desires."

My eyes bulged at the thought of this. "And we could live in a tent, and cook hot dogs on a fire, and live like the gypsies?" As I pleaded, he rubbed my hands, pressing my fingers between his, squeezing them hard and then releasing the pressure as he worked the Goop toward the tips.

"Happily ever after." He thought for a moment. "Providing, that is, that we figure out what to do about Mommy."

"What should we do about her?" I was troubled, unable to disconnect the two of them even in fantasy. "If she came with us, she'd just be an old crankpot all the time."

"We shouldn't object to a cranky mood once in a while."

"Yes we should." Then, after a moment, "I would anyway, Daddy."

"Call me Pierre."

"Pierre."

"You're afraid of your mother, aren't you?"

"Sometimes."

"Really afraid?"

"More afraid even than of the bogeyman."

"Well, in that case, we won't take her along; we'll have to find something to do with her. What do you say? What shall we do with her?"

It didn't take me long to find a solution. "Throw her in the sewee hole!" I was delighted with my fantasy.

"And Kyle?"

"He goes in after her!"

"So it's just the two of us?"

I felt a convulsion of joy that made my chest heave. "Yes, Daddy, just you and me."

I have this dream. I am trying to scream, but no words come out; I open my mouth—nothing comes out. As I get older, a more frightening variation: I open my mouth, but nothing comes out because my mouth is jammed with a wire brush, a stiff cable or a wire brush, like a prickly paint brush or a wire rod, which moves back and forth in my mouth so that no words can come out. The brush is so big, it makes me feel as if I am about to choke; the brush is so large, I feel as if I am about to die.

In Connemara, we cross over green moss and black mud to the sea. On our right, mountains covered by hot lava, on our left, bubbling veins of gold ore. We dive into the warm belly of the sea from a cliff; then we dry ourselves on rocks made smooth by the water.

She traces a salt ring that has formed on my body. She says it makes an eye, an O, a round cavern of pleasure, a brand-new beginning, a harbor of safety.

"You don't know how lucky you are." My mother, dressed in a polka-dot housedress, is unloading groceries; I am at the opposite end of the table, protected from her by six feet of solid pine. I am sitting in my father's chair, resting its back against the window ledge, ensconced with a twelve-pack of Twinkies and a diet soda. Four, maybe five years have passed since my father and I used to paint together in the basement.

My mother is telling me that my father is a very responsible alcoholic, that my brother and I are lucky to have a man like our father for a father. This, his alcoholism, is the one problem we talk about as a family, the only one we discuss openly, which oddly, during my teenage years, gives us a reputation in town for being a remarkably stable family. And my father's alcoholism does, in a way, serve to stabilize us, for the scope of the disease is so enormous and its influence so tyrannical that it prohibits consideration of any other problems. As a sort of side benefit, it also provides my mother with a way of keeping her obstreperous and irrepressibly vagrant husband in what she considers his rightful position: dominant and at the center of everyone's attention.

As she speaks, her voice only slightly agitated, she checks off groceries from the receipt; she will keep the receipt, this testament to her frugality, as part of her hidden armory to be used against my father. She will tuck it away in her top drawer, between the lilac sachets that scent her brassieres and the ornamented Bakelite case she uses to hold her gloves, the case that was later replaced with a locked box for her jewelry when, just before the divorce, she began to suspect that Shep might, as she said, be losing his mind. The receipt will join forces with the children's meager shoe bills, the statements from the pharmacist at the discount drug store, and the canceled checks from the local missionary societies and drug rehabilitation centers—an entire arsenal of vouchers testifying to her sheer perseverance in the face of what she was frequently to call, with a sweeping gesture of the hand, "all this."

When she starts to speak, I begin to rock the chair on its two rear legs, banging it softly against the window ledge. My mother will be so absorbed in her testimony that she won't notice, this time, the marks the chair leaves on the sill. As I listen to her, I shove one Twinkie after another into my mouth; by the time she's done, I will have finished off half the box and will be reaching for another diet soda.

"Your father," she says, staring at me as if leveling an accusation against the perpetrator and not the victim of the crime, "is really a very responsible man. He's an excellent provider. He works, every day of his life, at a job he'd just as soon not have, just for us. He keeps food on the table, clothes on your back, and never once—not yet—has he ever beat his wife." The profile continues: his attendance record at work, his mathematical dexterity, his kindness to animals. "A lot of people have it worse off than we do," she tells me. And then it begins, the usual catalogue of spectacular stories about mothers and children who have it "worse off" than we do: Bobby, whose father choked once and for the last time two months ago after mistaking the rat poison for the vodka; Cindy, whose father left to buy a pack of cigarettes two years ago and hasn't returned yet; Andrea, who has to carry both her parents up to bed; and Janet, whose husband came home last week and didn't like the way she had cooked the pork chops so he let her know it with the frying pan.

"Up and down the stairs, she was screaming bloody murder. But the more she screamed, the more he whacked her. She was black and blue from head to toe before she could get out and call the cops."

My mother pauses for a minute, lost in the sordid depths of this bloody scenario from which she will, when she returns, feel nearly ineffable relief.

Joining me again, her torpid eyes barely discernible behind the thick-lensed, blue-rimmed, Harlequin-style glasses, she says, "You haven't the slightest idea how irresponsible other alcoholics are." She has regained herself now, pulled herself back from that tawdry scene in the blood-soaked living room, and starts working again on the chores in her own home.

"I really feel sorry for him," she says, her voice wavering a little, "for all of them. It's really a terrible shame, a real pity; it's just awful to see what they go through. They must suffer very low self-esteem; I know your father does. It must just be awful living like that, without any respect for yourself."

A sigh, deep and long, puts her back in full swing and she hurls a handful of canned goods from the bag onto the shelf.

33

"Did you hear about Marsha's daddy?" she asks as she knocks the cans about, swatting them with her hands until they fall into place in the alphabetized rows on the second shelf of the first cupboard to the left of the stove. "Last Wednesday, he didn't like the way the meat loaf was cooked, so he threw his entire dinner plate—Frisbee style— across the room; Marsha's mother is still trying to get the stains out of the wallpaper."

She pauses for a minute to send four boxes of pasta flying into a space above the refrigerator, an area that would more comfortably accommodate three. Then, cleaning products, which overflow the wicker basket she recently bought for herself as a "splurge," are forced down until a small tear, barely noticeable, appears in the side.

"And you know about Sandy's daddy; he's been off and on the sauce so many times, even if he does ever really sober up, nobody will hire him. Why, Roberta told me just the other day that he went out to a site and the contractor told him that his reputation had preceded him." As I reach for another Twinkie, she jams the last of the perishables into the hydrator drawer. "I feel sorry for them, I really do." She jiggles the drawer once or twice, then rattles it again, hoping to make the vegetables squash down. "No one wants to be an alcoholic. Nobody wants to live like that." When the drawer still refuses to shut, she adds, shoving the food back, "Sooner or later, they all have to hit bottom. They all come to their senses." With a kind of missionary zeal, she gets down on her knees and rams the vegetables down, trying to force them into a space where they don't belong, where they'll never fit. Then she yanks at the drawer handle, trying to make it go back in its place, when suddenly, the handle tears off in her hand.

Squatting on her haunches, she turns to me, the handle extended, like an offering. There are tears in her eyes. Like a painter whose canvas has just been dashed before her, she looks at me, her pleading eyes searching my full mouth, my young eyes for something she can sling back at the offending vegetables, something powerful and incisive that would compel them to fit, to do what they're supposed to.

I rarely see my mother like this, out of control, and am embarrassed by the scene, by her troubled face, by the tears, the handle.

Seeing my discomfort, or perhaps more painfully seeing her own helplessness reflected in my eyes, she stands, turns full force on the refrigerator and kicks the drawer savagely with her foot, guillotining the heads off the new stalks of celery.

Leaving the fallen leaves, the necks, the stems where they lie, she slams the refrigerator door shut and, turning, says, "Don't you have anything better to do today than to just sit there watching me?"

My brother doesn't remember being privy to such scenes; he was not asked to bear witness to the delicate stilts upon which our family balanced, just barely, above the encroaching tides. He was assigned a different purpose.

They say that when he was a child, Kyle used to draw little black boxes, over and over again. It started in nursery school. While other children brought home blue and green and red rectangles and triangles and circles, which they had arranged, with the help of snub-nosed glue dispensers, in cryptic patterns on butcher paper, Kyle used only black crayon and refused to draw anything but carefully outlined and meticulously scribbled-in boxes. His teachers, not alarmed but definitely concerned, told my mother, "He seems to have no interest in color." My mother thought this was just as well. She was as proud of Kyle's boxes as other mothers were of their children's stick-armed potato creatures, and taped Kyle's "drawings" to the refrigerator between the grocery list she had divided according to the rows at Kings into eight sections (meat, dairy, fish, poultry, veg, fruit, dessert, household) and the THINK THIN sticker she had put up in the hope that this admonition might restrain her from vicariously, if pleasantly, satisfying her displaced desires. She convinced herself that his artwork, far from being regressive or a sign of disturbance, was, rather, a mark of genius, and told her friends that he had skipped a stage in his development: even at age four, she exulted, he was loath to bother with the mundane realities of the world—trees, house pets, suns—and had instead gone straight into symbols.

Except for his stubbornly sealed mouth, which made him appear, even at six, the most exacting, the most unsparing of taskmasters, Kyle looks, in his school photos, like the most ordinary boy in the world—a carbon copy of the ten-year-old Beaver Cleaver. His head was round as an O, his hair was always butch-cut; his eyes were soft, dark ovals; and his skin, which was completely unmarred, seemed, at times, almost translucent. With pride, our mother always noted that his height and weight never exceeded, in either direction, the norm mark on the school nurse's chart. In the fifties, Kyle wore cowboy shirts; during the early sixties, these were replaced by Henley-necked shirts, and then later, after the Vietnam War began, he and his girlfriends made tie-dyed Fruit of the Looms. By the first grade, he was required to wear glasses, which he hated but which my mother said made him look more like a leader, a man of distinction. My father agreed in a way, remarking, as he stroked the boy's shoulders, that the "spectacles" certainly made Kyle look "singular."

When he was very young, it's said that Kyle liked to bounce up and down on the balls of his feet, but, for reasons that weren't then apparent, by the time he entered the first grade, his feet had become firmly planted. As he grew older, he lost his interest in art, even in his little black boxes, and devoted himself instead to things he felt could be brought more to a point. Disliking anything physical, he sought out situations in which he could exercise his skill for dispassionate analysis. Referring to a cornerstone of the Al-Anon philosophy, my mother always said, "Kyle never needed to learn detachment; it was something he always had."

And it was true: teachers adored him, for he was a sober and painstaking student, and they marveled at his ability to offer an answer they were not even sure they were looking for until they heard it fall, somewhat ponderously, from my brother's taut, stern mouth. By high school, he became known as a sort of moral libertarian, defending another's right to speak, even as he disagreed morally, ethically, and politically with what that person was saying. Because he had memorized *Robert's Rules of Order* by the time he was thirteen, he was appointed the first student representative to the Board of Education, whose members felt comfortable turning to him whenever there was a question about who should go first or what document should be read next. He was repeatedly invited to the homes of teachers and guidance counselors, where local journalists and town historians delighted in his ability to articulate both sides of an issue.

Perhaps because it interfered with his thinking, or maybe it was his detachment that was at stake, Kyle stopped reading fiction after he graduated from high school, finding it too fantastical, really awfully specious, he said, to say nothing of misleading. (Recently, he told me, with a troubled and portentous sigh, that his five-year-old son has begun to "escape" by reading stories before bed. "There's a point at which one simply has to accept that one has no influence," he said.) He prefers solid nonfiction, especially the Germans who, he says, cut straight to the bone. I once offered him Sartre's *No Exit*, thinking it might capture his interest, but he said he'd prefer not to waste his time on things that weren't real.

As a teenager, Kyle dated girls who wore sensible shoes, pleated skirts, and strict features. They were some of our community's finest, no-nonsense types who finished their work at Smith and Holyoke and Wellesley, good girls who knew what to praise and when. As he got older, he veered more toward girls who, like Deborah, were adept at wielding a great deal of control over the mundane realities of life, girls who, for example, had been taught to ball the socks, girls who remembered to restock the shelves, girls who knew how to organize a laundry cabinet—girls who, unlike some of their more frivolous confreres, didn't hesitate to soil their hands with the daily dirt of human existence. My brother liked to keep his hands clean, and so he found Deborah, a woman who could whip up a grocery list in no time, shortly after he left for college; they were married two years later.

(Many years later, after it was all over, my brother confided one night over bourbon that he felt he had found something in Deborah which might help him overcome his habitual "evasion of life," a sense of personal aridity of which he felt, at times, only vaguely if disturbingly aware.)

Recently, Kyle questioned whether we were as lucky as my mother would have had us believe, and remembered a time when our father had also told him we were lucky, lucky because he had taught us the evils of drink.

"In a way, the old guy said, his alcoholism really was fortunate for us—a lucky break—because it taught us lessons he was deprived of. I puzzled that one out for days; I wondered if he really did have a point—I suppose from his perspective it probably was true. But from mine, you see, it seemed absolutely mad. And it was then that I realized that were I to tell him that I considered his logic faulty, really, in fact, crazy, I would have had to consciously entertain his craziness for a moment; that is to say, I too would have had to become crazy, at least for a moment, in order to refute his assertion, which I thought was crazy. So as I recall, I said nothing so that I wouldn't go crazy, so that I wouldn't become mad—crazy—like him."

I knew I was lucky the nights I got to stay with my mother's mother in her pink and white apartment with the peonies in the bathroom and the Callard & Bowser butterscotches always within reach in the cut-glass jar on the cherry wood butler's table. My grandmother occupied her pretty pink and white apartment on the other side of town only infrequently. When the Doctor died (they said it was a heart attack, although recently my mother's suggested that it might have been cirrhosis of the liver), my grandmother did three things. First, she retrieved the scarlet Chesterfield from the back of the spare closet, where it had hung since the Doctor had banished it there, four hours after she bought it and ten years before he died; she gave "the help" three months' pay and sent them on their way, and she called her college roommate, Clara Ackermann. Within a week, she and Clara were on a freighter bound for Tahiti; she spent the rest of her life— forty long years—traveling the world over with her dear and closest friend. They went to Lebanon and to Guatemala, to Turkey and Venezuela, to the Netherlands, the Philippines, Taiwan, and Majorca; they went to Israel and to Georgia, to St. Martin and Saudi Arabia, to the Greek islands and to Portugal, but never once did they return to Waukegan, not once did they ever set foot in Illinois again.

When my grandmother returned from her trips, she seemed different and looked somehow depleted, washed out. For a week or so before she left, we were the recipients of a seemingly boundless largesse and received, like little birdies, chocolates and bonbons and kisses which she dropped, from two fingers, into our mouths. But when she returned, it seemed she hadn't anything sweet left to offer; having invested so thoroughly in Clara, her gifts were reduced to the bare minimum demanded by her role as maternal grandmother, and these paltry offerings were doled out, silently, absently, as if we were draining her pockets of the last of her vital accounts.

When I visited her, my grandmother enrolled me in "charm school"; she always reported my grades for attendance, attitude, and skills to my mother when I returned. It was there I was taught to avoid seeing or playing with crumbs on the table, to sit up straight even when I had a stomachache, and never to show my host that I didn't like what she'd cooked. I was an exemplary student: I never lifted my milk glass until I had placed my fork, tines down, at the edge of my plate; I never gobbled my carefully measured portions, those small circles of pressed beef, mashed potatoes, and frozen peas; and I always asked to be excused before I left the table.

I did all this because I loved my grandmother. I loved her not so much because of the sweets in the jar, or the cracked wooden dominoes she kept in a Sunshine biscuit tin specially for me, or the lovely and lurid fairy tales about Chinese ogres and dumplings that she read to me before I went home, but because of something overheard, something I once thought I heard my mother say to my brother, just shortly before I first entered charm school.

"Something terrible once happened to your grandmother and it had to do with a man."

It was at that moment, when I was, say, seven or perhaps eight, well before I could articulate my own distress, that I fell headlong into love with my grandmother, promising to obey even the most objectionable rules of charm school. I cared for and cherished my grandmother as if she were a little girl; in my dreams, I held her in my arms and rocked her to sleep; when I lay next to her in bed, I imagined holding and comforting her, stroking her hair, hoping that my conscientiousness—my love—would not only save her but also serve as an entry ticket into that other part of her, not the socially acceptable part, but the part my mother said she kept secret. I wanted her to tell me about her anger toward men, the anger that made her say, not two weeks after wiping the dirt from the Doctor's grave off her hands, "Once was enough." I wanted to know if she too had nightmares about wolves dressed in top hats and tails, chasing her around her bedroom, and if she, like me, only woke when she felt the hot animal breath on the back of her neck, when she felt it condense into little rivers of moisture that trickled down her back, tickling her as they fell. And I wanted to know how she struggled, how she felt sometimes as if she couldn't even speak, how she felt sometimes as if she were choking, as if her mouth were all full, and she couldn't talk, couldn't scream, even if she wanted to.

Years later, after she died, when I came upon her travel diaries in my mother's basement, I finally thought I had found the stories I sought, but instead I found nothing: no tales of passion or longing, no confessions of dizzying erotic fantasies, no wolves that came after her in the night, just a niggardly recitation of dates and places, spotted, when she got older, with an occasional reference to the indigestion she suffered from the garlic on the escargots in Cannes or from the oil covering the fusilli in Rome. There were no dreams, no secrets, no shameful yearnings, no need to confess to her diary what she couldn't have even told to her god. Instead, the entries were flat, stiff and formal like the portraits of herself that she liked to give out, those artful compositions in which she stood just off center, directing, with her hand, the viewer's attention to the skillful arrangement of Baccarat and Wedgwood, the pink trim of her silk dress carefully pulling the composition together, directing your eye in a circle from the bodice of her dress to the pink daisies of the linen covering the buffet table, around to the pink edge hanging just over the horizon in the Hiroshige prints on the wall behind her, down to the pink velvet bow that adorned the edge of the table lamp, and finally back to her, her lipstick a pretty pale pink that starts your eye around the picture again. Like a Dürer engraving with color, everything in these portraits is perfectly contained; there is nothing excessive, no baroque overtones, no disruption; the hors d'oeuvres, her dress, the china, the prints on the wall—all are superbly managed, enclosed in subtly outlined and independent units, not one touching the other, and yet all form a magnificent composition of beauty and harmony with her at the center, a pillar of pink perfection.

It struck me to the quick the day I read those diaries, stripped me of a protective outer layer, when I realized that there was never anything to hide. Holding those diaries, I felt embarrassed, as if I had imagined a friend poor and then had suddenly discovered that she owned a Rolls-Royce, my mistake making my used Cutlass Supreme seem even more shabby and cheap. Her ordinariness, her lifelong composure, her lack of anything to hide, somehow served to highlight the shoddiness of my own pitiful twenty-year life, making mine seem even more conspicuously vile. It was as if I had suddenly put a huge orange feather in my hat at a recherché angle or had run naked into the middle of Grand Central Station and begun flapping my arms, up and down, to make sure I had gathered everyone's attention, to make sure that no one could remain ignorant of my glaring imperfection, my sordidness, my secret.

I stayed in that basement a long time, hugging myself, afraid to come up, afraid to come out into the light.

PART TWO

Every night, I hear my mother undressing upstairs. I hear her feet go down, hard soft, hard soft, as she hobbles from the bed to the closet and back to the bed. I hear the muffled plop of her furry pink slippers as she drops one, then the other; then I hear the slight scuffing sound as she pushes them next to the snub-nosed Hush Puppies at the side of the bed.

I hear her when she turns out her light. I hear her shift in her sleep. I can hear her as she exhales lavender-colored blossoms into the air, her mouth rounded as if expecting a kiss.

"If you haven't anything nice to say," my mother used to say, her emphasis on the upcoming conjunction, "*don't* say anything at all."

"Don't say anything now, nutmeg; keep your eyes shut."

My father's voice dropped like soft syrup into my ear.

An hour before, I was sitting in the family room, on the chintz-covered couch, knocking magazines and mail-order catalogues, one by one, with my foot, off my mother's old German coffee table. Kyle is bent over some lines of verse at the bridge table, chewing the tips of his fingers as he struggled to memorize the words before his next English class.

It was 1962, a winter evening. My mother had settled her lush body within the deep folds of my father's leather club chair and was darning some socks for him while watching President Kennedy's State of the Union address. Shep was not in the picture.

It had been a very cold day, too cold, my mother had said, even though the frigid temperatures had canceled school, for sledding or playing outside. In the morning, she drew the curtains across all the downstairs windows, and they had stayed that way all day, making me feel as if I, and not the house, had been closed off. I was nearly exploding with pent-up frustration and unable to sleep when I padded around the stairwell and into the family room, the rubber-bottomed soles of my Dr. Dentons striking the polished oak floor with insolent little slaps.

"Mom! I can't sleep."

"What, dear?" she asked absently, as if I had awoken her from a dream.

"I *can't* sleep!"

"Did you try shutting your eyes?"

"Yes."

"That didn't help?"

"No."

"Did you try counting sheep?"

"Yes."

"That didn't help either?"

"It gets boring." I was nine and felt no need to conceal or disguise my petulance.

"Well, sit right there and when this is over, I'll get you some vitamin B," she said, pointing to the couch on the opposite side of the room.

It was not what I wanted—her sweet placebo—but I sat there

46

anyway, tapping the edges of magazines with my felt-covered toes, trying to see just how far I could push them before they actually fell to the floor. I had heard this, it seemed, all my short life: when this is over, when Kennedy is over. "When Kennedy is over, when Kennedy is over," I chanted under my breath as my attention was drawn to Kyle. He had inserted the pointer finger of one hand between his upper and lower front teeth and was chewing on the tip, gnawing on it really, which he continued to do until it bled. Then he moved on to the others, nibbling at them all, tearing off little pieces of flesh until the tips all looked like rough upholstery, sun-faded and damp. It was when I heard my mother say, "That's right," to the TV that I resumed my knocking. I was tapping the magazines more impatiently this time, not really nudging but pushing them when suddenly an entire stack slipped to the floor.

"You stop that right now!" My mother glared at me.

"It just happened! I didn't do it!"

"The one time all year I want to watch TV!" She paused, regaining her breath. "Settle down right this minute and listen to your president or I'll send you right back up those stairs without any vitamin B!" Then, perhaps in response to my foot, which was suspended above another stack of magazines, she demanded, "Kyle, can't you do something with her?"

"Meggie, come into the kitchen. You can help me with my homework."

So I trudged after him, unwillingly, trying, as I walked, to see just how loudly I could make the soles of my pajamas sound against the floor. When I sat down, he placed a glass of milk and two Oreos in front of me as if they were a bribe.

I was staring at his upholstered fingertips when he said, "You have to help me. I have to say this by heart." He pushed the book toward me. "You have to make sure I don't miss any words. You think you can do that?"

I shoved a cookie into my mouth and nodded.

"No, stupid, anybody knows that you can't do it with your mouth full. Hurry up."

I swallowed what was left of my Oreo whole and concentrated on sucking the residual sugar trapped between my teeth as he began:

> "My pulse as yours doth temperately keep time,
> And makes as healthful music. It is not madness
> That I have uttered. Bring me to the test,
> And I the matter will reword, which madness
> Would gambol from. Mother, for love of grace,
> Lay not that flattering unction to your soul,
> That not your trespass but my madness speaks."

"What does it mean?" I asked when I was sure he had finished.

"It's Prince Hamlet; he's the prince of Denmark. He's talking to the queen. That's his mother. Did I make any mistakes?"

"I don't think so," I said timidly.

"Want to hear me do it again?" But before I could answer, our attention was drawn to the front door, which was opening slowly, furtively, as if by a ghost.

And there was our father, his eyes forlorn, looking like a forty-year-old child who had just lost its mother. Seeing him work his way around the newel post, my mother hollered, "Thank God you're here. *You* do something with her!"

Catching sight of me, Shep seemed somehow renewed.

"Little butternutter, what are you doing up so late?"

"She promised to give me vitamin B!"

"Dad, do you want to hear my lines?" Kyle asked, turning his eager face up to our father.

"Not now, son." Smiling at me out of Kyle's sight, he said, "Maybe later. Maybe I'll come back down later." Then, without another word, he turned to me and spoke so urgently I felt my knees quaver, "Come on upstairs, little nutmeg. Come upstairs. Daddy has something better."

After climbing the stairs, Shep tucked the sheets tightly around me, then leaned over me, supporting his weight on his arms. "Don't talk now, little runt. Shut your eyes, chucklehead. That's it. Think of something nice. Think of something like the gypsies."

"The gypsies?" My heart swelled as it always did when my father invoked these mysterious and happy renegades.

"Yes, the gypsies. Shut your eyes and think of the funny gypsies with their tambourines and how the fire smells good and makes your hands feel toasty and warm like a peanut. Keep your eyes shut now. You have to keep your eyes shut if you're going to see the gypsies."

"Daddy?"

"Call me Meko."

"Meko?"

"Yes, little nomad; it's a gypsy name."

"Could we really live with the gypsies?" It was the question I asked eternally.

"Why not?"

"And we could eat hedgehog and rat?"

"Of course."

"And catch chickens all day and never wear shoes and never comb our hair?"

"That's right."

"And we could sleep on the floor?"

"If you wish."

"And we could eat with our fingers?"

"Yes; if you're a gypsy you can," he answered, smiling.

I paused for a moment.

"Have you forgotten, little gypsy, the best thing we do in gypsy land?" Meko asked, loosening his tie and confronting me with a glinting smile that left me feeling especially embarrassed.

"We sleep on the floor, and we eat with our fingers, and the fathers . . ."

"Oh yes! And the fathers dance with the daughters," I said, clapping my hands.

"Yes, and the fathers dance with the daughters." Then, his tone shifting just slightly, "Can you hear the dogs?"

"Yes," I answered, straining to hear the mangy beasts that my father said always surrounded the gypsy camp.

"You know, they're fiercer at night than they are during the day."

"Really?" I don't know if it was Shep's provocative tone or my dread of the dogs that made me more afraid.

"Yes."

"Do they hurt young children?"

"No, not if the children stick with their fathers, that is."

Reassured, but still somewhat frightened, I turned my head and, with one eye, peeked out at the stars. I was fascinated by the constellations and felt somehow less alone when I looked at them, knowing that they were the same stars people saw all over the world, even in China, that unimaginably far-off place which Kyle and I hoped to reach when we went digging in the backyard. And I suppose I imagined that someone in the sky knew, and knew that I had once been innocent. But then, almost before realizing I wanted to speak, I shouted, "Dad! A shooting star!"

"You're not pointing out shooting stars, are you my little Bedouin?"

I squeezed my eyes shut, hoping that the darkness might erase whatever misdeed I had just unwittingly committed.

"Open your eyes, Megan. Look at me. You're not to do that again if you want to be a good gypsy." Then, after a pause during which he gave me a look that made me feel very very sure I wanted to be the very best gypsy I could, he said, "You do want to be a good gypsy, don't you?"

"Yes, Meko. You're going to be one, aren't you?"

"Well then," he said, ignoring my question, "you mustn't call attention to shooting stars. You must never do that. Every time a star falls, that means a gypsy thief is fleeing, and when you point to that star, you make it easier for the authorities to catch him." Then he added, "And telling on a gypsy is the worst kind of betrayal in gypsy land. You know, it's only by stealing that we gypsies survive."

Fearful that I might already have betrayed a gypsy friend, I turned my head to the wall, conscience-stricken, as my father began to form a spit curl with my forelock.

"Dad . . ." I asked finally, contritely.

"Meko."

"Meko?"

"Yes."

"Sleeping on the floor won't hurt your back, will it?"

"Not, of course, if someone with hands as soft as yours was there to rub it in the mornings, little nutmeg."

"Are my hands softer than Mommy's?"

"You could say so. In a way," he added mysteriously.

"I'll be there to rub your back, Meko."

Then, as I felt a wave of sour bar breath waft over my face, burning my nostrils and my eyes, he suddenly shifted direction and asked, "How have I managed so long without you?" After exhaling, he added, "I assure you, my life with your dear mother has not always been, well, as gay as one might have wished."

"Because of her hands?" I asked.

"Not exactly."

"The gypsies and me can make you happy."

"Yes, I think you can. You'll rescue me. You'll be my savior. That's it," he repeated, his voice low and urgent, "you'll save me."

With that, I felt his arms around me. And I remember that at that moment, as I allowed myself to be crammed against his chest, I felt conscious of a sudden rush of responsibility, one with which I was not completely comfortable. At the same time, I experienced a certain secret rapture, believing that I might indeed be the one to save him. My father seemed disturbed in a way I had not seen before, and I realized that he was quaking, and his quaking against me made something within me shudder. I knew neither what we were doing at that moment nor what I had done to provoke this kind of behavior, and I felt embarrassed and trapped, realizing, only semiconsciously, and for the first time, that he needed me for reasons that I, at age nine, could barely imagine. I had turned my face back to the stars and was concentrating on Cassiopeia when Shep, grabbing hold of my chin, declared, "You know, my dear inamorata, my dear Jezebel, you're lethal for me."

"Is that good or bad?" I was trembling, fearing his answer.

He remained silent, stroking my chin.

"Is Mommy that way for you?"

"Not quite, or rather, not quite in the same way."

"Is Kyle?"

"No, dear, boys don't have that power."

"He doesn't need it anyway. He's got all the privileges," I explained smartly, stumbling over my new word.

"What do you mean?"

"His teachers always give him A's and Mom lets him have more cookies than me at snack time." As if this weren't enough, I added, "And he can stay up later than me besides."

"But you don't need A's; besides, cookies are hard on the figure."

"Why don't I need A's? Mommy says everybody does."

"You've got me. I'll be your A," he added cryptically.

It made me giggle to think of Shep as my A. "Will you always love me, Daddy?"

"Forever; providing, of course, that you love me forever, dear chuck."

"I do love you," I cried, throwing my arms around his neck.

With this, he blushed. I wasn't sure if he was about to say something when we both pulled away, suddenly aware of the sound of my mother's lumbering footsteps on the stairs. My father, smiling, quickly put his finger to his lips. "Shhh!" he hissed as the door slowly opened.

"What are the two of you doing in here?" she demanded.

"Just putting your daughter to bed, my dear. As I recall, you were too busy with the boob tube."

"My daughter! You're the real culprit!"

"Pardon me, my dear wife, my helpmate, my, well, shall we say squaw, or perhaps I meant squall, but I do believe it was you who advised against arguing in front of the children. . . ."

I remember, as I watched the two of them sparring that night, framed by the light in the hallway, that I was never more aware of my insignificance in the face of their wars. My mother was easiest for me to see, and I watched as the icy blue of her eyes became even more frosty and cold and the skin on her face, pulled tightly across her cheeks, turned alarmingly pale. Then, after she slammed the door, I remember how my father and I turned back to each other.

I have this dream. It takes place nearly every night when I am a child, less frequently but just as intensely now that I am an adult. I am lying on my bed, stiff as a board, my face pressed into the mattress, my clamped fists tucked tightly under my shoulders, when suddenly I discover a shiny red carrot lying right in the middle of the floor. I am fascinated by the carrot, so much so that I climb down from my great big white bed and tiptoe toward it. I reach for the carrot, but as I do, it jumps one more foot toward the window. After a few more reaches, the carrot comes to rest on the windowsill; it teeters on the edge. I grab for it, but the carrot is too quick. It jumps out the window, I tumble out after it, and fall deeply—irresistibly—into the arms of a thin, hairy man who tickles me with his prickly black whiskers. The thin winking man whisks me into a car. We race to the city dump and drive around in circles, endlessly.

My mother always comes after us. My mother always chases around us in circles. But my mother can never catch up with us; my mother is never fast enough.

Con-ne-ma-ra. Con-ne-ma-ra. Con-ne-ma-ra.

"At least he never touched the college fund." Two weeks after the trial, my mother says, "Thank heavens for that."

Ten years before the scandal broke, my mother says, "What you don't know can't hurt you." Boring reproachfully into my eyes from across our kitchen table, blind, it seems, to the Mallomars I am cramming into my mouth, two and even three at a time, she says, when I get just a few years older, maybe I'll understand; maybe when I'm sixteen or maybe seventeen, I'll understand that ignorance is, for some of us, quite frankly, bliss.

It was, at least in part, my mother's reliance on hackneyed expressions like these that made Shep feel that he'd found the ideal mate. Incisive expressions eluded my mother like phantasms, fairy dust before a dreamer's eyes; words were to her like resistant clay, some intractable stuff that refused to submit to her awkward attempts to make them yield. She much preferred platitudes and clichés, phrases that, as she might have said, were tried and true, expressions that, like a good article of clothing, were preshrunk and ready to wear. These were phrases that had demonstrated, by their frequency of use and universal application, their enduring value; as the sexually retarded individual feels when aping the social skills of a soap opera star, so too did my crippled mother feel when using clichés: they were, for her, proof that she had, in a way, made it. As her marriage continued to falter, her use of clichés increased proportionally: my father, who had once "warmed the cockles of her heart" and had been "the light of her life," became her "cross to bear," and her dreams of a happy life with him but a "will-o'-the-wisp." After it was all over, she regularly reassured herself by remembering, as she brushed away her tears, that "there was no use in crying over spilt milk."

Shep took as much pleasure from this disability as from her physical disability, and was thankful he had married the girl they called Gimpy in college. He liked to put his skills to the test, but never so much that he'd run the risk of embarrassing himself. He grew up the only child in a maze of adult relationships that demanded the early cultivation of a certain physiological and psychological dexterity. "Somehow," he'd muse, "your mother made me feel on top of the world." Then he'd add, stroking my ears or the back of my neck, "My family was . . . different."

It's said that as a boy, my father was spry and cunning with skills in mathematics and accounting. Fear of finding himself less able than he wished made him consider himself somewhat quicker than he was, but this only further endeared him to his teachers. For a short time he fancied himself a shipwright and built lavish, impossible structures with twigs, scraps of carpenter's wood, and nails from his uncles' roofing business. He ended his college days writing bawdy limericks on napkins and the backs of envelopes, and working a brief stint as a blues pianist and then as a sales representative for a board game manufacturer before finding himself a job in the accounting department of Premier Products.

By the time he met his wife-to-be, a charming evasiveness had somewhat replaced the earlier cockiness. Evelyn liked him from the start and appreciated his buffoonery, his interest in her leg (it was really almost solicitous, she thought), and his calculating mind. She was pleased that he was a few years older than she, for she had never got on with men her own age. Shep was an excellent strategist: his ability to psych out and anticipate the moves of others thrilled her, a notoriously imprecise observer, and she felt it right down into her bones when, at the bridge table, he led them to victory. "All I had to do was follow," she'd tell me with pride. So she sat, during their courting years, always on his left, experiencing, at least vicariously, the unaccustomed pleasure of winning. Barely aware of other options that might have been available to her, she agreed to his appeal almost before he had asked.

Once married, they received little financial support from their families—both fathers died young (his, he discovered when the newspaper clipping arrived, died in a car crash outside a now defunct dog track off the Santa Monica freeway)—but my father soon won a position in the advertising department of Premier Products ("Your Old Kipper could sell the Brooklyn Bridge," he'd crow), where his shrewd mind and savvy with numbers earned him a top-ranking position and a commensurate salary. My mother stayed home, of course, having no interest other than ensuring, to the best of her ability, our domestic bliss.

They expected to have a large family: she wanted at least six children, he thought five was right; however, they were unable to conceive for the first six years of their marriage. Then, one morning, having lost hope of ever having a child, Evelyn woke knowing she was pregnant. It wasn't a physical feeling, she once told me, nor was it pride and she wouldn't have called it joy, but something more like relief. When finally a boy came and then, a year and a half later, a girl, it felt, despite their earlier inclinations, quite like enough. Small families, both agreed, surely provided more options for intimacy.

As her mother traveled and his kept to herself, my mother raised my brother and me almost singlehandedly. In fact, we saw my father's mother no more than five times, I think, in my life, and he talked about her and his past even less. I remember only two stories he told of his childhood and only one involved his mother. He had woken, as he tells it, early; he said he knew by the dull gray light streaming into his window that he still had hours before anyone else would get up. As if he were dreaming, he found himself—he says he doesn't know how he got there—standing before his mother's faux alligator bag. He remembers the sound of the click as he opened the clasp; he says he can still smell the rich mingling of skin and scented sachets rising to greet him. He felt dizzy looking at these lipsticks and emery boards, tortoiseshell hair combs and pocket handkerchiefs, loose change and mechanical pencils—all kinds of stuff which seemed to him immeasurably valuable, almost untouchable, simply because they were contained within this private and prohibited space. Then he found it; before he even knew what he was looking for, he had crumpled her monthly bus pass into a tight ball and climbed the stairs where, hidden behind his shut bedroom door, he ripped the pass into pieces and dropped them, one by one, behind the walnut clothes dresser set into a nook in the wall. His mother discovered the pieces, but, he adds, disappointed, only after he had grown and moved out.

When the Old Kipper tells this story, he is embarrassed. He doesn't know why he did this, he says; just to remember it makes him feel ashamed in some vague way.

"That was an odd thing for a kid to do, wasn't it?" he asks. As if he were suffering from some kind of chronic ache, a mild but constant pain that only just then had caught up with him, he crumples over a little and searches my eyes.

"That was a funny thing for a kid to do. Don't you think my little ginger spice, don't you agree, my little nutmeg?"

When I first told my mother that I thought Shep's public crimes—whatever they might have been or however odd they might turn out to be—paled when compared to his private ones, she began to cry. Lifting a copy of *Advertising Age* from the kitchen table, she read, "The alleged collusion between the Premier Products' executive and

Branner began in 1969 and continued until Mr. Arbuthnot was asked to resign in 1978. In exchange for alleged payoffs, Mr. Arbuthnot agreed to purchase spot advertising time solely through Mr. Branner without seeking competitive bids, the suit said. 'We do not yet know exactly how much his actions have cost us,' Dean C. Carter, assistant general counsel at Premier Products said, 'but we do know that it's in the millions. It's somewhere in the millions.' " Then, she snapped, brushing at her tears, "You always did think the world revolved around you."

"Kyle saw kitty cats again," my mother announced to Shep, pulling Kyle closer.

It was a decade and a half before anyone, *Advertising Age* included, began trying to fit together the pieces of my father's professional career. Kyle was perhaps ten; that made me eight and a half or nine.

"They were *tigers!*" Kyle hollered, breaking free of her grasp. His eyes, hard and dark, stared back at her from behind his glasses.

"I saw them! They weren't kitty cats! They were big and yellow and they had big stripes!" he shouted, jamming the stub of his right forefinger into his teeth.

Shep smiled, wan and superior, as I buttered his toast. He had just come into the kitchen from his bedroom and was wearing his army fatigues over khaki pants. He's up for something manly, he's saying with his clothes, up for something tough. We will probably end up at the dump today, shooting BBs into old lightbulbs and tin cans. Each time the bullet hits and we hear the delicate sound of falling glass or the sharp ping of a BB ricocheting off thin metal, Shep will say "Wow." He will say "Wow" and then he will say, distantly, "That was a doozy."

But at that moment he said, "Again, Kyle?"

"Again, Kyle?" I repeated in the toughest, most dismissive tone I could find, as I placed Shep's breakfast before him.

"I saw them. I saw them. I saw them," Kyle chanted as he circled the kitchen table.

"What exactly did you see, Kyle?"

"There were hundreds of them!"

"Kyle—" she said, trying to catch him.

"They were everywhere," he shouted, parading feverishly around the kitchen table.

"Megan doesn't see tigers," my mother chided.

Delighted with this opportunity to gain our mother's affection, I didn't tell her about what I did see in my room at night, but rather, moved to the edge of her chair and, with my hand resting on top of her arm, I said scornfully, "Who would want to see any old tigers on the ceiling, anyway?"

"You don't know anything about anything, Meggie, so why don't you just shut up."

"Scaredy-cat," I shouted, holding on to my mother's arm.

I knew Kyle was probably still angry with me from the night before, when I had inadvertently kicked over a bottle of Johnson's liquid shoe polish upon entering his room without knocking.

"You're so stupid, Megan," he had said as he sopped up the spreading red liquid with a sock he'd found on the floor, "nobody's ever going to marry you!"

"Oh yeah?" I had yelled back. What Kyle didn't know is that when I'm eighteen I'm going to marry Daddy and we're going to have two children, a boy named Shep Junior and a girl, probably named Meggie, and we're going to live like gypsies and have fun and not go to school or anything. And we will live in a place where we don't even have to think about Mommy and we don't even have to think about Kyle and it will be just the two of us, and our tent, and maybe a dog. Daddy says it's our little secret and no one can know. Not even Kyle. Not even my mother.

"Kyle," our mother beseeched, catching him as he rounded her end of the table, "be rational; we count on you to be rational. We're not going to pay attention to you unless you calm down right this minute. Is this the kind of behavior President Kennedy would like to see?"

"I *am* in a rational tone of voice!" Kyle hollered, crossing his small arms over his chest as if hoping to keep his small frame from coming apart.

Holding a slice of toast in the air, Shep said, "You always know when little Miss Beggin' Megan, our very own chucklehead butters the toast . . ." Then, looking right at me, he added, "Not enough grease, not enough lubrication, not enough, if you will, anointment." This was a new game of Shep's, a new trick, to enlist me in my own humiliation, to make me laugh with him at my "defectiveness" whenever I don't do something exactly the way he likes it; and, despite my anger, I remember I did, at that point, laugh nervously, anxious to please, as I began thinking of new ways to regain his affection.

"It's really nothing to worry about, son. We all see things that aren't there once in a while," he said, stroking Kyle's shoulders, looking down kindly.

"You see them, too, Dad?"

"Sometimes . . ."

"Maybe it's just a stage," I shot forth in my most adult tone. "And we'll just have to wait until he grows out of it."

"I will not!" Kyle broke free of my mother and continued march-ing around the kitchen table, clinging to his tigers as if they were something he'd sooner die for than give up.

"Kyle, I'm telling you right now; we are not going to speak to you until you modulate your tone of voice," my mother reiterated, the words superbly enunciated.

"I'm not going to," Kyle yelled, circling the table, circling the benches, bouncing himself off the edge of the counter when he rounds the bend as if to push himself back into orbit.

"Kyle," our mother said, "by the time I count to three."

"What's 'modulate'?" I asked as I opened the refrigerator door. I fanned the door, letting the cool air wash over me, trying to decide whether I wanted a sour pickle or chocolate cake to complete my breakfast.

"Megan, every time you open that refrigerator door, you are costing your father money."

"What are you trying to do?" Shep asked as he caught me at the door, pinning me against the hard steel with his hips as I struggled to wriggle free of his grasp. "Put your dear father, your dear paramour, your little honey bun out on skid row?"

"Let me go!"

"Not till I'm done with you, my pretty!"

"They were there!" Kyle broke in. "And you can't take them away, and they're going to come down some night, and they're going to eat me. They're going to eat all of us," he cried, trying to catch his breath as he fell into my mother's arms.

"Scaredy-cat, scaredy-cat," I sang.

"Megan, not another peep out of you," our mother warned.

"Megan," I repeated snottily, holding on to Shep and delighting in my ability to imitate my mother's impotent voice, "not another peep out of you."

"Mom," Kyle cried. "They're going to eat me."

"Kyle Thomas Arbuthnot," our mother charged, holding him by the back of his pajama collar as if he were some foul thing she had just discovered in the hydrator drawer or the cheese bin.

"You change your tone of voice right this minute, young man, or I'm going to send you over to your father."

"But Mom—"

"No more tears. No more screams."

"But Mom-mmm!"

"But Mom-mmm," I whispered snidely so that only Shep could hear.

"One, two—"

"But Mom," Kyle appealed in a softer, more dulcet tone.

"Kyle, the voice of the censor hath spoken. You must tell your mother what you know," Shep said.

"Tell your mother, Kyle," I echoed, hoping to sound like Shep.

"Mom? Do I have to?"

"Two—"

"OK, OK," he said sadly, surrendering into her arms.

"Tell us what you know."

"I know they were car lights on the ceiling," he said, as if reciting a catechism. "And I promise not to see them ever again. They looked like tigers, but they weren't really tigers. They were really just car lights."

"That's a good boy," our mother cooed, stroking his hair, tracing her finger along the edge of his ear, petting his temples.

"Are you sick?" she asked, holding her palm against his forehead.

With this touch, Kyle began rubbing his back against our mother's rich-smelling breasts and her doughy stomach as he sank into that huge open space of my mother's affection which was reserved for him. His eyes clouded with relief, he looked as though he would have liked to stay there forever, to move without any sense of intrusion or obstacle from one pleasant thought to another, enjoying a quiet and boundless infinity. As his breathing gradually slowed down, I watched as he sank further into her love until finally, they were breathing in unison, together at last.

"I'm sick too!" I announced, breaking free of my father and running to my mother's side.

"OK, ginger spice, my cinnamon buns; that'll cost you."

I grabbed my mother's arm before confronting his grin. "I hate you," I mouthed silently, surprising myself as I turned these new words around in my mouth as if they were stones in need of a polish.

"You're not sick," my mother snapped, interrupting my thoughts and shoving me to the side as if I were a second portion of mousse she couldn't bear to swallow. "It's Kyle who needs the TLC."

"Don't baby him, Evelyn. You're always babying him," Shep shouted as he threw down his toast and got up from the table.

"I'm not babying him," she responded, loosening her grasp.

"You coddle him," Shep repeated, downing the last of his coffee and pulling on his hunting jacket.

"You coddle him, Evelyn," I declared in my most disgusted voice as I moved back to my father's side of the kitchen. "You coddle him."

"He doesn't need babying," my father said, scooping me closer to him with one arm. "You'll turn him into a—uh-hum—a, well, shall we say—no offense to you, my dear pet—a girl."

"Yeah, Mom," I imitated. "You'll turn him into a girl."

"I am not a girl!" Kyle shouted, wrestling free of our mother's arms.

"I think he may have a fever," our mother offered quietly.

"The boy doesn't have a fever, do you, Kyle?"

"I don't have a fever, Mom," Kyle announced, moving toward our father. "Stop babying me."

"You're not sick, are you, Kyle?" Shep said, clapping him so hard on the back that his teeth clacked together.

"Dad, are we going to shoot BBs today?" Kyle pleaded.

"If you get your clothes on right now we are. Hurry up, matey. Your sweet sister and I will be out in the car."

I remember then, just for the briefest second, catching a glimpse of my mother sitting at the opposite end of the kitchen, holding her coffee cup aloft, looking as if she were not sure how it had got there, before I gave way to the pleasant pressure of Shep's grasp and followed him across the lawn and into the car.

In Connemara, my mother and I wear white eyelet dresses. We lie on a bed of imperishable white lilies. She holds a horn in one hand, the moon in the other.

When she says, "It was lonely without you," her voice is sweet and soft. When she whispers, "Come closer; you're too far away," her arms reach out to hold me. When she presses my face into her bosom, she repeats my name, again and again, lingering over each syllable, making them last as if they were sweets too delicious to swallow.

Many years after I stopped shooting BBs with my father, when I was about fifteen and asked my mother why she had dropped out of Michigan six credits short of a degree to marry Shep, she said, her usually impassive eyes coming alive with the brilliance of knowing something for sure, "One didn't go to college in my day for an education, dear; one went for a ring." Then, after correcting the way I was ironing Shep's shirts ("The cuffs and collars first, dear; then the sleeves. You want to do the shoulder panel and body last"), she continued, "When your father asked me, it was like being saved. A girl never wants to be an oddball." She then added, "It's not too smart for a girl to be too smart."

People have said this is all because I live too much in the past, and there are times when I convince myself that it's all been a dream, that none of it was real. I tell myself it was the kind of dream people sometimes have, the kind that you believe for a long time was real, even though you know that none of it actually took place; the kind that's so vivid, so graphic, that you can taste and feel and smell everything in it for years to come. I tell myself: just because it seems real, doesn't mean it was real; just because it seems vivid, doesn't mean it really happened. Some days, in fact, I'm sure it never really happened; everyone tells me it couldn't have happened. I must have made the whole thing up—nobody believes it, so it couldn't possibly be true. What kind of a girl would suggest that her father had done such a thing? It's unheard-of, a scandal. They say they don't know what makes some children act that way; it's hard to imagine how a child could come up with a story like that. They say some things just defy explanation, defy belief. They say we simply have to accept the fact that it's something that we can't, and most likely never will, understand.

They say that and they rub their hands, one over the other, and that's the end of it. It's vanished. Poof. Just like that, into thin air.

. . .

"They screwed me, they really screwed me this time," Shep garbles, chewing his words as if they were pieces of overcooked meat. He has come home unexpectedly, appearing without warning out of the late autumn mist. It is November 1963 and we thought he was in Chicago. Last week he had called from the airport; it was a Mickey Finn at the bar, my mother reported: he got all the way to the airport, but then he had to turn back; he didn't know—had no idea, he'd said—who would have done such a thing. In a rare moment of self-assertion, my mother had slammed down the phone, refusing his lies; but then, perhaps shocked by her own vehemence, or perhaps fearing she had falsely accused him, she called my brother away from his books in the library, called him to help her make sense of the various threads of the story, the innuendos, the tone, the implications. Perhaps he could help her reconstruct from the bits of information known, those only suspected, and those clearly unknown, her trust in my father's dependability and steadfastness. Slowly, my twelve-year-old brother helps her to do so; together they carry the pieces, each equally burdened by their weight, until finally the pyramid is remade, apparently steady, secure.

But tonight, like a monster suddenly reared up from the sea, Shep arrived at the doorstep, his rumpled Burberry tossed artlessly across his shoulders, his shoes crusted with salt from icy roads, twenty-four hours before he was due to arrive. He has no explanation for this. He is shabby and cold-looking, shaking when he rings the bell. After quickly scanning the paper in vain for a public meeting to attend, my mother reluctantly forms another hamburger patty from the meat in the bowl.

When Shep returns from business trips, we usually hear about the mistreatment he suffers at work from his lapsed and loose-moraled colleagues or about the way blackhearted airline officials miscalculate his fare ten dollars in their favor or about the way dissolute TV

moguls try to bribe him with Audis, with beachfront apartments, with
box seats at Yankee Stadium—all stories in which Shep maintains
his innocence in the face of a devilish world bent on tempting him,
stories that win my praise for his good work, his sheer willpower when
confronted by such desirable and glittering lodestones. Shep can do
no wrong, he is saying with these stories, Shep is innocent; Shep
deserves congratulations for his sheer fortitude, his moral fiber, his
courage in resisting temptations to which other men, being mere
mortals, would certainly succumb.

We also hear about stretch limousines and obsequious servants,
the huge diamonds on VIP fingers, the Peabody Hotel's steam bath
and the Turkish towels in the deluxe suite; we hear tales of extrava-
gant and opulent things—fourteen-course meals, car bars, and ruby-
studded money clips.

"Every morning at six," he'd told us the month before, "they roll
out the red carpet and twelve brown ducks waddle from the elevator
into the fountain in the middle of the lobby. At five-thirty, back they
march, across the red carpet and up into the penthouse suite."

And we hear especially about money, dollars, figures and costs,
accounts and dispersals, money of all kinds, money that could
buy everything imaginable—time, space, cars, women, even personal grandeur, your own sense of emotional and psychological afflu-
ence.

Today, however, perhaps because Shep hasn't any stories to tell,
he reaches for the bourbon as my mother flips the hamburgers. We
watch him, silently trying to decipher signs we are as yet unsure of:
the day-old beard, the dark puffy rings under his eyes, the way he tries
to muffle the sound of the liquor falling into the tumbler by cupping
his free hand over the mouth of the glass. Then, after placing the
tumbler on the floor, out of our sight but next to his chair, he takes his
place at the head of the table, crossing his left forearm in front of his
dinner plate, supporting his entire weight on his arm as if he were so
exhausted he barely had the energy to carry his food to his mouth and

swallow. (Only when he begins what we imagined to be his final
descent, will I, compelled by my sorrow and especially my guilt,
spoonfeed him while he will refuse the food until I have first chewed
it.) "Woe is life, woe is me," Shep is saying with his stooped shoulders, his sighs, his groans. Of course, I felt nothing but sorrow for him
at those moments, and not a small degree of anxiety: I was then ten
and the thought of living alone with my mother and brother so
terrified me that I would have done anything to keep him alive. When
finally we had all convened at the table, Kyle asked meekly and with
sympathy why he had come home.

Something about this question tickles my father. Perhaps in this
feeble gesture toward intimacy Shep perceives a threat, or even a
humiliating reproof. Regardless of the reason, it launches one of the
most dazzling displays of verbal pyrotechnics I've ever seen, a display
we later became habituated to. We are carried into a labyrinth of
bizarre and meaningless details, inventions and forgeries, dissem-
blings and confabulations. It is an expert con—double entendres,
scatological puns, malapropisms, and jokes—the sheer, playful cor-
ruption of language makes me woozy as I struggle to follow this rush of
words looping in and out, twirling like acrobats before our eyes,
swinging their arms and running in circles. Years later, as an art
history student, it occurred to me that Shep was, at those moments,
not unlike a Victorian villa, the kind you might see in any one of a
dozen candy-coated seaside resorts: full of corridors, porticoes, arch-
ways, niches, verandas, half-landings, balconies, balustrades, hidden
closets, anterooms, dumbwaiters, and parlors—all of these features
combining to entice and, at the same time, confuse any curious
intruder. Yet, there is my brother, his black eyes like small seeds
growing dim with concentration, receding farther behind his wire-
rimmed glasses as he struggles to keep up with our father, if only for a
second.

When finally Shep's head falls forward, my brother no closer to
the answer he sought, we are jolted from our fascination by the sound

of my mother's chair scraping across the lineoleum as she gets up to leave the room.

John F. Kennedy, she says, is giving a speech.

Later, as if defending herself against some unspecified crime, my mother would say, "You were the only one who could get along with him at those moments." And Shep and I did get along, I suppose, as I directed him, my small hand in his, up the stairs and around the hall corner, into his bedroom. The room was square, but the flamboyant polyester spread and curtains made the room seem to reel. There were reds and oranges and contrasting blues and purples, big colors, loud colors that my father loved, colors that made the room look, my mother once said, as if someone had thrown up in it. On the walls, pictures of himself and testimonies to his success: his B.A. from Michigan dated 1944, the photo of him and Ann Landers at a reception given eight years before, a thank-you letter from a man he had once helped retrieve his hat. Over the desk hung, framed, a copy of the Gilbey's ad he had accidentally appeared in. And there was the picture from *Advertising Age* taken when he'd accepted an award for ten years of loyal service, and another in which he is sitting to the left of some marketing honcho at a publicity dinner. And there was the newspaper clipping, slightly faded and yellow, announcing the last victory of his "grandfather," the famous blind chess champion, a man whom he had never met, a winner to whom, his mother once suggested, he was related. And later, as he began to disintegrate, he added, next to a cheap heraldic sign suggesting a bogus British ancestry, pictures of me, pictures taken everywhere, on every occasion: in a snowstorm at three, dressed at age five as a gypsy for Halloween, eating clams for the first time at age nine, hiding from his camera at age fourteen, my hand extended from the tub to cover the camera's prying eye at sixteen, my middle finger raised in contempt at eighteen, and me in my maidenly white gown, feeling momentarily

triumphant at age twenty-one, graduating from Vassar, my arms outspread like a defiant exhibitionist's. And there were clocks everywhere, clocks that he'd bought, clocks he'd been awarded, clocks he'd
found in the dump, brass clocks, rusted clocks, clocks in the shape of
ships, Cartier clocks and Timex clocks, all sorts of clocks that ticked
away the time in chorus, like the detonator on a time bomb.

And there, in that spectacular, garish room, as if he were a child I
would sit him down on the edge of the bed. Still excited by his own
verbal dance, an occasional demon still flying from his mouth, he
would tremble as I stroked his sweat-soaked Brylcreemed hair until he
quieted. Then I would unlace and remove his shoes, strip off his
socks, loosen his tie, and begin to unbutton his shirt, slowly, my
fingers faltering a little over the starched placket. As if on command,
he would then stand, and I'd reach into his pockets, removing car
keys and cuff links, collar stays and paper clips, fountain-pen tops and
pennies which he always said I could keep. Then he'd ask—
laughing—it was always the wrong kind of laughter, a different kind
of laughter, hard to describe—if I wouldn't reach in again and see if
there wasn't anything else that I wanted. He'd give me a look that left
me silent and embarrassed and he'd ask me to reach in again. He'd
wink and smile at me like the Cheshire Cat, and here I lose sight of
the memory. Like when the film tears in the middle, the screen
suddenly goes blank.

In Connemara, I never do anything that displeases her. In Connemara, I know that we will never live apart.

"Cunning? No, I can't say that I ever thought of Shep as cunning,"
Kyle says, smiling.

It was 1980, a dark night, neither clear nor cloudy. I had agreed
to join Kyle on his balcony overlooking the Pacific for a few double

bourbons, a ritual he has become accustomed to, without admitting it, in order to ensure a sound sleep. Earlier that day, Kyle, who was then twenty-eight, had confided that he had been working to develop a reasonable as well as a philosophically and morally acceptable way of understanding our father. It plagues him to think that we must act, that we have no choice but to act within the radical uncertainty of our knowledge about Shep's behavior.

But now he falls silent, apparently unable, for the moment, to find within his elaborate systems of logic and order a way of coming to terms with this seemingly systemless man who, if found guilty as charged, may be sent to prison within a very short time. Deborah, who is putting Aaron to bed, has encouraged him to clear his aura so that he might make his body more receptive to the vibrations necessary for healing, necessary, she says, to facilitate his movement onto the next chapter of life. Watching him return from the kitchen with one glass filled almost to the brim, the ice clinking seductively, I can't help wondering if he doesn't consider bourbon the most effective stimulant, the most powerful and certainly the most expeditious way of lubricating the passageways, irrigating the arteries of health.

"But I'll tell you what I do think—what I sometimes think . . ." He pauses, coloring. "Well, it's like a fantasy or a dream. Sometimes I have it when I'm awake, sometimes when I'm asleep. I'm walking along a dark street, and suddenly, down an alley or a side street, I see my father, my real father, the father we've never met, the one who is to replace this stand-in, this poor imitation we've dealt with all these years. He is standing there waiting for us. For me."

Dropping back down into his new leather club chair, almost an exact reproduction of our father's, he seems unsure whether or not to continue. Then, after a long swallow, he turns his head away from me, looks out over the Pacific, and says, "Sometimes I think it's just that I haven't looked hard enough, that I haven't done enough. If I could just figure out the one thing that I'm supposed to do that I haven't done, the one thing he wants from me, then I could find him there, at the end of that alley, his arms outspread, opened out, to me."

On November 22, 1963, Mrs. Günsel, a stolid matron of herculean proportions who might have found a more congenial arena for the exercise of her natural endowments in a South American prison camp than in the fifth grade of Wilson Elementary School, let her charges go two minutes before the bell. This was an unheard-of transgression. But by the time I reached my bicycle, I knew why the principal had called her from the room: President Kennedy was dead.

President Kennedy was dead! I was deliriously happy. I jumped and twirled, hardly able to control my trembling fingers as I fumbled to unlock my blue Raleigh and point it in the direction of home. I wasn't even out of the parking lot when I raised my hands and, waving my fists, shouted, "Yeah! Kennedy is dead!"

I raced home, riding dangerously fast down Beekman Place, jumping over potholes as if my bike were Pegasus. The wind, tearing at my skin, pulled at my clothes; as I got closer, thistles and thorns scratched at my face, but they did not hurt; there was no blood. I was riding too fast, yet as long as I kept her in my sight, I felt utterly, absolutely protected.

As I turned the corner of Country Club Drive from Passaic, I see her even though we were still some miles apart: she is standing at the doorway, wearing lavender and white gingham. The house is surrounded by hills, hills so green and so soft they look like giant velvet cushions. In one hand, she holds a horn; in the other, the moon.

When I arrive, I know my mother will hold me; barely able to contain her joy, she will rub tears from her eyes, and then she will smooth my hair with her hands, again and again, trying to make herself believe that I am actually there, secure in her arms. She will wonder where I have been and why it took me so long to get home; don't I know, she will ask, how precious I am to her and how hard it is to live without me, even for a few hours? Then she will lead me inside—it will be just the two of us, just her and me—and she will feed me: sweet raisin bread with lots of butter, hot tea, and oranges for dessert.

I dropped my bike at the door, careened around the newel post, and leaped into the kitchen, my arms outspread, hollering "Mom!" as if her name were a trophy, something I had just won.

"Mom-mmm!"

But she was not there. I shot into the living room, through to the family room, into the back porch, but she was not there either. I raced back through the kitchen and on up the stairs from the green and brown hallway; I bounded up the steps two at a time, my short legs just making the jump. I was almost to the top, just four more steps to go, when suddenly I stopped.

There was a long, low cry, horrible and plaintive, like the sound a dog makes when it is locked in the dark. On tiptoe, I turned at the landing.

And there she was, at the top of the stairs, sitting on the toilet in the bathroom, holding her head in her hands as if it had just come off and she was trying to screw it back on. Her lips were open, even though no words came out. And her eyes were puffed up, and her nose and cheeks were covered with red splotches, making it look like her skin had turned inside out.

Never during the entire course of my unsuccessful attempts with her had I had to take such a stare. Curling her lips, shaking her hideous head, she snarled, "Stop looking at me as if the world had just collapsed." Stop gawking at me as if this were the end of the world, she said, rolling her eyes back in their sockets.

I flipped the TV dials again and again, frustrated because I couldn't find anything good on. JFK was on all last night and then again all this morning. We have been kept home from school to honor this dead man; I kept turning the dials, but I couldn't get rid of him.

Last night, my mother emerged from the bathroom only long enough to throw some TV dinners into the oven; then she returned to her room. When Shep arrived, Kyle muttered sullenly, "Mom's not coming down."

"Not coming down? Dinner without Mom? It's like God without apple pie, stars without stripes, you without me," he said, seizing my hands and swinging me in circles again and again. "There's only one thing to do, then: I'll be your mother." He then tossed the frozen dinners into the garbage and prepared our favorite supper, what he called an Irish banquet: peanut butter on Silver Cup with salt, ginger-ale-and-milk spritzers, and Rice Krispies and chocolate ice cream for dessert. It was delicious.

But this morning, the Old Kipper was gone and JFK had taken his place. My mother remained in her room most of the morning, unable to pull herself away from the jigsaw puzzle showing four different views of covered bridges in New England.

I turned the dials again, but there he was, even dead, still taking up everybody's attention. Desperate to find some distraction, I turned to our public broadcasting station, thinking that it, at least, wouldn't show him, but, of course, there he was with the whole family: Jackie and Caroline and John-John, crisp and clean, sharp as yacht sails in the midday sun. Despite the man's death, they were still one big happy family, exuding for all the world to see their extraordinary harmony and grace, exempt, even in grief, from the banal cruelty, the mundane miseries of ordinary life.

It was when I saw Jackie take Caroline's hand that I kicked the TV as hard as I could, smashing Jackie's impassive face. I kicked again, furiously trying to knock that celestial grace from her face, wanting to kill her for her self-control, her composure. At that moment, I was sure I had never hated anything as much as I hated that family, that celebrated reminder of the monstrousness of my own family. I kicked her face again, harder and harder until finally, I saw it smashed to bits, that ease and grace now a smear of brain matter and blood. I then turned to Caroline, banging her with my fists, pounding that pert freckled face until it was unrecognizable, a mass of splintered matter where once a girl had been. I kicked the TV again, hard enough that I hurt my foot and the dial selector cracked. "I hate you! I hate you! I hate all of you!" I screamed, as I pounded Jackie, pounded John-John and Caroline, pounded until I suddenly felt something seize my shoulder.

I turned my head and my mother squeezed tighter. My brother, his eyes glowing, stood beside her.

"What's wrong with you? What's gotten into you?"

"You only care about him!" And then, I got what I'd longed for: I pulled her hand from my shoulder and sank my fully formed adult front teeth into the deep, firm flesh at the heart of her palm.

With her free hand she slapped me on the ear and pushed me to the floor. Staunching the blood with the edge of her nightie, she sent me to my room; my brother was employed to escort me.

I was not permitted dinner that night because of all the damage I'd done.

I would like to bury that resourceless little girl, disconnect myself from that angry child who could not cope, that thin-skinned girl who stood night after night at the big bay window looking out expectantly into the driveway, pressed against the window ledge in her red and pink poodle dress and black patent leather Mary Janes. I would like to make it so that that little girl had never been, I'd like to start all over again, to make it seem as if it happened to someone else, someone I've never even heard of, to make it so that all I have to do to make the whole thing disappear is to open my eyes and then watch it fade away; like a dissolve in a movie, it will erase itself, leaving hardly a trace, not even a memory behind.

Upon leaving the dump late one Saturday, Shep, referring to some errand my mother wanted us to complete, remarked suddenly, "No, let's not do that—let's do something else." Once settled in beside him, I asked where we were going, to which he replied, "You'll see." I waited and wondered as I saw first the leaves and the trees disappear, and then the pretty steel cables draped like long necklaces from the top of the bridge, but it wasn't until we drew up at a towering steel and glass structure in the dark heart of the city that I clutched his arm and broke out, "Your office?"

Within seconds we were there. With a quick jab at a button, my father's plush office came into view and I gave out a short little cry. Amid the tropical plants, banks of TVs, and leather club chairs was an enormous brown figure stretched out on top of his desk.

She stood and I saw that she was nearly as tall as my father.

"Of all the wickedness!" she exclaimed, holding me steady with her heavy black stare.

She was magnificent. Her bosom, which rose as she spoke, lay partially concealed beneath a wealth of trinkets, that had produced a soft tinkling sound when she stood. Her dark hair and skin, the purple and gold she was swathed in, the dazzling jewels that glinted in my father's overhead light made me think of *The Arabian Nights*, and I imagined her spending her days on a divan, surrounded by leopards and llamas while sucking sugar from dried apricots or figs laid on her tongue by bare-chested boys with gold rings in their ears. Her burnished hair, the spectacular coral of her lips—her gorgeous, violent splendor—astonished me, and I gripped my father's fingers with both hands. She was one of those women my mother would later identify as one of my father's "floozies," but at that moment, I considered her by far the most shining presence I had ever shared space or time with, and I took silent pride in my father's knowing someone so grand. Something in her pageantry, her resplendent sumptuousness, made up for something fallen in my father, some slight tawdriness of which I was becoming only slightly aware.

"My dear butternut"—Shep smiled showing deep dimples— "meet my clerk, my scribe, my amanuensis, the recorder of all my misdeeds, the accountant of my wrongdoing, the scorekeeper and stonecutter, my chronicler and secretary, the Princess—uh-hum— Cecilia, also known in these parts as the Lady Roundbottom. Lady Roundbottom, my sweet petite, my daughter, my angel, my cinnamon bun."

"Have you no shame?" she brought out, adjusting a gold sash around her firm hips.

I was struck by her dramatic intonation, the sound of glass that emanated from her chest as she spoke, the way she stood there, so broadly, her hands on her hips, facing my father full front.

"Is she a real princess?" I whispered, curling in closer to Shep.

"Sure she is, butternut. In fact, she's as real as they get, in Alabama."

"Why, she is just a real little goddess, isn't she?" she asked, laughing as she negotiated, unsteadily, the deep-pile carpet with her gold and white pumps. She then practically swooped toward me, calling to mind an osprey I once saw at the dump, its flight so urgent I wasn't sure its intention was to feed or to kill. Her trinkets reached me first and clattered against my forehead; then she lay a thick, sticky kiss on the top of my head. I admired her firm bosom and was feeling warmed by the heavy, hot heat of her when she rose and announced, "Well, I, at least, think you're lovely."

"Well, whoever said that she wasn't?" Shep lowered his lips to her ear and draped his arm around her wide butt. They stood there, enmeshed for a brief moment until, pushing him back, the Princess cried out, "You ought to be ashamed!" Turning to me, holding me by my shoulders, she added, "If ever he ever says anything like that to you, why, we'll both have to go live like the nuns."

At that, Shep's face seemed to jump. "That would put things together for you!"

Casting her head back so that we could see her beautiful dark neck, she met him on the same note. "I should have been born Catholic!"

"That would only give you a motive," he chided, flashing all of his beautiful white teeth.

"One, at least, ought to offer *you* a motive. If I were any better, I would have already worked one out for you."

"A motive?"

"You, of all people, ought not to be without one. Think what you stand to lose."

"Oh, that?" Shep laughed.

Affectionately bending over me, she drew her tongue along the length of her lips. "Your father is a vast liar, you know. But what can you expect from his rotten-to-the-core sex, and it is a rotten little sex, don't you think?"

"No reason butternutter here might not act as our chaperone," Shep mysteriously threw in, pulling me to him. "Don't you think you'd make just the perfect accessory?" he asked, tossing me back toward the Princess.

I felt my cheeks color. "Yes, of course I would," I replied, burning with the desire to show how little was lost on me.

"It would be nice, really, if only we did have a little monkey like this to help us out here," she responded, flinging me back over to Shep.

Smiling, Shep pitched me back. "Oh yes, she'd be a great help to us here."

"Indeed she would. She could help us get on." With that, she sent me flying once again to my father, whom I noticed exchanging a quick, strange look with the Princess.

Flurried by my own high emotions, I didn't pause to question but rather called out, "I'm a very good helper." I laughed in a way that made me think I had pursued the subject with an agreeable rejoinder.

"Don't you think, though, she's a little small?" the Princess continued.

"One can't help what one's got."

"Well then, you can help us get on," she cried, pulling me toward her and hugging me furiously. "Providing, that is, her mother doesn't drop in."

"Oh no." Shep laughed, pulling me back. "Not for anything would *she* find herself here. She has her son, you know."

"Well then, she's mine."

"No, she's mine."

"Mine," she retorted, gaily pulling me down beside her onto the couch.

I felt confused and, for some time after, conscious of a vagueness that felt slightly embarrassing when I thought of their game of monkey-in-the-middle that day. I was pleased, if somewhat bewildered, at being the cause of so much raucous amusement, but the impression of their exchanged glances remained, confronting me with notions about my father's behavior of which I was growing increasingly curious. But my reflections were cut short when the Princess, making a corrective adjustment of my bangs, confided, "Your papa has been so kind to me; he'll talk to me all day long about you."

"Won't I just now?"

Emboldened by my father's jovial tone, I asked, "Could the Princess ever come visit us?"

"No," Shep said kindly, stroking my hair, "it's not the same for her to visit us there. But we can always visit her here, as we're doing today."

I thought for a moment, nodding, while wondering where the difference might lie, when a small slouching man with overhung eyebrows and a damp rosy mouth appeared at the door.

"Mon dieu!" He clapped his hands. "Isn't this a treat," he shouted, making his way toward us. "How do you do, miss?" He adjusted his tie and smoothed his hair with his palms while winking at Shep. The office was further heated by his presence, by the sense of overflowing cheer that was, I thought, a sign of happy maturity explicitly associated with adults and which I felt privileged to be a part of.

"The guard said you were in, but I had to see for myself. He's always talking about you, but I couldn't take such a mythical creature on trust." Planting a wet kiss on my lips, he remarked, "You're just what one would expect."

"I tell everyone about you," Shep said, turning to me ingratiatingly.

"He absolutely bores us with you, darling; he bores everyone," the Princess announced, playfully nudging Shep on the shoulder.

"You're a charming one, just like he says, ain't she Celie?"

"Charming," she said, her voice going down, making me wonder if there wasn't something besides my smallness that was, after all, deficient in some way.

"Charming," my father agreed as he clapped the small man on the back and turned toward the door. The next minute the Princess and I, heaped on the couch and looking curiously at each other, were shut in the office by ourselves.

"It's criminal," she said finally, nodding toward the door, "the things your father gets away with."

"Criminal?"

"That's what I said." She lifted the glass she had left on Shep's desk. "Don't get me wrong; he's all right in his way," she continued, lighting a cigarette and drawing the smoke deep into her lungs.

"Do you like him as much as my mother?"

"Your mother?" she shrieked. "From what I've heard about her, she's beyond even a joke."

I failed to understand this response, but wanting to meet her on the same plane, I offered, "They have their quarrels."

"Oh, one would expect so," she said, rising and refilling her glass from a bottle concealed in the case behind Shep's desk.

"Why?"

"Are they quite fearful?" she asked, ignoring my question.

"Atrocious," I offered, hoping to impress her with the word Shep had just taught me when he'd described the diabolical wickedness with which my mother prepared stew.

"Well, for one thing, she doesn't get paid," she said, turning her lovely chin to the ceiling and blowing a soft ring into the air.

"Yes, I know."

Smiling prettily, she then said, "Perhaps you'll understand—

when you get older—how terribly bold a young lady has to be to do the little things that I've done."

I looked directly into her eyes, hoping, by meeting her straight on, to impress her with the extent of my understanding.

"Good thing for me your father appreciates it. He appreciates it enormously. Even though, he does say I'm horribly expensive." Throwing back the rest of her drink, she asked coyly, "Does he say the same thing about you?"

She looked so pretty with her head turned down to me, her round chin almost touching the tops of her plump breasts, her eyes glistening with some moisture I perhaps mistook for love, that I thought I might lose myself in her gaze, before she confided, bringing me back, "You know, I'm saving your father."

With this, I felt the full, hot rush of an emotion more mature than I had ever experienced flood over me.

"From misery," she continued, resting her hand on mine. "He leans on me."

I colored, remembering Shep's promise that I'd be the one who would save him.

Undaunted by my red cheeks, she gave a small sigh. "You'd never be able to guess the rest." She took her mirror out and was adjusting her trinkets when Shep, flushed but not excited, reentered the room. He glanced at us both and then crossed toward his desk; it occurred to me that he wished not to be looked at.

"I was just telling your daughter, your sweet little thing here, about your ideas," she said, pushing her lips out as she drew an orange lipstick across them.

"Oh, I'm in for it now!" he responded, laughing at the same time he averted his eyes from my stare.

"You've been in it, you scoundrel!" The princess laughed, spitting out the accusation along with some of her drink.

"Oh, my dear daughter! Profanity before the virgin," he chuckled, sweeping me toward him, his hands covering my ears.

And then we were out, down the cool corridors, past the mottled plastic of cubicle walls, and into the elevator, before I even had a chance to question him. I watched the numbers descend and then raised my still hot cheeks to his face. "She says you lean on her," I began, gulping back emotions I didn't have words for.

"Oh!" he barked, throwing his face upward. "Is that what she says?"

"She said it was your idea." I felt my eyes fill with tears. "She says that she's the one who saves you."

"Well, of course she does, my dear little donkey." He grabbed my shoulders with his hands and then asked, perhaps more warningly than he had ever asked anything, "What is there for me to do when you're not here but to just love her?"

He appeared to watch for a minute the effect of his emphasis before holding me out, he added in an even more ominous tone, "You must be nice to me now, nutmeg, nicer than you've ever been. Wipe away the tears." Bearing down on me as if threatening me with a spanking, he held firm. "Remember, little nutmeg, certain things little ladies keep under their hats."

Something about the way he said that gave me my first small glimpse of something that I hadn't known to expect from him. I looked straight into his eyes, hoping to find something that might relieve my sense of his possible inconstancy and, as important, my nascent awareness that for perhaps the first time I was fully aware, my father had dodged me.

Recklessly passing one car, then quickly dodging another, Kyle, tilting back his head, threw off a laugh. We were driving across the invisible black ice that made the highway along the Columbia River Gorge a patchwork of danger, and Kyle, who seemed in an odd way titillated by the perilousness of our situation, stepped on the gas.

"He's one of those guys who think they can get by on a smile and a shoestring, like some poor sales rep who believes there's a continent waiting for him, just outside his front doorstep. Isn't that what Willy Loman says, Meggie? You're the literary person; that's something you should know. Isn't that what Willy says?" But then, before I could reply, he slapped his hand against the steering wheel as if he had just heard a good joke.

"You know what he's like? He's like one of those guys who believe that everybody—even a skinny little shit like him—has a greatness in him. Isn't that rich, Meg?" Pressing on the horn and laughing, he whipped us around a truck that had swerved into our lane. With tears leaking slowly from beneath the rims of his glasses, he laughed again. "Don't you find that unbelievably rich?"

My mother, through clenched teeth, says she doesn't see what's in the least bit amusing. It is about 1965 or '66 and we are on our way to Cape Cod, about halfway into Connecticut, and just a minute before my father's last crack, she announced that she wanted to go back and check the burners.

It is a day like all the others when we've gone to Cape Cod: high sun, stifling humidity, close air, traffic jams. We, as well as half our kitchen appliances, a suitcase full of Kyle's books, three boxes of beach towels and rubber rafts, two weeks' worth of pedal pushers and tennis shorts, and the rudder for my father's Sunfish, which is strapped to the roof of the car, are crammed like sardines into Shep's black and yellow Chrysler New Yorker, which, eight years after he bought it, still looks shiny and brand-new.

Earlier this morning, while my mother stood before the stove, her hands on her hips as if defying the shut-off burners to turn themselves on, and my father sang witty, if somewhat off-color, sailor chanteys as he secured his boat to the car, Kyle and I sat shoulder to shoulder on the porch, forming a small parapet between them. In response to my question about the sheaf of papers next to him, Kyle looked away from our father, who, tucking a small flask into his back pocket, had declined Kyle's offer of help. He explained that he had enrolled in Numen Mind Control classes, an extracurricular summer course designed to help students develop a systematic approach to self-control. It was guaranteed to dispel anger, manage hostility, and, most important, he read from the brochure, "banish confusion and ambivalence."

"It's supposed to put you in touch with a higher intelligence," he explained.

"Higher than what?" I asked, genuinely confused at the thought of any intelligence being higher than my brother's.

"Don't ask stupid questions, Meg."

Kyle said that the program gave him a scientific way of knowing and expressing his feelings; it's "mathematically correct," he announced, showing me the chart and guides that enabled him to take objective measurements of his daily emotional fluctuations. The more even the line, Kyle explained, nervously folding and refolding the edge of the paper, the better off he was. He then offered me his nearly straight graph from last week as proof of his increasing skill. He practices two hours a day, alone in his room, inhaling his thoughts, disciplining them into strict submission with his newly standardized desires, before exhaling them in carefully measured and clearly articulated phrases.

But now, in the car, Kyle is silent. Shortly after we began our trip, Kyle inserted the middle finger of his left hand into his mouth. He is chewing on the tip now; as is his habit, his teeth make their moves rapidly around the edge of the nail. He stops only when Shep asks, looking first at him and then at my mother's hand stroking his knee, if Kyle has the foggiest notion of how to spell "minion."

I am practicing curling one finger over the other, the middle over the pointer, the fourth over the middle, the pinkie over the fourth, so that when I'm done, I look like I've got claws instead of two hands. My father doesn't seem to mind at all what I'm doing.

The rule, announced with demonic zeal at the beginning of each jaunt to the Cape, is that whoever drives gets to pick the station. Shep and I, knowing that my mother and brother loathe country music, have found the only nonstop country station our side of the Mason-Dixon line, and we are singing, crowing really, along with Roger Williams: "Trailer for sail or rent, / Rooms to let fifty cents, . . . I'm a man of means by no means, / King of the road," while my mother, stripping off first her windbreaker and then her sweater, asks why anyone didn't tell her it was going to be 110 degrees and humid. My brother, sitting in the back with my mother, has his chewed-off fingers in his ears when my mother suddenly says we have to turn back. Leaning her head against the window with such force that it seemed she might actually break through, she says she's not sure, but she can't remember clearly whether or not she actually turned off the burners. She's almost positive, but she's not completely sure; so, she says, she would really like it if we could just turn around and go back—it won't take more than a minute. Perhaps catching both the smirk and the wink Shep tosses me across the front seat, she says, stonily, she just wants to make sure that we still have a house there, when we get back.

Perhaps it was during one of those endless, sweltering days at Cape Cod that my father told me the second story he says he remembers from his childhood—the one that doesn't have to do with his mother. It's a story about how he learned to swim. He was dangled, he explained, by his uncle, his mother's brother, Rip, who stood reeling at the edge of a pier in Atlantic City, held by his back belt loop over the sea for a few minutes while everyone on the shore—Polonius and Ali and Edith and Rory and Tootie and James III—watched. They watched while my father begged his uncle to let him go, till his uncle finally said, "Sink or swim," till he was dropped from a height of ten feet into the darkness, into a space so deep he didn't think he'd ever come up.

I remember my father, the Old Kipper, shrugging his shoulders as he told that story, then brushing one hand over the other, as if he were trying to get rid of some dirt.

As if about to speak, he then cleared his throat.

It was my mother who taught my brother to swim at Cape Cod, after he had been stricken with polio. My mother had never been allowed to admit her polio: admission of disease in the Doctor's family was considered not only a defeat, but an intolerable embarrassment as well; hence, the mandate to return the orthopedic shoe my grandmother had purchased once they were sure my mother would regain at least partial use of her legs. Instead, my grandfather trained her to walk without aid, one foot flat on the ground, the other up on its toe, as if she were a ballerina about to pirouette, *Achtung*.

My brother's case was not nearly as severe and never crippled him the way it had my mother, but throughout my childhood my mother reminded us of what she called "the curse of the blood," finding in this bogus attribution a number of gratifying benefits. It could, for example, allow her to comfortably and publicly expiate "sins" for which no one could justifiably blame her, hoping, it seemed, that this assumption of genetic responsibility might engender our respect, if only for what she considered her failure. And she carried her "burden" with Teutonic flair, back straight, nostrils arced, cooing to and coddling my brother, caressing his diseased limbs long after it was necessary, apparently hoping to call attention not only to her undying and superhuman maternal efforts but to her own needs as well.

But most important, this "curse" allowed her to lay claim, in some smothering way, to my brother's achievements. When my brother succeeded, my mother felt it straight down into her bones; it was as if the deadly microbes they had both suffered were, to a degree, a measure of some microscopic interconnectedness. She rewarded his early achievements with special attention and small favors: kisses for walking, swimming lessons for A's, cupcakes and sweetmeats for academic honors and awards, allowing herself, as he grew, to move with him, at least in fantasy, into a world that had always tantalized, at the same time it had prohibited her entry. And so she pushed my brother and soothed my brother—with a vengeance—making him kick, kick, kick as if his life depended on it, acting at times as if her own life depended on his ability to remain afloat.

Shortly after my mother taught Kyle to swim, he began sleep-walking heading always toward water. The first time he set out, Shep found him, just after three in the morning, holding his short, pudgy fingers under the water streaming into the downstairs tub. When Shep touched his shoulder and asked, always with kindness, what he was doing, my small sleeping brother said, "I'm going to take a bath." Shep then reached over the boy's shoulder, turned off the faucets, and stroked his head. Lifting him up, he told him he could take a bath in the morning. That night, he stayed with my brother for perhaps an hour, running his hand over his hair, singing him lullabies and sailor chanteys, until finally the boy's breathing evened out and Shep was sure he would not rise again.

Toward the end of every month, like someone mandated by a periodic cycle, my brother would be pulled as if by magic through moonlight to water—once to the kitchen sink, once to the utility tub, once, my father found him splashing his arms in the bird bath— and each time my father would kiss him and caress him and lead him away from whatever attracted him in the water.

The last time it happened, my brother was older, perhaps fourteen or fifteen. We were at Cape Cod; Shep says he was alerted by the slap of the screen door at the front of our cottage. By the time he was up and had pulled the drawstring of his pajama bottoms fast around his waist, my brother was halfway down the sand trail to the pond, moving as steadily as a foot soldier toward the water lapping the shore. He was just twenty feet from the pond's edge when my father put his hand on his shoulder and asked, "Son, is everything all right?"

My brother said he just wanted to go in for a quick dip, that was all. No big deal; he just wanted to get wet. He spoke as if his desire were the most ordinary thing in the world, not worthy of question. He seemed not to understand what could motivate my father to keep him from sinking his body into the water's cool and sympathetic depths when, perhaps in response to the increasing pressure of my father's hand, perhaps it was the screech of an owl across the pond, he woke, suddenly aware of the darkness, the sand underfoot, the wind etching deep creases between his eyebrows. As if stung, he jerked his head toward the hand holding his shoulder, then back to our father. Moving his gaze back and forth over Shep's eyes, he looked in them and across them for something that might help put the pieces together.

"Would you like to see the water, Kyle?" Shep asked as he brushed the bangs away from the boy's eyes.

My brother blinked; his still pudgy, baby-boy face grew red in the moonlight.

"Why would I want to do that?" he answered, flicking Shep's hand from his forehead as if it were a mosquito. "Why would anyone want to do as stupid a thing as that?"

My mother knew nothing of my brother's nocturnal missions, these appeals to the water; she boasted that she could sleep through anything, "even an A-bomb." Besides, Cape Cod was her time to relax, a time when she too explored the pleasures of the bottle, hoping, she once said, that if she could just get over her slight squeamishness about other people's drinking, everything would be all right.

And it was all right, in some ways. I see my parents dancing in the front room of our cottage in South Dennis. The Andrews Sisters'

"Don't Sit Under the Apple Tree" is on the radio and they are dancing as if it were 1944 and the war had just ended. My father turns up the volume and tilts his head to the sky as he begins to hoot and holler like a cowboy. Then he pulls my mother close—my happy, beautiful mother—and they hold each other tight, looking deeply for one split second into each other's eyes, and then my mother spins out, twirling like a top, her polka-dot skirt like a pinwheel forming swirls of color in the breeze. As he snaps her back to him, her ponytail leaves a trail of light behind her that fractures in the afternoon sun; splinters of blue-and-red-and-green-colored light fragment the sea-soaked after-noon air. Out and back, out and back, my brother and I are en-chanted with their motion, with the love that radiates from them, warming the room, warming our lives, like a tropical breeze in the springtime. Outside, it sounds as if the whole world has joined in their dance; we hear people whooping and hollering and we can see confetti falling through the air, and streamers and open kegs of beer. Everyone is cheering our parents as if the victory were theirs to celebrate with this happy mongrel dance, part lindy, part Charleston, part dervish gyrations. When the song ends, they collapse into each other's arms, happier than they've ever been in their lives, over-whelmed by their joyous love for each other. They sink down into the wicker couch, wrapped up in each other, unable to imagine anything better than this. They are laughing so hard that it almost looks like it hurts, laughing so hard that we're not sure if they'll ever be able to stop. And that makes my brother and me laugh too; holding our sides and our stomachs, we collapse into their waiting arms and they pull us together—one big happy family—as we all laugh, laughing until we think we will burst.

But is that really a memory, or is it something I've just now made up? If I try to think about what really happened, I see something different; the picture has a certain intensity, a movie-like sharpness that makes it seem almost unreal. It is about 1962 and the brother is not in the picture. The man has just wiped his hands on the towel by the sink; he has already opened the clams and covered the table with a cracked plastic cloth, white with blue cornflowers. In the center of the table, a plate of cherrystones, twenty-four eyes staring up at the girl, open, wet, and dripping. There is a bottle of bloodred hot sauce on the table, a saucer of lemon quarters, three plastic tumblers, and two half-empty bottles of Muscadet. When I see this scene, I see the man squeeze the juice from one of the lemon slices onto the purplish flesh that wobbles in the shell; then I see him dare the nine-year-old girl to put it into her mouth. When this happens, the girl, her anger shown only in the deep red of her ears, stares at the clam which retracts as if stung and then slowly begins to respond, its flesh oozing over the side of the shell. When I get this far in the scene, I then see the man, like a priest offering the chalice, holding the shell before the angry girl's mouth, teasing the girl with his eyes, and I hear the woman sitting next to him start to laugh. The woman's laughter sounds canned, like on *I Love Lucy* or *Father Knows Best*; she throws back her head and laughs so hard that peals of laughter fly from her throat and catch in the blades of the shiny brass ceiling fan rotating silently above. The girl, it appears, feels a little woozy; she draws her hand over her eyes, then turns to the woman, now back to the man.

I see this scene again and again. I hear the girl's father, his voice soft and cooing, "Don't be afraid, little shrimp," and then he adds, his voice corrosive, his eyes like magnets, "It's not going to bite you." And then I can feel his hand, the heat of his hand on the back of her neck, pulling her closer; his hand presses her head toward the wobbling white and purple mass as her mother throws back her head and laughs.

In this scene, I hear the girl's father and mother laughing without being able to stop. They are laughing so hard that it almost looks like it hurts.

．．．

In my dream, I feel as if I am choking, drowning, as if I've got hot liquid in my mouth. It's like hot liquid silver, and I am trying to get it out. I can't stand it in my mouth, but the more I try to spit it out, the harder the silver gets; the more I roll my tongue, the more it solidifies until finally it becomes so big I feel as if I am about to choke; it becomes so large and hard, I think I am going to die. Later I spit out a huge chunk, but a lot of it still remains in my teeth, clinging to the sides of my mouth.

Could I ever have told my mother? Could I ever have told the woman who now says that if she had it to do all over again, she'd never have done it in the first place?

Bacon cracks and pops; my mother stands over the frying pan, a huge black cast-iron one, just large enough to make a deep gash in the side of an average man's skull. She is singing the refrain from a zippy little love song over and over again as she moves the bacon slices around in the pan.

I have been called to the table by the smell of the bacon; I am the first one down this morning, beating my brother, who will probably sleep until noon and then disappear until Monday, and my father, who we will probably not see until tomorrow. It is Saturday and my mother and I are going to B. Altman's to buy a forty-third-birthday present for the passed-out man upstairs. My mother likes to take me along because she says I know what my father likes best.

The eggs are cracked into the frying pan, one at a time. I watch her use the spatula to flick bacon grease onto the top of the eggs; it's the way my father likes them. She'll make up an entire plate for him: two fried eggs, lacy around the edges, three strips of bacon, a sliced tomato, and three well-buttered pieces of toast. I watch her as she makes my father's breakfast first, even though she knows he won't be down until after we go out, and then it won't be to eat but rather to fix himself a vodka milk shake to help him get over the vodka from the night before. I watch her drop the tomato wedges into an artful arrangement around the eggs, watch as she readjusts first the bacon, then the tomatoes, watch as she makes things beautiful, does all this, for him.

My mother passes close by me, tucking the aluminum foil tightly around the edge of my father's dish; she is heading for the hot plate, which will keep his eggs warm while we're out. I can smell the perfume of her soap as she passes—it's like the lilacs we grow in the backyard—and it's so intense I'm embarrassed and I turn my head away. I want to tell her, I want to say it so badly it hurts, but I can't get the words out, nothing comes out of my mouth. I feel strangled, choked nearly to death by my twelve years of anger and longing for her, my desire for her to protect me, my wish that someday she will care for me and feed me and take all the pain away. I want her to erase it so that it's completely canceled out, to reverse the film—make the whole thing go backwards. She is moving away from me, getting closer to the hot plate, and I want to say something, I want her to look at me, I want her to hold me in her arms the way she does on the steps of our cottage in Connemara and bring me into her, I want her to enclose me within the steaming hot dark flowers of her flesh, to press my head against her bosom and let it rest there between her sweet-smelling breasts, buoyant and shielding. I want to say something, I have to say something, but instead I watch her flip the switch on the hot plate.

Without looking at me, she asks if I'm ready. We can get breakfast on the road, she tells me.

Halfway up Country Club, she says that maybe if we're lucky one of these days, that hot plate will set the whole house on fire. Wouldn't that be loverly, she asks. Wouldn't that just be loverly?

PART THREE

I have this fantasy. I am sitting at my mother's knee, or sometimes I am standing behind her, leaning over her shoulder. She looks the way she did when I was about ten, maybe twelve; her skin bright and smooth, her chin firm and square, her voice rising from her voluptuous breasts, snugly held and full. She is replacing the things in my hope chest, the old pine one with the red hearts and moon shapes and angels painted on the sides, with the inscription (translated from the German) that reads, "Now join hands to share your life / Through joy, sorrow, wealth, and strife. / May God's sweet angel guide your feet / While you your blessed vows do keep." She is folding the things she has taken out to clean and air, pressing the various cloths, smoothing out wrinkles over her knee while she tells me stories about each piece. For example, when I was born, my grandmother said she had never seen eyes as blue as mine and so bequeathed me her entire set of delft; to go with it, my mother embroidered a white linen cloth, which she now holds up for me to smell. It smells like lilacs, like the smell of her soap, her hair; I can still smell its intoxicating sweetness even after she puts the cloth back in the chest. Then she lifts the little red and white gingham apron that she made with my initials M.A. stitched on either pocket; I wore it the first time I used my miniature tea set to serve hot chocolate to my brother and his friends. And there, still inside, are my report cards, and my ribbons won in school jumping contests, a mysterious horn my grandmother gave me, and a drawing I once made of my mother and father: Idaho potatoes on sticks. My mother recounts the stories of these homely, hallowed objects one at a time; she tells me about all the wonderful things in my life as many times as I wish to hear them. I look up at her from where I am sitting on the floor and see her white teeth flashing in and out of lips that look as red, as firm as a movie star's while she tells me stories about myself and smiles.

"You were just an unlovable child."

When I am perhaps twelve or thirteen, my mother calls me into her room for a private tête-à-tête. "Shut the door," she demands as she picks at an African violet Kyle gave her last week for her forty-second birthday. Without her saying so, we could tell that Kyle's gift infuriated her almost as much as the card Shep gave her, the one that said, "Some people don't have to worry about getting older . . . or prettier." Each year, Shep gives my mother a "funny" birthday card—he has stopped buying her presents. Perhaps feeling unworthy of them, she has never complained and each year she caves in, tears cascading down her cheeks, and asks why my father can't ever buy her a "real" card, to which he responds, always winking at me, his eyes like flypaper, "I was only joking. . . . Can't you take a joke? One must have a sense of humor in this world, old matey." The judge will suggest later that this period of Shep's "jokes" was the beginning of the end. For me, the end was already in sight. My relationship with Shep had become one of imprecise gestures, muddled restraint, ambiguous if slightly salacious asides, the alcohol helping to render him a slobbering and ineffectual parody of the salty seducer he once was. I can still see him now, in what Kyle later called his "bad" period (as if that was, in some way, different from his "good" periods), careening about the house like some wild creature. He bumped blindly from room to room, dazed and only semiconscious, his sterling tumbler always in hand, while we, in other rooms, pretended that we did not hear the liquor sloshing over the rim of the glass or the crash of the ice cubes that got away from him, leaving slippery traces for us to mop up in the morning. He repelled me and yet, in a way, I did love him. Over the next few years, as he sank into a mire of alcoholism, I alternately gave way and resisted, not knowing whether it was better to sink or to swim.

"You had tantrums and you didn't like to be touched," my mother says, eyeing the violet suspiciously. As with all the plants given her, she will leave this one on the window ledge, too embarrassed by her queasiness in the face of this—yet another living thing demanding her care—to chuck it immediately. Instead she will watch it die slowly, saying all the while that she had nothing to do with it, that it wasn't her fault, that she never asked for it in the first place. When the leaves begin to brown and drop, she will pluck them off, the finger-nails of her thumb and forefinger forming neat, lethal pinchers, while telling herself that it won't be long now, that it is losing its life, and that she will therefore, once again, have hers. Finally, when there remains nothing but a brownish yellow stump, she will say, "Well, it looks to me like there's nothing to be done; it's dead." And then she will carry the remains as if they were contagious, between two fingers, and drop them from a height of ten inches into the garbage bin. Brushing her hands together, she will turn to me and say, "Well, that's that." She will brush her hands on her skirt and say, "That's the end of it."

But now she turns from the violet to adjust the butterfly pin indicating her tenth year in Al-Anon. "Lord knows, I tried," she says with a sigh. Her tone, vacillating only slightly, is that of a soldier who feels she needs, in the interest of world peace, to describe her part in the struggle, but who, at the same time, refuses to assume any responsibility for the atrocities committed. As she tells me she's told her friends, she had tried—Lord knows, she had tried—like a re-sourceful guerrilla, a Che of the suburbs, she had taken hours out of her day to listen to guest speakers on television and radio shows, she had solicited the advice of paid professionals (she would show me the bills if I wanted to see them), she had even purchased a small library of child care manuals, but no one—not a single source—could ever tell her what to do with a child who had, quite simply, made herself unlovable. Never finding "unlovable" in the index, she said she felt she had to go it alone, stoically, back straight, nostrils flared, reciting the Serenity Prayer like a mantra, and ignoring, to the best of her ability, what she hadn't the ability to change.

"It's a good thing your father loved you," she concludes, replacing the pin at her neck. It really was lucky, she says, about my father. Wasn't it?

In Connemara, it's hard to know who falls asleep first. We dream of magnolia and dogwood and lemon verbena. We float through the darkness to flowers together, connected, unable to part, even in sleep.

Having wolfed down our Cheerios, Kyle and I were thrust out the door by Shep, who, planting neat kisses on our slick pompadours, begged us to remember always to curtsy and never to fart.

"Do you think Mom will let us play outside today?" I asked as we trudged down the drive. I rerolled my softcovered math book which had already grown moist in my palm.

"I doubt it," he panted. His determination to make it to school on time, despite the humidity, bloated his already red cheeks. "Besides, who would want to? It's too hot."

He was right again. It was too hot, it would be too bright. The sky was already so pale it looked as if it had been bleached by the hot morning sun; even at this hour, 8:30 A.M., the leaves all drooped, sodden with the oppressive wet air. Everything lay still; even the

Atwoods' dog, usually such a menace at the top of the hill, lay limp across their uneven front stoop. Even its tail didn't move.

Despite the heat, I walked cautiously, avoiding the cracks my brother had convinced me could break our mother's back; he, I noticed, avoided them only irregularly.

"Hurry up," he insisted when I lagged a few steps behind.

I ran to catch up with him.

"Hey," he asked, his glasses reflecting the sun's glare. "You know that one-eyed creep who hangs around the playground? That sick-looking guy who's always at the swings when the bus comes in?"

"Yeah?"

"The guy with the goofy grin who looks like Quasimodo?" he asked, grotesquely pulling his mouth to one side and lifting one shoulder up to his ear. "The guy with the pockmarks all over his face?"

"What about him?" I eyed him suspiciously.

"Want to know what he did over the weekend?"

"I don't know," I said honestly.

"I'll bet you didn't know he was in love with the bus driver—that's why he was always hanging out at the swings. So he could see her when she came in."

"So?"

"So on Saturday, he saw her kissing another man. You know who it was? The guy who owns the candy store in town."

"Mr. Fielding?"

"Who else do you think owns the candy store, Megan?"

I lowered my head to the books clutched to my chest where I caught a vague whiff of the still new smell of perspiration. I pressed my arms closer to my sides.

"So he saw her kissing him so later that night he snuck into Fielding's house. Then he tied him up with this really thick rope and stuck a rag in his mouth—a rag that was all greasy—and then he took him in the trunk of his car to the railroad tracks. You want to know what he did next? He tied his head to the tracks and then he took his shoes off so the rats would get to his toes before the train got to his head. So the rats came and ate all his toes and then a train came and—wham bang slam—his head squashed open just like a watermelon. When the cops finally found him there was nothing there— just all this blood and guts. The rest of him had been eaten away by the buzzards."

"I think the sun has fried your brains," I hollered as I dashed away from him and up the side of a mountain of dirt on our neighbor's lawn. Something about being on the top made me want to yell or fly. I thought if I could just stay up there, I could think for a while. The sun, so white and so hot, made everything on the ground look shimmering. "Death on death," I thought as I began carving my initials into dried clots of dirt. Starting in on a second set, I decided that when I turned sixteen and was famous, I would write my initials on everything, and everybody would know who I was. I would have lots of pink clothes with lace, and chauffeurs, and when I stepped out of my white limousine, everyone would be waiting to applaud me.

"I'm telling Mom you were late," Kyle yelled as he moved farther along the road.

I eased myself down the other side of the mountain and raced to catch up with him.

"Mom says that Shep lies," I brought forth suddenly, my lungs congested with the wet air. "And that I can tell him for her that he does."

"So?"

"So I just thought I'd tell you." Trying to catch sight of his eyes through his glasses, I prompted, "That's what she says anyway. And that he's a cheat as well."

"I hadn't heard about that," he said, wiping the sweat from under his nose with his shirttail.

"Which?" I demanded, keeping my eyes on him.

"What you just said."

"Well, does he?"

"How would I know?" he answered belligerently, slapping at a deerfly that had settled on his bare arm.

"His secretary says that he's a vast liar. She's a princess," I added, hoping that this privileged information might provoke a response in him. "A real princess," I repeated when no answer seemed forthcoming.

"Meggie, you're so stupid. She can't be a princess."

"He said that she is. From Alabama."

"Meggie, they don't have princesses in Alabama. Or even in New Jersey. They only have princesses in New York."

"How do you know?"

"My teacher told me. He said he married one."

"Does he know that he lies?" I pursued.

"Where do the two of you go all the time?" he suddenly put in.

"Just to the dump."

"What do you mean, 'just to the dump'?"

"What have you got, potatoes in your ears or something? I said just to the dump." Then, after a pause, I continued, "Even if he does lie, it doesn't keep him from loving me. He loves me tremendously. He's told me our affairs are immensely involved," I boasted uncertainly.

"That won't keep him from chucking you. He'll chuck you when he's done with you."

"He won't chuck me; he'll chuck you!"

"He can't chuck me, stupid. He already has," he murmured, kicking a crushed Coke can into the street. "How do you know her anyway?"

"He takes me."

"Oh sure, he takes you. You're a great cover!" His vehemence propelled him after the can into the street.

I followed him with my gaze as he kicked the can across the street and up onto the sidewalk. I didn't fully understand his words and I didn't dare ask. But the effect of his mysterious pronouncement was to confront me with an increasingly critical view of my father's behavior, and I felt not so much frightened but rather detached as, for the second time, a slow, curious realization that Shep might yet betray me gradually broke over me.

"Sometimes I think you just want to hold on to this. That your whole goal is to get back at us by dredging this whole thing up," Kyle charges as he taps the edge of his mug with a spoon.

We were in my apartment, the four of us: Kyle, Deborah, Aaron, and myself. It is around 1980, maybe fifteen years after Kyle made his awful pronouncement, shortly before the divorce but after the scandal reports began appearing in *The Wall Street Journal*. My brother is saying that he loves my father, that as he has gotten older he has learned to love him even more; he is protesting that it is something he can't do anything about; his love, he says, is as impossible to alter as the weather. This is the way it is, this is the way it's always going to be.

I am looking after Aaron for the evening while he and Deborah go to a Core Energetics intensive during which time they hope to find out, through a process of releasing energies trapped due to misconceptions about life and the self, just what loving, healthful, joyous, trusting, and happy beings they can be; to experience, Deborah has told me, "the unifying, transformative, and healing inner core" at the same time they "relinquish the illusions of the ego." She is, I can tell, a little leery about leaving Aaron in my unregenerate hands, but has resigned herself, perhaps assuring herself that it's a risk she's loving enough to take.

Kyle is on sabbatical in Princeton, the place he took his Ph.D. just four short years after taking his A.B. with honors, and so the four of us see each other frequently. By his tone, I can tell he thinks I'm an idiot for not understanding the intensity of his love for our father. It does no good to tell him that, in a way, I love our father too.

I tell him I don't want to take away his love for Shep, that that's not what I'm trying to do.

"I know you're not," he snaps. "I'm just telling you how I feel, that's all."

Deborah reaches across the table for his hand; feeling her touch, he recoils and folds his arms across his chest, inserting his hands into the tight folds of his armpits.

"You asked me to be honest with you about my feelings; I'm only doing what you asked me to do. You're the one who brought the whole thing up. If you didn't want to know, you shouldn't have asked me in the first place."

He is sitting up very straight now, speaking very fast, as if he had a fever. He is facing me, his eyes pointed in my direction, but although they appear to connect with mine, I know that he does not see me. I touch his shoulder and feel the muscles contract beneath my hand. He winces as if stung.

"Dad! Dad!" Aaron hollers from the bathroom.

"In a minute, son," my brother says, assuming his most beneficent and paternal manner. Someone has got to take control here, he is saying with his tone, someone must serve as a reminder of decency and reason here. "As soon as I'm finished talking with your Aunt Megan.

"What do you want me to say? That I don't love him? That I don't have any feelings for him? That because of what you've told me, I should just stop loving him, just like that, as if I never cared for him and he never cared for me, make believe a relationship between us had never existed?"

"That's not what I'm saying, Kyle. Did I ever say that? Have I said that yet?"

"No, you haven't. But then you go and you tell me about all this, you tell me about . . . the way you behaved, the way it happened when you were a child, and what do you expect me to feel? Huh? What do you expect me to do after you tell me about all this? I didn't even know what was going on."

"Well, now I've told you. Now you know exactly what happened."

At this, my sister-in-law sighs and shakes her head. She calls to Aaron, she wants Aaron to come out of the bathroom and sit on her knees, she wants that blessed child to take her head between his immaculate hands and hold it—his innocence protecting her from the deep penetrating remorse that permeates this room vaguely, like an odor.

"Daaad!"

"I *was* sorry for you," he snaps. "And maybe I did know something was wrong—I just didn't know what," he announces, spitting his words back at me.

"Damn it, Kyle, get it through your head—I'm not asking you to do anything about the past. I'm talking about right now." Then, biting back my tears, I ask, "Aren't you ever going to be able—be willing—to help me?"

"Da-aad!"

Deborah, rising, says she'll see what he wants. But my brother jumps before her, arms extended, palms forward. "No, no, it's my turn; I'm his father," he says as he walks toward the bathroom.

Returning a second later, he announces, "Aaron's bottom hurts." And then he just stands there, rocking back and forth on his heels, his hands in his pockets, looking like he can't think of anything else to say, doesn't know what he ought to be doing.

"Kyle?"

He looks up, his eyes unfocused.

"Check the medicine cabinet," I tell him. There should be something there, I say, that can help you help your son.

A photo I remember or perhaps have made up. My mother and I are standing within a foot and a half of each other outside the Hibben Magie Apartments in Princeton. We are visiting my brother the year he took sabbatical there. I appear to be about twenty-seven; that puts my mother near sixty.

I am on the right. My hair is cut very short, almost like a crew cut, and I am wearing an oversized black jumpsuit, very spare, very plain. Over my left breast I have attached a clay pin in the shape of a star. If you look closely, you can see the red, angry beast painted on it that appears to be ramming its head against the single impervious star in the sky.

My mother is on my right. She is not wearing lavender, but instead a classic beige shirtwaist with a coordinated black and brown bargello belt, clear hose. Her breasts, not buoyant, hang flat, almost reaching her waist. Her weight rests on the right foot, her good foot, so it appears as if she is leaning away from me, almost as if she were afraid of crowding me, and her arms are bent behind her, either because she is afraid of some inadvertent contact or to give the impression of openness. I have bent my right arm so that the hand, folded into a fist, is on my hip; as if it were a warning, the elbow is pointed at her. My free hand grips one rail of the steel fence dividing the apartments from the lawn so tightly you can see the white of my knuckles; it looks as if, for some reason, I were afraid of falling, of being pulled in the other direction, the direction of my beautiful, stern mother.

The photographer has captured us at the moment we are looking straight into each other's eyes. We look as if we were in some kind of standoff—something you'd see in a movie about the Wild West. My mother's face is partially bleached out by the sun—there is only darkness behind her glasses—but her mouth is set, like wax, in a half smile, waiting, it seems, to see if it will be returned before she will dare carry it further. I am not smiling, nor am I frowning. I imagine her eyes, like mine, are blank.

But what if the photo were different? What if my mother's arms were not behind her, but were instead extended toward me, as if she were hoping I would move in toward her? And how would it be if, instead of hugging the rail, my body did lean forward as if to fall into her embrace? What if we'd met in the middle and the photographer had captured us holding each other?

But the real photo is different. In the real photo we look as if we were challenging each other, defying the other to come any closer, even as it appears that neither of us will budge or risk making the first touch.

"Mom, when I have a cold, do I '(a) take aspirins, drink fluids, and think it will pass; (b) see the doctor—it could turn into pneumonia; or (c) ignore it and hope for the best—I think colds are mostly psychological'?"

I looked up from my magazine to my mother, who was sitting on the edge of the tub in her everyday bra and girdle, rubbing the back of her heel with a stone. It was Friday, "Personal Day," the day of the week when my mother "pampered" herself—made herself over—after, that is, she had mopped and polished the kitchen floor and washed and folded the laundry. "It's a well-dressed woman who shows her man off at his best," she'd say, hanging her apron on the hook in the cleaning closet.

It was an hours-long process of self-alteration, self-mutilation, one she hoped would permit her association, by proxy, with what she called "power." When I was very young, she preferred I not watch. As if we were schoolgirls vying for the same man's attention, she would point to my "Cleopatra" eyes, my "bedroom" eyes, and say, "You've already got what it takes; you don't need any help," and then she would shut the door between us. But now, perhaps thinking that the ugly manifestation of nearly a decade and a half of discontent—the furrows, the extra fat, the perpetually downturned mouth—negated any threat I once might have posed, she swings open the bathroom door as if welcoming guests to a party.

I would watch, fascinated by the transformation that took place. "How do I look?" she'd ask, groping like the small sister after her big sister's approval when the conversion was finally done. "Like a million bucks?"

And I always thought she did.

It was late afternoon, say, 1966 or '67, around 4:30 or 5:00, that queer, indecipherable time of day when it's hard to tell if it's still daytime or night. I waited for her answer while I watched curled little pieces of flesh fall to the bottom of the tub, forming an amorphous heap at her feet. I was sitting on the closed toilet, leaning against the cool porcelain tank.

"Give them to me again," she asked brightly.

"Do I '(a) think it will pass; (b) think it could turn into pneumonia; or (c) ignore it and hope for the best'?" I repeated, clucking my tongue. I felt conflicted and tired, unable for the last day or two to figure out how the earth could be spinning so fast without our even noticing. I began kicking the edge of the tub with my foot, banging it to see when it would hurt. It all seemed very odd, the way things just happened, without explanations, without any sense, and without your feeling as if you had any control.

"It seems to me, dear, that you don't get colds," she answered, lifting herself up from the tub.

"But imagine if I did. It's for the sake of the quiz."

"Well, I'd say you probably wanted to see the doctor—you're always imagining the worst." She heaved her crooked leg up so that the bent foot rested on the edge of the vanity. "Plug this thing in, will you?"

"I do not," I said, pushing the plug of her Lady Gillette into the outlet at the side of the mirror. "I probably want to take two aspirins and hope it will pass," I shouted over the steady buzz of the razor.

I watched her for a few minutes while her dark coarse fur fell into little piles in the sink. When the crooked leg was as smooth as turned wood, she said, "May I sit there, Her Highness?"

I clucked my tongue again, louder, as I positioned myself side-saddle over the rim of the tub.

"When my plans are rained out, I feel '(a) challenged to try to be creative in the house; (b) glad—I need a chance to mellow out at home'—yuck!" I shouted wanting to show my disdain for even the fantasy of staying home a day—" 'or (c) depressed and restless and stuck inside.' "

"What is this for, dear?" she asked, pulling her razor along the inside of her thigh.

"I told you. It's a quiz. 'How You See the World.' It tells you if you're an optimist or a pessimist."

"Oh, well, that's useful." She straightened herself up. "What are you?"

"That's exactly what I'm trying to find out! How do you think I can know before I even answer all the questions and begin figuring out my score?"

Ignoring me, she layered a thick line of white gunk across her upper lip.

"You look like Santa Claus, Sandy Claws, Santa Claus," I repeated idly, rhythmically, as she leaned toward the mirror, tweezers in hand.

"Just you wait." She smiled, yanking the "walrus whiskers" from under her chin.

I put the magazine down, resting it precariously on the edge of the tub, and took my mother's teasing comb from the counter and began dragging it across the thin hairs on my arm.

"Mom?"

"Don't do that!" she snapped, grabbing the comb from my hand. "Do you want to make them longer? Your father wouldn't . . ." Then, her tone softening, "I had hair there once too. You don't want to look like a gorilla, do you? You don't want men to call you the hairy ape, do you?"

Embarrassed and feeling vaguely ashamed, I lifted the magazine and began flipping through ads for minimizers and straighteners, lotions and potions, polishes and conditioners, laxatives and aspirins and diet pills—a whole array of camouflages and strategies for flattering and dissembling, all things I knew could never conceal my real badness, things that I feared, despite their promised potency, were powerless to help me. My eyes fell on a series of schematized female figures, each of which looked the same in the center—a black outline representing the "ideal" figure. The dotted lines surrounding the solid outline of each figure showed the contours of the "less than ideal" thigh shapes; there were jodhpur thighs, obese thighs, complex-fat-syndrome thighs, all kinds of thighs and all kinds of sizes, but none like mine. I became immediately alarmed: neither the solid outline nor any of the seven dotted contours corresponded in any way to my own body shape. It was one of the many moments during my adolescence when I felt convinced that I simply didn't fit, and so I began pounding my thighs with my left fist.

"You know, Megan"—my mother paused, smiling, as she looked from the magazine to me—"I think you look pretty just the way you are."

"Do you really think so?"

"I always have."

Then, without going further, she peeled down the front of her girdle and sprayed a white powder on her vaginal area.

"Did you finish your quiz?" she asked.

"What's that for?"

"It's to keep them coming," she answered, winking. Then, her eyes gazing out the front window for a moment, she added, "That is, if they come at all." Heaving a sigh from her chest, she replaced her smile and added, "You'll understand when you get older."

I couldn't imagine not understanding anything more than I already didn't understand. I turned my head toward the window and looked outside at the fading sun. If it's moving around in circles and we're moving around in circles, how come I'm not dizzy?

"I want to know whether you're an optimist or pessimist," my mother asked brightly.

I began calculating my quiz score, plumping it up in a few spots where it seemed especially low, but when I was done, I still had only enough points to be classified as a "Hurricane Alert." "You're likely to see the lemons instead of the lemonade," I read silently, "and you blame yourself when things go wrong. This self-defeating thinking cramps your opportunities—and it can even affect your health."

"What did you get?" she asked as she began pushing her cuticles back with a stick. My mother was especially proud of her nails and worked assiduously to cultivate ten perfectly shaped tapers, equal in length and shape and color. For her, polished nails were proof that she could triumph over her shortcomings, that she could wax floors, polish furniture, clean scraped knees, iron shirts, and still remain feminine, worthy of a man's attention.

"Well," she asked again, pinching my cheek, "How'd you do, old sourpuss?"

"They say I'm mixed sun and clouds," I lied, hiding my own nails that were dotted with white spots that my mother said came with telling "little white lies." "They say that sometimes I'm down, but mostly I'm up. They say I'm one of life's philosophers: that I see the world for what it is, and try to make the most of my opportunities. The plus is that I'm likely to have an easygoing nature—"

"Hah!" my mother interrupted as she unfurled her shoulder-length hair from the electric rollers. "That'll be the day."

"And that I might be playing life too safe. They say I should take a few risks—get a new friend, or a new hairstyle. They say the fun is in the adventure."

"There you have it," she said smartly. "I'm not the only one, then, who's telling you to get out and have some fun. Sometimes I think you're just like your father with those creases between your eyebrows and that downturned face. You know," she began a recurrent chorus, "it takes fewer muscles to smile than it does to frown."

"Daddy always smiles when he's with me."

"That's because you're Daddy's little girl," she said, with perhaps a hint of bitterness in her voice.

"I'm not anybody's little girl," I yelled.

"Look at this," she said, drawing my attention from the cuticles I was picking to her new full-size faux tortoiseshell mirror compact, which included eighteen powder eye shadows, two dual-tip applicators, a kohl eyeliner pencil, three powder brushes, one blush brush, three lip glosses, a lip brush, three matching lip pencils, a "lush" mascara, an under-eye concealer cream, a translucent powder, and a free copy of *World of Beauty* magazine.

"You know, in Russia, they only have one color." She drew the mascara wand over her top lashes. That was one of the rules I had memorized from other Personal Days: use mascara only on your top lashes if you want to open up your eyes; bright shades make your eyes look bigger; dark shades add depth and dimension; only people with blue eyes should wear blue eye shadow; outline your lips with a slightly darker shade if you want them to look smaller; brush your base with the tips of your fingers and always in the direction of your facial hair; never shave your moustache . . .

"You know, we could do something about that mole," she said as she finished dabbing Erace over her "crow's eyes" and around her nose. My mother had always had an aversion to the lump on the side of my neck and had tried for years to persuade me to conceal it, along with the brown birthmark in the center of my back. "Let's make it look like a daisy," she said the first year I wanted to wear a two-piece bathing suit. "Then people will think you did it on purpose."

"Forget it. I don't want to," I said sullenly. Then, reconsidering, I asked, "But how about my freckles?"

"That could be arranged." She approached me with the putty-colored marker.

I shut my eyes and felt the gentle pressure of her cool, bony hands as they rubbed the thick, waxy paste over my cheeks, around my chin, along my nose. And as she rubbed the paste in, a memory suddenly surfaced of times when I was very young and my mother and I would bathe together on the nights my father didn't come home.

"How about a bubble bath?" she'd ask gaily.

Once in the warm water, we'd take turns lifting her thick natural sea sponge, squeezing it over each other's backs and shoulders, letting the bubbly rivers run down, as strands of our hair, like little tongues, curled around our throats, our shoulders, the tops of our chests.

"Doesn't that feel like silk?" she'd ask as she let the water trickle down over my back, my shoulders, my neck. Then I'd lift the sponge and watch my mother relax as the water cascaded along the lobes of her breasts, around her wide stomach, down to the furry moss at the V of her groin.

But now it seemed odd having my mother's hands on me after so many long years, and I braced myself.

"What do you say, Elizabeth Taylor?" she asked, turning my face to the mirror.

I was astonished by the face I saw. It was a face that looked childlike in its purity, its chasteness, a face without any sign of shame or wrongdoing, the makeup having erased my physical inadequacies, as well as any manifestation of my discontent, my anger, my guilt.

"Don't hog the mirror," my mother said coyly as she applied base to her cheeks.

"Can I borrow your blush brush?" I asked, now impatient to test the rest of her gear.

"Go ahead, honey; use anything you want."

"Think you've got enough on?" she asked when I had finally put the brush down. Then, without missing a beat: "You want to create a sensation, make a grand entrance," she continued as she aimed the Shalimar atomizer at her breasts, her ears, the edge of her wrists. "Want a little?" she asked gaily.

I shook my head and we moved to the bedroom, where I sat on the edge of her bed, aware only of an aching sense of inferiority. My mother had always said that I was the Beautiful One, la Bella Donna, and that's why my father liked me so much, but at that moment, I couldn't for the life of me imagine anyone more beautiful than she.

"Suit yourself," she said in response to my silence as she adjusted some foam pads in her jet-cone brassiere. Watching me watch her, she explained, "Every woman knows how much she needs to bring her bust up to ideal."

"Maybe I need a bra," I asked hopefully.

"Well, there's only one way to find out," she said, passing me the short yellow golf pencil she kept at her bedside next to the smile face notepad. "Put this under your breast," she said as she readjusted her own within her enormous brassiere, "and see if it stays."

I lifted my T-shirt and placed the pencil under where my left breast would be if I had one. When I let go, the pencil clattered to the floor and I watched it roll into the dust under the dresser. I turned to my mother. You could have fit a dozen pencils under her breasts.

"There's your answer," she remarked cheerfully as she peeled off her girdle. She will replace it with a special black lace one that matches her bra and slip, thus completing her underwear "ensemble." "Every woman wants to match not only the outside but the inside as well," she once told me. Then, patting the place just above her waist where the "everyday girdle" had dug purple rims, she announced coquettishly, "I've been bad, I've been letting myself go. I'll be more careful in the future," she promised, sounding like a Catholic schoolgirl to her confessor.

"Mom, do you think anyone will ever like me?" I asked, covering my mouth with my hand. I watched her pull her tight-fitting black cocktail dress over her head. My mother liked to wear black because it was "slimming." "It's *the* color for the full-figured woman," she'd say. Only later, when I went shopping for myself, would I remember the other rules about dress that I had been taught on other Personal Days: horizontal stripes make you look wider; vertical stripes make you look longer; ribs can help reveal a full figure; a deep V neck keeps a long line going; bright colors give a boost to your bust; dark colors whittle your middle; pleats always look classic; hair combs and ankle bracelets are tarty; high colors are unacceptable on older women, as are skirts that come above the bottom of the knee; high heels lengthen your legs; panty girdles smooth embarrassing lumps. . . .

"Daddy loves you," she said, cinching her waist with a wide, shiny belt. Our eyes met for a second, and then we quickly turned away.

"Daddy's weird," I said, perhaps testing to see if such a switch in allegiance would induce a similar switch in her.

"Your father is not weird, dear; he's an alcoholic," she said as if scolding me for a crime I kept committing. "There's nothing wrong with being an alcoholic. What your father has is a disease, just like when you get a cold. We don't say that you're weird when you get sick, do we? You ought to be happy that even when you get sick, he can still love you so much." She was fumbling with the clasp of her charm bracelet which she said was her "trademark"—"like Jackie Kennedy's hats" she once told me.

"Megan?" she asked in an unfamiliar tone.

I lifted my eyes to meet hers.

"I think I know what . . ."

But then, as if to mark some change in register, the bracelet fell to the floor. After staring for some seconds at the fallen charms, my mother turned to me.

Perhaps to conceal the intensity of the longing I felt for her at that moment, I lowered my head and looked at her shoes. They were swank black suede pumps with three-and-a-half-inch heels, one a size seven, the other size five and a half. Because of her shortened leg, my mother always bought two pairs of shoes in order to end up with one pair that would fit her two differently sized feet.

"Go ahead," she said, having finally fastened the bracelet. "Give them a try if you want to."

I pulled off my sneakers and slipped my hot, sticky feet into her shoes.

"You've got to stand up. A man has plenty of other things to do than to pay attention to a wallflower."

I stood and immediately thrust my arms before me, trying to maintain my balance. But it was no use; I fell back on the bed.

"Up, up, up," she said. "Nobody likes a quitter. Come on," she said, hoisting me up as if I were a rag doll. "You know what they say: practice makes perfect."

"It hurts!" I yelled, angry at her, angry at my incompetence.

"You'll get used to it," she said as she sprayed her hair with a sickly sweet-smelling varnish that she said was every woman's "finishing touch."

"Help!" I yelled when I realized she wasn't watching me.

"You'll do fine," she said, her back to me, as she gazed at her own image in the mirror.

My arms akimbo, I wobbled across the room, gradually gaining confidence as I heard a vague suggestion of the sexy clickety-clack-clack, clickety-clack-clack that I associated with my mother, my elementary school teachers, my father's secretaries, movie stars— with all the glamorous grown-up women I admired and longed to have love me.

Seeing my fanny begin to wiggle and my breasts—what there were of them—begin to shake, my mother said, "That's the trick." Then, approaching me, she threw the black lace mantilla her mother had brought her from Spain over my T-shirt and put a plastic rose from the bouquet on her dresser between my teeth.

"You want just a little more jiggle," she said as I moved toward the mirror.

Staring at my reflection, I couldn't tell whether I looked more like a crazy lady or a beautiful lady. I lifted my hand to the mirror and touched my waxy cheeks, my lips smeared with color, my soot-blackened eyes. But my thoughts were cut short when my mother, as if in answer to my silent question, declared, "You look like a knock-out!" Clapping her hands, wrinkling her mouth in a way that made it clear to me that pleasure was not all she was feeling, she said, "Wait till your father gets home and sees this. You look like a million bucks."

I am taking a shower before I go to bed. My mother is at a meeting for some liberal cause, my brother is working with his friends downstairs on The Commune, the underground newspaper he began a year ago to publicize alternate views to "the party line." I'm going to bed early because I have a big biology test in the morning. I am practicing spelling "mitochondria" as I lather my hair—I like the sound of the word. Maybe that's why I miss the creak the door always makes when somebody opens it slowly.

"Peekaboo, I see you."

"What do you want, Dad?" My body stiffens as I try, without

moving, to disappear into the darkest corner of the shower. Just for a minute, I catch my brother's voice, outside, downstairs. He wants the cover graphic—a middle finger held in disrespect against a backdrop of war scenes—made larger, more prominent.

"I wanted to see how you were doing, matey," he announces in his old treacly voice.

"I'm fine, Dad. What do you want?" For perhaps the first time, I had the sense of looking up at him as hard as he was looking down on me and felt almost capable of violence in thrusting my question back at him. "What do you want from me now?"

"I told you. I thought we'd visit." Then, after rounding his lips with his tongue, he smiles and asks, "What is there for an old goat like me when your mother's not here but to just visit with you?"

Something about his response reminded me of our afternoon, years before, with the "Princess," and I colored suddenly understanding more of what had happened that day. His tone wasn't new—I had heard it often enough—but it now struck me with a sharpened sense for the latent meaning of our previous contact.

"How'd school go today?"

"Fine, Dad. We can talk about it when I get out."

"Did you have any tests?" he asks, showing his greenish teeth, his mottled tongue.

"No, Dad." I stood motionless, frozen except for the strange tingling I felt in my fingers.

"Must have been an easy day, then."

"It was, Dad." I reach for the soap, but my hand is too tense and the bar drops to the bottom of the tub, where it slides from side to side before finally settling on the drain. I watch the blocked water as it collects at my feet, rising, forming soft pools of detritus—the muck of myself—which swirl around the drain and cling to my ankles. The tingling now feels like a pain in my body and crawls up from my feet into my shins and then into my thighs and onto my groin, where I feel it would burst if I let it.

"All days should be so easy, right, kiddo?" he asks, shutting his eyes and leaning his head back. A few seconds later, the Cheshire Cat grin returns and he winks. "Where were we, darling?"

"We were at 'easy,' Dad. Easy."

"Ah yes. I wish my days were so easy."

"I'm sure you do, Dad."

"Wish they were as easy as yours," he repeats as he opens the curtain farther with his right arm while extending his other to the opposite end of the shower, forming a wall with his body—his eyes—as the obstacle between me and the rest of the world, between me and my brother, me and the stars, the trees, the night sky, which I can see through the window behind him. I am trapped, unable without leaning toward him to reach a towel, and too embarrassed to step from what I hope is the concealing darkness of the shower into the revealing light of the bathroom.

"My days aren't so easy," he slurs, opening the curtain still farther.

"I'm sure they aren't."

"Did you see your friend Carlton today?"

"I've told you, Dad. He's in my biology class."

"I just wanted to know whether he was in your classes or whether you saw him outside, at home, after school. That's all I wanted to know," he insists as he leans farther into the shower and rubs the back of his head against the cool, slippery tiles.

Seeing my fourteen-year-old self in that shower now, at a distance of almost two decades, seeing myself watch the way you rubbed your head back and forth against the hard, wet tiles the way Kyle used to roll his head against Mother's breasts, your eyes distanced like his were, your face a mask of private pleasure, I ask myself why I didn't just throw you out. Why didn't I just tell you, Daddy, to leave me alone, to get the hell out? Why didn't I scream bloody murder right then and there? Why, when you said, "What's the matter, sweetmeat, cat got your tongue?" didn't I just lean toward you and take your skinny old neck between my strong young hands and strangle you right then and there? Why, when I couldn't respond and you just stood there gazing at me, running your tongue over your lips as if admiring a chop you were about to devour, didn't it even occur to me to slap you? Why, when you indicated by your collapsed shoulders and downturned mouth that you were irreparably wounded by my rejection, didn't I say good riddance? Why didn't I sing "Hallelujah! Hallelujah!" so that everybody—my brother, my mother, the whole world could hear? Why, when you started to leave, saying with your offended sighs, your shuffling feet that you would never recover from this one, didn't I kick you in the behind, boot you out of the bathroom, out of my heart, once and for all?

Why? What made me so thoroughly incapable of defending myself, of protecting myself?

"It's not that your father is a bad man," my mother explains shortly after this shower, "but rather that he doesn't know the difference between right and wrong. As with any alcoholic, we have to pity him, detach ourselves from the situation.

"In Marsha's church, the minister calls them lost angels. And that's what I think they really are too: lost angels."

On a different night, years later, my mother, interrupting my brother and asking him with an imperious wave of her hand to pour just the teeniest bit more brandy into her tea, declares, "I knew nothing about the Lincoln Continentals."

We are having another one of our endless roundtables complete with strong tea, cheap brandy, and Pepperidge Farm cookies, which always remain untouched except by our mother, who hates to see good food wasted. We talk, the three of us imagining, as usual, that we can find an explanation for everything, thinking that we can forge connections for all of it, hoping that distance can somehow be transformed through these arbitrary words into proximity. As always, our talk seemed premised on a belief that somehow our words could serve as an acceptable substitute for what we felt was missing, what we imagined we hadn't had. And so we feasted on our words like cannibals, like vultures, chewing them over, gobbling them down, hoping that they could restore to us everything that had eluded us, that they might return to one whole our small, unhappy family.

And now they are talking in counterpoint, my mother and twenty-eight-year-old brother. As my mother reaches for another cookie, and while I try to stroke another headache out of my temples, Kyle, making a somewhat oblique reference to yogis who sleep on nails, tells us that pain is not necessarily pain. After a brief pause, he then picks up, as he did last time, his lesson on the various types of attribution of causality.

"That is to say, Mother, that in some circles, our blessed Shepherd's actions—his alleged actions—are really no more scandalous than the tax evasion we all engage in at the end of the year."

At this point, her voice rising, my mother interrupts to say that she has never cheated on her income taxes; in case we had any doubts, she adds that she thinks it's a serious crime; whether the rest of the world thinks so or not is their own goddamned business.

That's when Kyle begins to describe the consequences of reification, the difficulties that one encounters when one tries, as she seems to be doing, to determine anything for certain. Holding *The Wall Street Journal* article entitled "Premier Products Suit Accuses Former Exec of Taking Kickbacks and Bribes" as if it were a sheet from a lesson plan he had prepared for a class, he tells us that "the nature of our present knowledge prohibits irrefutable pronouncements of our father's guilt or innocence." If Shep did commit the alleged crimes, then perhaps punishment is appropriate, although my brother will want to withhold judgment until a later date since prison, as he has told us before, has been shown throughout history to be a useless organ of rehabilitation. If Shep did not commit these crimes, however, that does not necessarily clear him of wrongdoing or expunge his guilt. Should that be the case, we need to consider more variables.

As we listen, his logic moves our father first into the dark confines of the jail, and then back into the light of freedom; he flirts with us, teases us and himself first with incarceration, moving Shep closer and closer to the forty-foot cement wall covered with barbed wire at the top, and then back to my mother's pretty and clean kitchen table, the brandy and tea. It's as if my brother can't make up his mind whether he'd rather our father were in jail or at home, free or confined. He moves Shep again in beyond the cement wall, past the gate with the steel doors and the guards on either side, into the glaring circle of the spotlight that, like an accusing finger, fixes Shep at the center of the prison yard; then he returns our father to his own kitchen, lowers him gently into one of his new plush and chrome dining room chairs in the spanking-new Hampton Village condominium where the clocks continue to tick in harmony, three or four on every shelf. In and out, in and out, my brother looks at our father sitting on a hard bench opposite a straw mattress, gazes at Shep as if he were a museum piece, and then he drops him back again into his new condominium. Maintaining the same detached curiosity, he examines his specimen in this different context, asking himself the same questions and trying to figure out just where he thinks this creature ought to be, hoping that these different locations will somehow help him determine his own feelings about this man who was almost always kind to him, this man who never hit him, this man who, perhaps he knows, did something to his sister, but who would stroke his head for hours after rescuing him from the water.

My brother takes off his glasses and rubs his eyes. It's hard to tell if he will continue. His face is blank.

Some time later that year, when the FBI first showed up, my mother refused to talk to their man. Like a crazy lady you'd see in a movie, she stood only half dressed, her worn, baby-doll nightie rumpled on the floor as if it were a skin she had just then sloughed off. Flapping her arms up and down, she shouted through the security porthole in her new condominium door, "I have nothing to say. Leave me alone; I knew nothing about it."

Not in the least daunted, the FBI officer returned the next day. Standing on her front step, wearing a nondescript blue suit, a non-descript haircut, and nondescript features, he looked for all the world, my mother later told me, like a parody of an FBI officer. Parody or not, he came back, first at 7:00 in the morning, and then, after my mother hollered from her bedroom window, "Get away from my front door, you bastard, or I'll call the cops," he tried again at 6:30, ringing the bell, leaning on it really, until my mother threw open her bedroom window and, like a Fury, threatened him as best she could, first with consciousness of his own odious behavior, and then, as she had before, with the local police. For a week she was awakened, each day a half an hour earlier, the same blue caricature standing at her door, displaying his badge, until finally, at 5 A.M. one day, my mother was forced to concede, the condominium board having received a complaint about strange men knocking on her door at all hours.

"Good morning to you too," my mother spat as she yanked open the chain lock and directed him to the dining room table. They talked, she said, for barely an hour.

Later she told me she didn't think he believed a word she said. "What do they think? That an alcoholic husband lets his wife in on everything he did? That he came home like a good little schoolboy every night and told Mommy all about his licit and illicit transactions? Don't they teach them anything about alcoholism at the FBI? They think I knew about any of this?!"

Her lips pull tight around her mouth, forming little vertical creases through her lips.

"Somebody ought to tell them," she says, "what it's like to live with an alcoholic. Maybe they want to stop by an Al-Anon meeting some night. Then let's see them have the nerve to go around inter-rupting an old woman's sleep."

The second time the FBI clown appeared, my mother shouted down from her window, "If I'd known, you think I would have stayed with him? You think I would have stood for all that?"

Later, swiping his coffee cup from its place on her table, she said, "What kind of a person do you think I am, blue boy? What kind of a person do you take me for anyway?"

Sifting through this dowry of images, identifying traces, parts of whole pictures that have been given to me, I feel, at times, like the witness of some horrifying tragedy—a gangland-style murder or a satanic mutilation—who's been asked to review photographs for the authorities: not shocked so much as numbed, anesthetized. At times I don't even recognize the people involved; no matter how long I stare, I can't make them out, I wonder if I've ever known them, if I know them now, if they have any relation to me at all.

Looking at them now, I see myself in a teacher's apartment, a young high school teacher's apartment. Lying back on his antique velvet chaise that way, I look as if I am shivering, as if a breeze had just passed over my face, gone through my tie-dyed shirt, and chilled me right to the bone.

The apartment is decorated in academic beige and brown, mostly natural fabrics and neutral colors that seem to provide, in their consistent, spare purity, a guarantee against any gaudy or imprudent pursuits. In the bookcase, volumes of Milton and Proust and Shakespeare and Scott and cut-glass decanters of whiskey and rye, a bottle of bourbon, and a glass bucket of ice. On the wall, next to the bookcase, hangs a photograph of the teacher, looking consecrated and inviolable, in black and white, marching in a procession of educated sons, hallowed columns of black and dark gray moving in front of carved pillars of stone, ornamental geegaws, bronze doors, and plaques. My eyes turn next to the water trickling in lazy rivers down the sides of the ice bucket; to the left I see the only color in the room—an elaborate blue and red and green and yellow Guatemalan tapestry hanging above the carved marble mantle. It reminds me of something, but I can't remember what.

When the teacher reenters the room, he is naked. I sit up and twist a little in my seat, making it impossible for me to see my face, but I can see my arms drop limply, loosely, as if I were waiting for someone to take hold of me.

He, though, is still on the opposite side of the room, rocking slightly on his naked white haunches, rocking against an unfinished-pine dresser. You can see his whole body outlined in the pale moonlight; as he lifts his long blond hair from his shoulders and pulls it back from his face, his biceps fill and his eyes stretch. While he holds the hair, he keeps his eyes, stone cold, on the girl on the couch.

Now he sighs and hauls himself up, his hands pushing his weight from the knees. The way he glides across the room, his thigh muscles compressed, his movements languid, he could be swimming through some invisible, viscous fluid. His embrace, as he lifts me, the girl on the couch, is intense, almost violent. One side of his face, bristly with hair, presses against my neck, the girl's mouth.

Lowering me onto the bed, he relaxes; you can see the arteries in his neck begin to get smaller. And you can see the girl, moving her head back and forth so fast on the bed that you'd think somebody had been fiddling with the speed dial on the projector. You can see him looking down at her, at her T-shirt pushed half up, her jeans zipped but not fastened, her head pressed into the mattress so that the neck seems bent backwards, doubled over. Then the teacher kneels on the bed, positioning his hips, his muscular buttocks so that they are directly over her head, her mouth, her open mouth.

And this is what the girl feels: she feels, looking at herself, as if she is at the movies, watching this whole thing happen to somebody else, someone who is not in the least bit connected to her, someone she hardly even remembers. Seeing herself distanced that way, she feels safe, feels as if she couldn't even imagine it happening to her. Instead it is happening to someone else—anyone else—a friend, her mother, a girl in a story—but not to her. It is happening to all of them, to any one of them, but she does not let herself think that it is happening to her.

My mother, bursting through the back door, says that she doesn't understand anger; then, adjusting her tone and letting me see with that shift a glimpse of the green hills within her, she says that if you want to know her opinion, she'd tell you that some people—like some of those people in Al-Anon—are just asking for trouble. Don't they know, she asks, wrenching open the refrigerator door, that they would be so much happier without it?

Then, reproving me with her eyes, she says, you're a smart teenager, you explain it to me. Through a mouthful of bologna and cheese, she says, you tell me why a person would go out of his way to make his and everybody else's life more miserable.

"Well," she asks, tapping her foot, crossing her arms over her chest, "aren't you going to answer me?" Then, as if suddenly ashamed of her volubility and hoping to find some way to stop it, she reaches into the refrigerator again and, pulling out a jar of gherkins, exclaims, "Aren't you ever going to say anything?"

"Well, aren't you ever going to answer me?" I demanded, trying to pull Kyle back through the distance.

We had been sitting on the balcony of his summer house on the Oregon coast, passing the time playing gin rummy on a foggy afternoon in 1980 or '81. Deborah had gone to a transformative therapy and visualization workshop in Portland; Aaron was playing on the beach with friends. We had exchanged few words, only occasionally trying to identify things we thought we saw in the distance.

It was his turn to deal and he shuffled the cards absently. Like Shep, Kyle was an agile cardplayer and could keep in his head both the score and an accurate record of the cards that had been played, but today he was playing clumsily and seemed to toss down cards without any calculation.

Without drawing it to his attention, I picked up the second queen he had discarded and tucked it between the two others I held. I might have knocked, but before I could speak, he pushed back his chair. Leaning across the wicker table, his finger pointed at me, he said, "If I ever had to tell our father what I thought of him—tell him my real feelings—I know the old guy would come completely unglued. He'd be so hurt, it would just kill the guy," he repeated.

"I could never do it. He wouldn't be able to take it." Then, as if surprised to find it in front of him, he stared at his finger for a moment, then put it back into his pocket.

A moment later, I picked up the third queen he had dropped, and knocked. Peevishly, he reached for the bottle of Jim Beam.

My mother and I have just come back from Edith's Shop, where we spent approximately seventy-two dollars of my father's hard-earned money to buy me clothes for the school year. My mother, using tips gleaned from *Redbook*, has helped me select four coordinated pieces: a burgundy jumper that zips in the front, a matching burgundy and blue-flowered blouse with a Peter Pan collar, a royal blue Villager skirt with pleats, and a cream-colored cardigan—four items that, when mixed and matched, will provide four different outfits and one repeat for the week. I have just turned sixteen and had wanted a deep purple mini dress with stars, but my mother did not think it appropriate and doesn't care for me dressing like "trash"; besides, and perhaps most important, it didn't "go" with anything else purchased.

My mother had hoped, she said, to buy more, but our clothes budget has suffered somewhat, along with everything else, because of my father's drinking. "He's sure to hit bottom sooner or later," she assured me, replacing her credit card in the torn leather pouch. We were able to eke out enough money to buy me my first real bra, though, a Playtex Cross Your Heart, now that my "little plums have blossomed into firm young tomatoes."

It is September, 1969. When we arrive home, the Old Kipper, his captain's hat on the table beside him, is waiting for us, reading *The Wall Street Journal* in his leather club chair. His sterling tumbler may or may not be on the floor on the far side of the chair. Shep rises and gives my mother a kiss on the cheek. This atypical gesture, part of a new game of Shep's, surprises her. She blushes a little and tells him that we'll be right back.

"I don't think he's been drinking," she says, clapping her hands as if she were the recipient of some unexpected good fortune. Noting the querulous look on my face, she giggles as she helps peel off my shirt: it's time for the annual fashion show I'm required to stage for my father. Everything, including slips and other undergarments, must be displayed for his approval.

But this time I don't want to. I have become embarrassed by my "blossoming" and blame myself for the way men have begun to stare at me. During the next few years I will do everything I can, including wrapping Ace bandages around my chest at night and starving myself on fruit diets, to keep myself from full bloom.

"Do I have to?"

"Of course you have to. After all, it's your father's money."

"But Kyle doesn't have to."

"That's because Kyle is a boy. This is what girls do. Someday," she added, winking, "it will be for your husband."

My mother positions me at the door to the living room, tugging at my hair, trying to make the straggles stay behind my ears, adjusting the satiny slip straps, pinching my cheeks to give them a "blush," and then she propels me into the room, as she begins singing, off-key, the theme song from the Miss America pageant. Shep chuckles, as he always does, and then he claps, not maliciously but in true appreciation. Each year, he says I become more and more beautiful. I walk in front of his chair toward the front door, through which I can see outside, a place beyond this place, a world beyond my home, when I hear my mother, in "the wings," telling the girl in the new bra and slip to "turn, turn." Just as the modeling teacher had when I was taking classes last spring at B. Altman's, my mother says, "That's right. Now tuck your bottom in, that's it, move your hips, that's right, one foot right after the other, there you go, there you've got it, keep it steady, that's it, now smile. Smile. You want to show the camera those pearly whites. Smile. That's it. That's a good girl."

It was only after I grew much older, when I found in my mind a collection of images, parts of pictures, and echoes all stuffed away into the same dim recess, that I was able to attach meaning to this assortment of curling irons and starched dresses, tea sets and aprons, visits to cosmetologists and dermatologists, ballet lessons and modeling classes, fashion shows and curtsy lessons, the whole white-glove routine, the training to make me over into a "proper young lady," a training that my mother, with her own barely conscious faith in her own value as a person was incapable of mastering. There I was, pirouetting before my father, lean where she was fat, long where she was short, fair where she was dark, pliant where she was resistant, and this was the payoff, the attempt made to disguise or at least divert my father's attention away from what she considered her recalcitrant self, her seditious heart, her feelings that she couldn't understand and which made her feel "odd" in a way that she never wanted to be. Standing on that runway, positioned before my father, I was to cover for her "flaws," to serve as a sort of replacement for her "shortcomings," her flat hair, her crooked legs, her big hips, her discontent.

Shep claps again and says, "Come here, Miss America, come on over here. Isn't the winner supposed to give Bert Parks a kiss?"

As I moved reluctantly toward him, my pointed young breasts pushing out through the shiny cloth of the new slip, I sank deeper into the realization that for Shep I was nothing but an ingenue or soubrette, some young docile thing to keep him amused. He calls again and I continue moving toward him, even though he looks, at that moment, for all the world like a frog; even though I do not feel like it is really me doing the moving, I move toward him where he, swallowing the bait, circles me with his arms and plants a wet, sticky kiss on my ear. Laughing, straddling me over one pumping thigh, he says, "Want to go for a drive, little girl?" Then, seeing my blush, he laughs again, wheezing a little through glittering teeth. "Aren't you my little girl, my little morsel, my little shrimp; aren't you my little nutmeg?"

"I am not," I say, slapping him more with intention than muscle across the loose flesh of his cheeks before I run from the room and bump into my mother still waiting and watching from the wings.

"Why do you always have to be so mean and rotten to your father?" she demands, raising her hand as if she wanted to slap me. "What's he ever done to you to deserve this? What's he ever done that's been so horrible that you have to treat him—a sick man, an alcoholic—like this?"

Seeing her hand raised as mine had just been raised to Shep, I suddenly understood something about my position with them that had never before come clear.

"Answer me!" she shouts as I race up the stairs. "Answer me!"

As I pull my taupe panty hose over my thighs, Shep watches, caressing his thighs. I am getting ready to visit my boyfriend, a ringleader for the Students for a Democratic Society and part-time

law student at Columbia. Stretching his legs wider, Shep sighs as I
fasten my new bra and shake my breasts into the cups; he whistles a
little tune as I pull my gray slacks up over the panty hose and the
transparent Indian print blouse over the bra. As I dab Tabu behind
my ears, between my breasts, at the edge of my wrists, he asks if I
like my boyfriend. Then he asks me how well I like him, how much.
When I reach for my thin strand of beads, he says, "Here, let me."
He ropes me with his eyes into some kind of private, tacit complicity, and then he fastens the clasp, stroking my shoulders when he's
through, whispering that there's a little bit of lint there. It'll just be
our secret, he says, picking again at the tiny piece of fuzz and
covering the clasp with my collar.

Fifteen years after that last fashion show, I feel, as I write, still
engaged in a kind of archeological pursuit, discovering fragments of a
structure I need to reconstruct. The pieces are there, floating just to
one side of consciousness, flickering as though they were part of a
motion picture being run through a faulty projector. I squint, imagining that if I adjust my vision, put on or take off my glasses, I will see
it—finally—one enormous and revealing tableau.

But even here, in my apartment on West Fifty-seventh Street,
when I shut my eyes, I can still see only part of it, the part that shows
him, a blackish, vaguely defined figure, denouncing the first floor
from the second floor landing, a headless broom handle in his hand.
He looks like Neptune; as if scales, the slithering Qiana sticks to his
thighs and his bare chest swells with latent power. To my young eyes,
he looks perverse and indefatigable, a wrathful deity pounding his
trident into the silent curse of the night. He shifts his weight, first to
the left foot, then forward and around to the right. He's not really
reeling, but close. He does it again, then hurls the broken shaft. It
crashes, caught between two polished spokes of the railing. He reels

again and I catch my breath, then he tosses bourbon-colored kisses down the stairs; they plop and explode, one on each step along the way.

He totters; on the edge of the darkness, circling the night like a plane awaiting permission to land, he lifts his hands from the railing and, with his arms outspread, presents himself silently, unsteadily, to the darkness.

In my dream, I see that someone has murdered my father; yes, murdered him. He is lying at the bottom of the stairs, a broom handle trapped beneath his chest. His legs, probably broken, are twisted beneath him, and his head is cracked open—it must have smashed against the edge of that old marble vase my mother likes to use to mark the bottom of the stairs. From where I am standing, I can't tell for sure, but there might be a knife in his back too. The contents of his skull—brain matter and blood—swirl together, forming a pool of gray and red at the bottom of the stairs. If the pool gets much larger, it will stain the rug in the foyer; if it continues to spread, it will get all over the floor; my mother won't be happy with the mess.

I wonder who did it. Who could have done such a thing? Was there anyone else upstairs at the time? I wasn't aware of anyone going up. It could have been a neighbor, I suppose. Or someone might have come in in the middle of the night without any of us being aware of it, someone we don't know, someone we've never seen who was just passing through, who's never been seen in the neighborhood before or since.

We have to wonder who could have committed such a grisly crime? Who would have had reason to push that old sot down the stairs?

. . .

We watch TV, the three of us, fascinated by the blood coagulating on the steps leading to the Chicago Hilton and McCarthy's headquarters. Shep is on a "business trip." The convention coverage is interrupted by a newscast: 535 Americans have been killed in Vietnam thus far this week. My mother's thin voice breaks through the bullets to ask what my brother, on the eve of his seventeenth birthday, intends to do about the draft. It is too late for academic deferral, and CO status, my mother's first choice, is risky.

"I've talked to Bill Doran," my mother says brightly. "He says if you want to go as a conscientious objector, he'll have one of his associates represent you. He likes you; he likes me," she says, animated by his apparently fond feelings for her. "He might even do it as a favor."

My brother, penetrating, insistent: "But does he know Judge Townsend's politics?"

"Well, I don't know; I didn't presume to ask." My mother is uncomfortable with this challenge; the emphasis on "presume," she backs away; then, recovering, she makes a slight, harrumphing sound meant to make certain to my inexcusably uncouth brother that proper etiquette prohibits the asking of such questions of such people. Rather, she feels she ought to be congratulated for having had the audacity to present our petty little difficulties to one of the town's preeminent lawyers. As it was, it took her three days before she gathered enough courage to open the phone book, then two more passed after underlining his name, before she could lift the receiver and dial.

"Well, I'd need to know that first before—that is, I made a commitment. I'm not interested in being any jackass lawyer's guinea pig."

"I really don't understand why that's important," my mother pleads, faltering a little over my brother's diction, and perhaps fearing

that she must make another call. Besides, she assures herself, goodness and decency are always rewarded. Not killing is good, killing is
bad; ergo, Kyle will be rewarded; he may even be given some kind of
special dispensation, a reward for having had the courage of his
pacifist convictions. When she pauses, however, to apply this logic to
her own situation, her system somewhat breaks down, for it is really
rather hard to fathom why she herself has not yet been rewarded. But,
she comforts herself, patience, like goodness, is also a virtue; she is
sure things will work out in the end.

Ignoring her plea, my brother says he'll probably have to cut his
hair before the trial; brushing the shoulder-length hair back from his
collar to reveal the FUCK THE WAR button he wore all that year, he
says he's not sure anything is worth that.

But my mother, disturbed by his flippancy, is suddenly consumed
by an image of this, her last hope, shattered to bits by a NLF grenade.
As the television shows last week's carnage, she holds the image
in front of her eyes as if to impress the direness of this possibility
upon her own not failing but rather frigid concern. Returning
from the squalor before her, she says, "There's always Dr. Stanton." Marsha told her last week that he is indeed falsifying mental histories for some of his patients, and "Who knows? He might be willing
to write one for you too." Perhaps, she suggests, Kyle ought to talk to
him.

My mother knows this is really risky business, a doctor falsifying
records—she has yet to make up her mind about Dr. Spock's conspir-
acy charge—and it makes her tremble a little to think of a medical
man engaged in such doubtful behavior.

Kyle seems intrigued by this. He says he'd love to hear his diag-
nosis.

But, on second thought, my mother is sorry she brought up the
whole thing. Who knows what it would do to his record? It might
mar it forever, like too many B's in school. "Besides," she adds,
lowering her tone to a discreet level, "we don't really know what he

says about those people; for all we know, he might even be writing that they're homosexuals," this last word choked off somewhere between her esophagus and the air.

My brother laughs and says he could always, as his classmate Tommy Toth had last week, chop off his forefinger with a butcher knife.

This really interests my mother; she hadn't heard about this. She wants to know how it happened, how he did it, if he had help or if he did it alone, if he sterilized the knife, if he marked the finger at the joint beforehand, if it hurt much, if he ended up going to the emergency room. And what, she wants to know, did he tell the people at the hospital, what did they bandage the stump with, what did he do with the finger? She is fascinated by this sordid tale of passion and, she imagines, righteousness; savoring the scene, she shuts her eyes, and sees a woman and a young man at a radiant temple, suffused with incense and organ music. Thousands are there, participating in a great religious rite of which the woman and the young man are the luminaries, one meant to restore all goodness and decency to the world; as they lift the knife that will hack off the finger that would kill, they cry hallelujah, and they cry hallelujah as they lower the knife, they sing hallelujah for the new Christ child who would not kill in Nam is born. Hallelujah.

My mother tells Kyle she's not sure this is such a bad idea after all; she tells Kyle that at least he'd have his life; she reminds him of the importance of being a role model for others. She says, staring down at her attenuated left leg, that he might look very distinguished with nine fingers, the way some men do with a patch over an eye—kind of mysterious and sexy. She says it's an option she'd like him to consider. It really couldn't be so bad if that goon Tommy Toth did it, it really couldn't be that awful, she says, losing sight, as she pleads, of what she is advocating in her desperation to keep this boy from death and, as important, to keep alive the hope that goodness will be, in the end, restored.

My brother laughs, wagging his finger. He wants to know what good one finger is anyway. He says, one finger—more or less—probably won't hurt his SAT scores.

I, for one, don't care what happens to my brother. I hate him and I'd like to see him dead, out of the way. I resent all the time devoted to saving his life and wish Shep were home; while they talk, I sit and bang my ankles against the rung of my chair; like a child, I bang them so hard that they hurt, hoping that the pain will distract me from the rage stockpiled in the munitions dump of my consciousness during the last fifteen years. I stare at my brother, out of reach, hidden behind his wire-rimmed glasses, his long, thin hair draping his face like a shroud, and I see him being carried away on a tank. He is only one among many piles of torn limbs, ripped skin. His face, which you can barely make out, is wrapped in a thick bandage. And there is an IV tube attached to a clot of guts and cloth on his chest; another soldier, unwounded, holds the IV bottle filled with a viscous yellow fluid above his head. Looking at him, you wouldn't be able to identify this heap of flesh and blood as the wunderkind of our local high school, the golden child who smokes marijuana and is complimented by his mother for his taste in incense, the little lamb who comes home late and is excused by his mother because she'd given him an unreliable watch, my mother's cosset, my mother's darling, our very own Übermensch who will soon be a philosophy professor at a prestigious West Coast university and who, she still claims, will be a presidential adviser, the only dove on the Foreign Affairs Committee, by the time he is forty.

It takes me years to recover my sympathy for this boy whose most intolerable characteristic was that he learned to get by, that within the war zone that was our home, he was able not only to survive but to succeed as well.

. . .

I was in a war, fighting a treacherous and inscrutable force, an enemy whose transgressions I hadn't any words for, when Shep's "diamond"-encrusted finger, tracing the edge of my ear, wakes me from my dream.

He joins us with his eyes and his knees pop as he lowers himself onto the edge of the bed. "We've been introduced, yes? Or perhaps you've forgotten; perhaps you thought it was only a dream. I asked our hostess who you were the moment you appeared on the scene. She didn't seem quite eager to reacquaint us, so I thought I'd do the honors myself. Allow me to introduce myself: I am Shepherd A. A. Arbuthnot, the Second or the Third, king of the Scottish high seas, a.k.a. Chef Louis, and I would be charmed, simply charmed—I haven't another word for it—if you would allow me to escort you to brunch this morning. I hear the chef has whipped up something superb for us."

And there was a lavish feast waiting for me when I arrived in the kitchen: pancakes and fried eggs and herring, Wheatena, granola, fruit, and yogurt; as usual, he's prepared to give me anything I want, he would die without me, he again reminds me with his attention.

Shep directs me to my mother's place at the table and settles himself on the bench next to me. After adjusting his weight, he puts one arm on the back of my chair and rests the other on top of the bench rail, thus forming a fence between me and the rest of the world with his body as the gate to the other side.

"Quite a little set-up, wouldn't you say?" he asks in his wet, pearly voice.

"Yes," I answer, rubbing the sleep from my eyes.

"It's just the two of us this morning," he tells me as if I didn't know. "Your mother banged off to some meeting—she ought to try church—at who knows what hour, and your brother—why, only the gods of the Liberal Democrats know where the devil he's gotten to."

"Kyle goes to the Fortune Society meetings on Sundays, Dad."

"Oh, right on. How could I forget? The brilliant young meliorist who needs all his daddy's money to set the world aright." Then, arching his back over the rail of the bench as if about to loosen his belt, he added, "Something told me—uh-hum—before I arrived, that this place had had its license revoked, so I whizzed around the corner and got myself restored at Eamon's before turning back."

I leaned away from the wave of sour mash breath that wafted across my face, nauseating me as it passed. The explanation is offered in response to last night's purge, during which my mother, in another desperate attempt to restore my father to his rightful angelic position, had drained every liquor bottle she could find, including the two tucked into the hip waders hidden in the back of his closet and the gin-filled coffee tin Kyle discovered under his bathroom sink, dutifully placed there by Shep "to help one catch leaks." Somehow Shep feels he is less at fault when he tells us he's had a "nip or two" before we tell him.

Fixing the strap of my nightgown that had slipped from my shoulder, Shep says, "You are most remarkable, my dear."

"Remarkable?" I ask, pushing his hand away. We looked at each other as never before. "You've contributed a great deal to making me so."

"Me? Why, I was thinking the same thing of you." Then, reaching for the strap that had again slipped from my shoulder, he says, "You know, you asked for it."

"Touch me again and I'll kill you."

Something appeared just then to fail in Shep and as he rubbed the back of his hand where I'd hit it, he seemed, for a moment, not to know where we were. But then, after casting about for a second or two, he started again, his lips only quavering slightly. "I've been wanting to ask you all night: just how old is the babe, the child, or did I mean child bride of the house?" he asks, fingering his fly.

"You know how old I am, Shep; almost seventeen."

"Seventeen! Good God! To look at you, you'd think you were twelve. Ten! Nine! Eleven!"

Then, adjusting his tone, "I'll tell you, when I first saw you up there this morning, in the bed you've had since you were my child bride, your eyes shut, your lips like young petals, I thought for a moment that I might just break into pieces, right there on your floor. That's what I thought. I thought this is an angel too, this is an angel I could tell every last nasty detail, every last lick and spit—no pun intended, of course, dear—of my entirely crooked career."

"You already have, Dad," I say, reminding him of previous breakfasts by Chef Louis, during which he had told me about his mistresses ("There are nights when a man needs some comfort"), about my mother's "frigidity" ("Colder, so to speak, than a witch's tit"), and especially about how, to be a good girl, a dutiful daughter, I'm supposed to staunch his despair, lick his wounds, revive his wavering sense of himself as an adman, as a father, and altogether resuscitate his ailing soul through my constant faith and attention. Needless to say, he had never said a word about the scandal, and at that time I had no way of knowing that there was anything to tell.

Then, holding up his palm which was sticky with syrup, he says, "You probably lick all the boys clean."

"Not quite, Dad," I say, embarrassed, despite it all, by this overt reference to my sexuality, which I have done my best to conceal, carrying my guilt, like my school books, close to my chest since my breasts began showing a year or two earlier.

Then, after a pause during which time he coughed and deposited a thimbleful of brown sputum into a pretty silk handkerchief, he steers his face, blotchy with conflicting emotions, toward mine and asks, "There's just one thing I need to know." Holding me with his eyes, he says, "Just tell me you'd be a teensy-weensy bit sorry if I was to croak right here and now. If I was to bug off right now. Just a little bit, just the teensiest tiniest little bit would do."

Then, folding his hand into the shape of a gun and raising it to his temple, he pulls the trigger and laughs. I don't know what he sees in my face that makes him guffaw and shout, "You are an angel! You are! You are!"

From *The Wall Street Journal*, 3 August 1978: "Premier Products' suit alleges that Mr. Arbuthnot received substantial cash payments that varied depending on the amount of time Premier Products purchased through Branner's broadcast-services concern. It is said he also received two white Lincoln Continentals, a small sailing vessel, clothing, at least five color television sets, two stereos, a foot massager, a video recorder, jewelry, liquor, and the favors of women."

It is 1970 and I am sitting at the head of the table at an ostentatious French restaurant in New York. I am sitting upright with my legs firmly crossed, my hands holding the hem of my red miniskirt down as if I were afraid the fabric might fly up my thighs, exposing me, exposing everything as we sit. My hair is cut very short, close to my ears, perhaps to defeminize me, perhaps to keep my father away.

The restaurant, Le Fond de la Mer, is one of Shep's favorites, the vertiginous effect created by the enormous art nouveau patterns perhaps serving, in some inexplicable way, to stabilize him. After pointing admiringly to the tangled designs, Shep turns his back to Kyle and my mother and leans his body into me; he presses his chest into the edge of the table so that the front of his suit jacket almost grazes the splendid cream sauce he's pushed to the side of his plate. He is trying to cordon me off with his eyes, to rope me with his mesmerizing stare into his glorious, spectacular pathos.

"We're off, the captain shouted as he staggered down the stairs," my mother rang out as we piled into my father's freshly waxed black and yellow Chrysler New Yorker. She is looking forward to her meal, to satiating herself at my father's expense. It is my seventeenth birthday.

It is my seventeenth birthday and I am now trapped and Shep is rolling back his sleeves; as we wait for our desserts, he is showing me his swollen elbows and the pinkish, slightly raised rash on the inside of his arms. Life is tough, Shep is saying as he pulls down his lower lip to show me the gums the dentist said were receding. Life is misery, Shep is saying as he lowers his arms and begins massaging his stomach. I have done all this for you, Shep is saying with his fingers as they press in and out at various spots on his belly. I am a wreck, Shep is saying as he reaches for the string of amber worry beads that he's kept in his pocket since finding them at the dump; an absolute wreck, he says as he begins caressing the stones with his fingers, leaving his Pear Daphne, like his main course, untouched.

At the other end of the table, my brother and mother are acting as if this were all normal, as if there was nothing unusual about the exchange taking place at the other end of the table. Kyle downs a glass of wine and reaches for the near-empty bottle to pour what's left into his and my mother's goblets. As he does, he says, "In response to your question, Mother, it was during the eighteenth and nineteenth centuries when it became more profitable to place certain people under surveillance rather than to extend some form of grisly punishment. As I'm sure you know, prisons then became production centers, rapidly manufacturing delinquents and professional criminals whose political and economic value was far from inconsequential."

When, instead of responding, she lifts her spoon, nearly toppling with chocolate mousse, to her lips, he continues. "Power is everywhere, Mother. There is no outside of power. Even if we commit criminal acts, we exist merely as deviations, defined against what is considered right and proper." Then, stopping to look around him, he makes a sweeping gesture with his hand, one meant to take in not only our family but the entire world—the maître d' and bartender, the other patrons, all of Manhattan. "We are all caught," he says, searching her swollen face for some sign that he might not even recognize were it to be there, "trapped in networks of power. Stuck," he concludes, draining the last of his wine.

"I see," says my mother.

And with that unastonishing rejoinder, a flicker of hope lit my brother's face, rounding off his harsh features and arresting, for the moment, the perennial diminution of his eyes. For just those few seconds, I saw the strange small boy with round cheeks with whom I had grown up, the boy who had once had hope. She would, he was saying with his relaxed cheeks, his suddenly sagging jaw, understand what he was trying to say, what he wanted her to see. As if an order of execution had just been stayed, a broad smile of relief broke over his face, illuminating, just for a second, the black pinpoints hidden behind his glasses.

Perhaps seeing this momentary relief cross her son's face, my mother leans her lush body back into the soft cushion of the chair at the other end of the table. It is as if she is saying with her posture, with her languor, that she has had *just* enough—an elegant sufficiency—as if the food, the sound of her son's voice, eloquent and assured, has been all she can take in right now; that the combination has made her feel snug and cozy, even a little sleepy; she bathes in this, her sense of the luxurious, infinite present as if she were a seal sunning herself on a sun-warmed rock.

Then, perhaps fearing that she is losing my brother's attention, she lowers her hands from behind her head and absently asks, "But what I'm asking, dear, is what if someone does something that is really wrong?"

With this, Kyle's smile drops and his face regains its characteristic austerity. He hails the waiter and orders a cognac. He seems suddenly exasperated, tangled by conflicting emotions which tell him both to remain at the center of her sphere, deep within the halo of her affection and, at the same time, to be thrown out, booted out like some bullying drunk at a bar.

Perhaps to regain my attention or perhaps because it's just the way he is, Shep snaps his finger imperiously at the maître d'. "Eggheads," he says when my eyes return to his.

As my father drones on, I look at my mother, patient and adoring, as she throws her head back and, turning her head toward the stereo speaker hidden behind a ficus, announces to no one in particular, "Mussorgsky does something to me," and it's then that I know I will eat when I get home, that I will eat after everyone has gone to bed, that I will eat in secret as if I were engaged in a criminal act because this has become my habit, to stuff myself with Fig Newtons, with pickles, with bologna, with coffee cake, with anything that will fill me—it doesn't matter what. It's the ingestion that counts, the filling up to the point where I feel finally full, the filling up till I feel almost as if I will choke.

"Looks to me like we have a real daddy's girl here," the maître d' says as he discreetly tucks a silver salver under my father's right hand.

With polished nonchalance, Shep signs the check, groaning histrionically as the slim gold pen cuts into his delicate fingers. There are no cards, no bills exchanged here. This is Shep's place, Shep is saying with his quick, graceful signature, this is Shep's territory, he is saying as he leads us, somewhat reelingly, through a labyrinth of tables set like little islands in the sea. Everyone knows me here, Shep is saying with his nods to other patrons, some of whom seem to recognize him, most of whom do not.

And for those few moments during which Shep led us forward, his usual grace marred only slightly by a momentary imbalance, the way a hiccup might interrupt speech, he rose enormously high in my estimation; in the time it took for us to pass through the restaurant and into the lobby, I convinced myself that he really was a success, that he really was a big man. These people just don't know a great man when they see one, I told myself; if they knew Shep, they, too, would admire him, they would have no doubt about his goodness. It took only those few short steps to convince myself that he wasn't just a puling drunk, a miserable old man with runny jowls and yellowed eyes—and to convince myself that if he wasn't a miserable failure, then neither was I.

He passes my mother's overcoat to Kyle and then opens mine to me. After adjusting the coat over my shoulders, he lifts an imaginary mane of long hair out from the collar and then, as he begins to smooth what's not there down over my shoulders and back, as he begins to rub my hips and my bottom, he turns his oily smile to me and grins.

He can't be that bad, I tell myself, turning away from his rotting teeth, his tipsy smile. He can't be that awful, I tell myself; he can't.

Shortly after that dinner, my mother tells me she doesn't understand what more she could have given that she didn't already give. She reminds me that a day didn't go by when she didn't wash, clean, or cook meals; she never once neglected us, not even when she had pneumonia. She reminds me that housework is boring and tedious. She says I'll know that when I have kids of my own; it's liable to bring on what they used to call—before the days of Betty Friedan's book—housewife headache. Making beds, putting meals together, acting as family chauffeur—doing the same tiresome routine day after day—why, it's a mild form of torture, she says. She only took barbiturates once; it was only once when she took barbiturates, right after the president died, that she forgot to leave dinner on the table.

She wants to know what I want from her; what I want that she hasn't already given. She says I should tell her now, have it over and done with, get it out into the air, once and for all.

. . .

It was my brother's faulty right knee that, toward the end of 1969, finally determined his military status. A month before he was to be classified, cartilage was replaced with a metal pin; the draft board agreed with my rather effusive and exuberant mother that the pin might well cause more trouble than my college-bound brother was worth. We celebrated that night, for once really one big happy family, all four of us, even our belligerent, disintegrating Old Kipper, contriving ways my brother's knee could dismantle the war machine, imagining how it could foil the National Liberation Front as well as the South Vietnamese and American detection systems, imagining my brother's defective knee so powerful that it could thoroughly foul up the international war machine, making it so that war would never again be possible. Peace would reign again and love would be restored. One of us, I forget who, put "All You Need Is Love" on the stereo and we danced, all four of us, drunk on Thunderbird and my brother's life, draping our arms around each other, our relief, like the smell of cheap wine, palpable in the air.

But now my mother is crying. We are at dinner, one of the rare times the four of us are together. My mother keeps dabbing her eyes, her Teutonic nose, her arced nostrils, with scented pink Kleenex; Shep, reeling only slightly, keeps getting up, oversolicitously, to replace her tissue, to touch her shoulders or the back of her neck, or to clap my brother hard on the shoulder, as much to show concern, it seems, as to test his ability to take further punishment. A piece of letterhead, embossed and soggy with tears, lies beside my mother's trembling left hand.

"He's the brightest young man to come out of our school system in ten years; his ninth-grade English teacher said so," she cries into the air.

Shep and I are struggling not to laugh; we are sharing this moment in a way we haven't for years. The brightest young man to come out of our school system in the last ten years has just been denied early admittance to Harvard, the only college to which he and my mother applied. I can't say that I don't think justice has been served; indeed, I think justice has been meted out in a way more keen, more exacting, more satisfying than I could have imagined. I am savoring this moment, licking the chocolate from our dessert cookies off my fingers, one by one, and smacking my lips when I get to the tips.

My mother lifts her head and takes Kyle's hand. (Years later, long after Kyle had received his Ph.D. and was directing the philosophy program at a prestigious West Coast university, he will tell me in his somewhat flat way that although he was shocked by that rejection, he was also aware of a certain sense of release; he said it was as if he had been, without realizing it, suffocating all his life and had only just then been offered relief.) She says she's going to write to Harvard telling them all what fools they are for not recognizing his potential; she wants them to know that they have done a very stupid, even a regrettable thing in rejecting her son, that she wouldn't want a child of hers going to that school anyway, that they'll be sorry in the long run, that there are plenty of other good schools her son can go to, plenty of other schools that would sign him up, this boy, her hope, in a snap. She rubs her eyes, then snorts once or twice, trying to control her despair.

Shep winks at me, inciting me as he used to when I was a child, and tells her it's going to be all right. He winks again, firing me up, then grins as he caresses her shoulders, telling my mother it will all work out in the end. There are plenty of good colleges, he says, baiting me with his eyes, for Kyle to go to.

But my mother will not desist. She cannot control herself in the wake of this challenge to her son's immutable and, until today, untarnished superiority. She is saying that she is going to write to the American Association of Educators. She thinks that perhaps the admissions director at Harvard ought to have his head examined. She

says she's going to put that in her letter too. She may even go to Mr.
Van der Veld, the school principal, and enlist his aid in her campaign.

I am about to burst; Shep and I both, through clenched teeth, are
struggling to control our laughter. Something in his gaze, just at that
moment, seemed to ask, quite touchingly, that I help him pretend that
everything was all right between us, that my understanding presented
no problem. And in the first moments of our recovered fellowship I
did, for an instant, picture us in the same dream. He is in a crowd, at
the end of a runway in the South Pacific or it could be the Caribbean,
maybe Mexico, and he is craning his neck, standing up on tiptoe,
bumping into people frantically without bothering to apologize. Now
he is pushing people aside, trying to get a look at me, trying to see if I've
gotten off the plane. When I begin to descend the stairs, he sees the
way my light-colored dress reflects the pure heat of the sun and his
arms open out to me. He directs me to a car—a platinum and chrome-
trimmed Bentley with mink and white leather seats—and as we drive
through hibiscus and citrus groves, I can smell oranges and mimosa
blossoms. There is no pain, no past humiliation; he is not drunk and I
am not his daughter; everything that doesn't work is bleached out by
the blinding light of the sun.

I turn to Shep triumphantly. Such possibilities of renewal bore out
at me from his smiling face that I needed nothing more than his wink
to make up for his omissions. I wink back at him and then, flaunting
our love, I turn my mocking gaze on my mother, my frustrated, pitiful
mother.

But she is not looking at me. Instead she has raised her head up,
catching a glimpse of Shep's pressed, ridiculing lips just before they
relax, the smirk vanishing so quickly that for the next few days, she will
wonder, dully, whether or not she actually saw it. And now my mother
turns her ashen face back to mine. Like a deer momentarily stunned by
the headlights of an oncoming car, she seems only vaguely aware that
something remarkable was about to hit her but couldn't quite figure out
what. She turns blankly back to Shep and then to me as her face

begins to go red, to bloom like a carnation steeped in red dye.

And then she begins shaking her head. She shakes her head violently and then she looks once more at Shep and then back down to me. She is staring in a new way, in a way I had never seen before; she later told me that she saw, at that moment, further than she had ever before allowed herself to see.

"It's your fault too, you know!" I spit out.

Hearing this, Shep makes a sound like a gasp cut short. Then he lunges for me, his sapphire-and-glass-studded fingers raised to strike me. Seeing him lunge toward me again, I tear into the hall, around the marble vase and up the stairs, with Shep, like a wolf, his breath warming my neck, right behind me. Turning into my room, I try to slam the door against him, but his strength is too much. The door collides against my body and then I shut my eyes.

With my eyes shut, this is what I see: I see a frightened young girl bracing herself—her shoulders curl up, forming a nest around her head, and her arms flatten to her sides. But it does no good; the face jerks back, stung by the fist crashing against her fiercely closed lips. Then, as if in slow motion, I see the girl drop like a feather across the bed, her back arched over the carved wooden frame.

And that's when the picture goes blank. I don't see any more. I just hear the sound, the soft, muffled sucking of young flesh, compliant flesh being struck by some kind of hard object.

When I open my eyes, my mother is there, sitting, her back very straight, her legs neatly crossed, at the far end of the bed. Except for her face, she looks ordinary and quiescent, a young Sunday school student trying to win divine grace. She wants to know if I'm all right.

I rise and touch my lips. It was then that I realized that I had grown to her height—we were sitting there staring quizzically at each other, almost as if we thought we might recognize each other, for the first time in our lives.

I rub my mouth again and see my fingers, so recently covered with chocolate, now smeared with red, dripping with blood. More blood falls from my face into my lap, and as I watch the red liquid form an anemone that spreads slowly into my shorts, I begin to cry.

Only later did I realize that I was experiencing, in an instant, the convergence of years of insight that shattered my complacent position in the family. It was as if Shep's blows had jolted me from a dream in which I had imagined myself safe, protected the way a little girl feels when she's in her daddy's lap, his arms, like a seat belt, wrapped tightly around her. Instead it all seemed suddenly a lie, my place in his heart disappearing faster than a star shooting across the night sky. It was as if I had been riding a car—a Plymouth Duster or Chrysler New Yorker—a car I may not have liked, but a car in which I thought I was safe, when suddenly the drive shaft fell out, forcing me to recognize in a way I had never before that something was fundamentally unsound. I was not going to save him, nor could he save me.

Groping desperately for a way of making things fit, as my mother had done many years before in the kitchen, I wipe my lips again, and then I open my hand to her; as if making an offering, I extend my red palm to her face.

And just as I could not receive her offering a few years before, when she, kneeling like a frustrated penitent, turned the hydrator drawer handle to me, she cannot now receive mine. Staring at me, shaking her head, she gives off some kind of low cry that comes from someplace deep within her. She is not crying but grappling, struggling as I am with some kind of new feeling, a new agitation that seems to prelude an awesome and uncharted future. Her face looks deathly pale and her lips tremble as she whispers, her voice sunk very low, her hands pressing down on mine till they hurt, "I'm sorry." For the first time in my life, I hear my proud Teutonic mother say, choking on her words, "I'm sorry."

And then, galvanized by some emotion stronger than our individual sorrows, we begin to sob, heavily, unable to find words. We tremble, trying to control our breath and then suddenly we are together, our heads fallen forward, our two faces in our four hands, our tears wetting each other's hands, diluting the blood, dissolving the pain. As if we had just survived some sort of wreck, we clasp each other in a way we never had before. But then as fast as we had fallen together, we move away, the space between us suddenly so strained it feels almost as if it is thrusting us apart.

Wiping my lips, her eyes, my cheeks, dabbing her nose, she says, groping like an architect desperate to find something, some ballast with which to restore a rapidly crumbling edifice, "You must have fallen down, hit yourself on the bedpost." Choking now, floundering as if she were slipping down a muddy hillside, she says, finding momentary footing, momentary security, in old words, old ways, "Maybe that's what happened. You hit yourself on the bedpost."

"Don't worry," she adds, rising, breathing in fitfully, unsuccessfully trying to staunch her tears, "it will be better by morning."

PART FOUR

Now, eleven years after that beating, it's hard to position myself there, hard to make sense of the queer deposit of images, echoes, half-remembered scenes that has collected around that moment, encouraging my realization that the clues, the power for what needed to be done were held within me. I don't think Shep ever knew or could ever imagine the repercussions his blows would have. Much later, my mother said the night of the beating was the one that took the wind out of her sails. For weeks we walked around the house as if in a dream, not certain what to do, what to say to each other, or even what to ask. Like travelers only vaguely able to decipher the signs and symbols of a foreign country, we moved about randomly, unable to orient ourselves on any of the available maps.

There were times when we did let ourselves get close, times when my hopes would rise as the arteries in my mother's neck began to bulge, only to be dashed when the strain became too much, when our talk seemed literally to threaten her life and I would watch, helplessly, as her breath was cut short and her heart began racing, beating at her ribs like a caged bird desperate to get out. This, my mother's tachycardia, happens over the next few years almost every time we are alone, every time we get close to talking about "it."

I now wonder: were those hits and misses, those abrupt transitions and long pauses some kind of beginning, a necessary part of the mending of our relationship, which, like a delicate fabric, had been stretched too far, torn almost before we knew it existed?

Shortly after Shep lunged at me, when my brother was en route to completing, after only three years, the philosophy program at Oberlin, my mother's mother, during one of her rare visits home, died. The doctors said something broke off in her heart.

For a brief time after, my mother began wearing my grandmother's clothes. My mother's weight fluctuated, wavering between a stately 145 and a majestic 175; my grandmother never went over 130. She had composed herself in rose-beige and pink, sometimes some red, colors that made her look blushing and healthy, colors my etiolated mother complained she could never wear "because of my skin." Even so, after the funeral, we folded my grandmother's clothes—the silk dinner dresses and tea gowns from the Orient, the embroidered chinchilla boleros from Argentina, the transparent chiffon sarongs from India, the silk lounging pajamas from Paris and cashmere sweaters from the provinces, even the painted wooden shoes from the Netherlands and the Tyrolean hats from the Alps—and packed them into eighteen large suitcases. Once home, we emptied them all onto her bed.

My mother's bedroom was in the front of the house, and her windows faced the street leading around the bend to the dump, but she preferred keeping the curtains shut, she once told me, because she didn't care for the seasons. When, shortly after I was born, she moved from the master bedroom into the sewing room, she chose a robin's egg blue and cream-colored calico paper to complement the white hobnail spread her mother had given her when she went to college and the milk glass hurricane lamps that illuminated, dully, opposite ends of the walnut dresser. Indeed, everything in her entire blue and white room seems to match, each part in agreement with every other and speaks of a special need for order, for some kind of grace that might ornament inconsistencies, plaster over unsightly cracks and fissures. The sprigged eyelet curtains match the eyelet dust ruffle and the runner on the dresser, forming a simple and pretty harmony. The two Wedgwood cachepots sitting on either side of the dresser match the two porcelain perfume decanters, the two mountains of women's magazines match in height and content, and on top of the two matching walnut night tables stand two Panasonic alarm clocks, one of which is set ten minutes after the other to galvanize her from her invariable return to sleep. And, of course, there is the horn-shaped crescent she inherited from her mother and which she uses to store odd things: bobby pins, nail files, garters, and tacks. On either side of the dresser, within padded calico-covered frames, hang four of her favorites: there is a Picasso dove with an olive branch in its mouth and a photo of Martin Luther King on the left side, and on the right, a sampler that reads, "Ask Not What Your Country Can Do for You; Ask What You Can Do for Your Country," and a print of a beach scene somewhere, the turquoise waves rolling serenely over an apparently endless beach, spotted only with a few starfish and tern. Scattered among the few Hummel figurines she's collected only sparingly and the earring tree Kyle made her in grade school are neat piles of books: *Jonathan Livingston Seagull, Love Story, I'm O.K., You're O.K.*, and Mark Twain's *War Prayer*. Stuck into the mirror frame is the button she wears to town meetings: ANOTHER MOTHER FOR PEACE. And, of course, there are the two recently installed Yale locks on the inside of the door, an anomaly in this house without locks, without limits.

When we returned from my grandmother's apartment, I sank into two calico-covered reading pillows and began rubbing my hands through thick velvets and stiff organdy, trying to get a sense of this rich stuff, the exotic and foreign material of my grandmother's life, and now I watch as my stocky and unsatisfied mother, on the eve of her fiftieth birthday, attempts to wrench her figure into my grandmother's chenille skirts and pink crepe de chine blouses. Squeezing her thighs together, she tries to tug the fabric up over her exuberant hips, she pinches her buttocks, her front teeth biting down on her lower lip in an agony of anticipation as she struggles to fasten the clasp at her waist, and then she pulls her stomach in and asks, through choked breath, if I wouldn't give the zipper a tug. I grab the pull and try to draw it up over my mother's bulging hips, struggling unsuccessfully to fit the metal teeth together with one hand while I jerk at the pull with the other. We try again; she holds the two sides of the zipper together while I try to yank up the pull with tweezers, with a paper clip, with a bobby pin, with anything within reach that might help me enclose one woman within the other. We try a different skirt, this time a houndstooth in dove gray and taupe. As we push and pull and yank and squeeze, she tells me that at least she had time to show her mother that she loved her even if, it goes without saying, my grandmother didn't have time to show my mother the same. In a way, she says, the stroke was a lucky break, her solicitousness last week in the hospital having granted her a sense of entitlement, a sense of her own unquestionable right to this precious stuff, this exotic cloth, this, the expensive and withheld fabric of my grandmother's existence. Yanking at the skirt, she allows herself to fantasize, perhaps for the first time in her life, an eternal place in my grandmother's heart; as she struggles to shut my grandmother's clasp over her flesh, she allows herself to envision a place or time when this will all make sense, when all that does not fit now will go together, like an outfit, and she will have restored what she feels is irremediably missing.

Finally, we find one, a soft lavender dirndl that will make it over her hips. Tucked in like that, my mother looks confused and uncertain, not sure how it feels, if it fits. She struggles with the hook for a minute, stretching the material as far as she dares, pulling it vigorously from around the back, desperate to find a way of making it stay.

Watching her tug, I fear she's going to tear the material; the seam on the other side looks dangerously drawn. I tell her to put her hands down; surprising myself, I say that with a belt no one will notice, no one will see that it doesn't quite work, that the pieces don't go together.

We find one in the closet, black patent leather. Fastened around my mother's waist, it really looks smart; it looks, I say, turning her toward the mirror, as if it was meant to go with it.

A sigh escapes. She smiles.

Tearing the lids from her shoe boxes, frantically pulling nighties and nylons and slips from her drawers, my mother turns to me, her eyes filled with terror. "Could *you* tell me what my mother looked like?" Moving toward me, her arms full of precious cloth, silk stuff, and chenille, she begs, "Megan. Oh my God, Megan. Do you have any idea what has happened?"

"Do you realize," my mother announced, clutching the area below her left breast an hour after I had arrived home from college for the '72–'73 winter break, "that this is the most I've seen of your father since you left?" She then supposed she ought to be thankful for small favors; shoving an empty dinner plate toward my place at the table, she said that at least she gets to see him sober once in a while.

The night I arrived, I was made to promise that Langdoc, my chauffeur, could take me back to school. The next day, my mother and I went to her health club for massages and then out to dinner— we thought Shep had passed out for the weekend—but that night, I woke to find him crumpled over on the side of my bed. My mother was in bed, having felt her tachycardia come on, just minutes before we got home.

"Good evening; may I introduce myself?" he said, anchoring me with his eyes.

"Dad, we've met before."

"It must have been our hostess, our hostess with the mostest. I fear, however, somehow, I have forgotten." Then, after a pause, "You went out."

"Yes."

"With your dear mother."

"Yes."

"Your mother used to scare you . . . Does she still now?"

"What do you mean?"

"Exactly as I said. Your mother, the female who bore you, who you bore tonight, does she, how shall I say, does she frighten you, alarm you, disquiet, startle, or unman you? Does she take your breath away, make your teeth chatter, make your blood run cold; does she, in other words, make you shit in your pants? That's what I wanted to know. If she made you crap in your crinolines."

"Not that I see it as any of your business, Dad."

"Call me Captain."

"Sure, Dad."

"Captain, please."

"Captain please."

"Now try Captain, sir."

"Captain sir."

"That's better. Now, how was your massage?"

"It was fine," I said, turning my head away from the sour bar breath that washed over my face, repulsing me like polluted air on a humid day.

"I've never had one, so I just wanted to know. I just wanted to know what they do to you."

"Well, I told you: it was fine," I said, as I tried to inch myself away from his arms. (Later, after the scandal broke but before my mother divorced Shep, when I detailed this conversation to her, she said that as far as she knew, my father never did have a massage in his life. As if the hill we had been pedaling up for the last few months were suddenly too steep, she tossed her bicycle to the side and, turning about-face, added that she probably would have known about something like that; beginning her descent, she said it's nice to know that at least at that point he was still telling the truth, that at least he wasn't lying, she added, one hundred percent of the time.)

"It hurts me when you turn away from me," Shep cooed, grabbing my chin. "And to think: your own father. Your own paterfamilias, your very own daddums, the prime mover in the case, the author of the work, the originator, the creator, the headwater—or is it waiter?—the mainspring, the instigator, the big what and wherefore; the all." He winked, reaching toward me.

"That won't work anymore," I snapped, trying to hold my eyes steady as he winked again. There was something in that wink, perhaps in the way it attempted both to tempt and to subdue, that reminded me of a Chinese fairy tale my grandmother used to tell, the one about the red-fanged ogre who drowned and then reappeared as a ghost—its hair, like my father's, wet and tangled, its skin, like his, opaque and bloated. It waited, winking by the water's edge, to seduce down a substitute.

"Now tell me I'll get to drive you back to school," he said, turning his bloated face down.

"Why do you want to drive me?" I asked as I turned away from the plaintive eyes, the imploring tone, the Cheshire Cat smile.

"Nutmeg, what has gotten into you? You mustn't, you know, turn away from me." Grabbing my chin again, he said, "You know you'll kill me if you do."

Then, after I remained silent, he demanded, "What has made you act this way?"

"Darling, let me put it to you this way: I started my job the month you were born. I deserve a return. I demand a return."

When, after I still hadn't answered him, he said, his tone shifting, his eyes struggling to meet mine, "I don't understand, *no comprendo.* I made you the friend and companion of my life. I loved you more than a father loves a daughter. Everything I've done, I've done for you." He thumped the left side of his chest, then paused for a second before adding, "Am I asking too much? Is it asking too much to ask you to love me, to not turn away from me?"

And I still don't know what he saw in my face, just at that moment, that made him turn his head away and ask with only some slight vindictiveness, "Has it all been a sham?"

Then, after clearing his throat with a delicate uh-hum, he asked, "Have I really no value for you—at all?"

A few days later, when it came time for me to leave, I still felt, despite my hatred, incapable of witnessing the disappointment in his eyes, the way his great broad shoulders would collapse, like air out of a balloon, were I to tell him that he could not drive me back, and so I had turned the ignition key, hoping he wouldn't hear the car start, all the while fearing that my decision to save myself, to preserve my own miserable life at the sake of his, might well send him into a void of disappointment from which he would never return.

But he did hear the car start and he did appear beneath the shroud of wisteria draped around the garage door, in his underpants, crying, a besotted ogre waiting by the water's edge, one finger raised, begging a substitute down. He was crying so hard I knew I would hear him all the way to Poughkeepsie; he cried so hard I knew I would hear him throughout the night—a wolf baying at my heart—and into the forever of the following morning. When I shut my eyes, I can still see his face in the distance like some kind of black hole from which erupted a sound the likes of which I'd never heard before, a wail that sounded desolate and inconsolable. It was when I saw his arms stretch, when I saw the hands that had caressed and betrayed me reach out that I could not bear it, I could not decide whose life was more valuable; at the edge of the driveway, I pressed on the brake and turned to my mother, who had joined me, only vaguely realizing that someone must bring the car back.

"Mother, what should I do?"

"Hmmm? What, dear?" Her voice rose and then fell, echoing down. She looked at me strangely, pityingly. She looked as if she did not know what was going on.

"Mom, please."

She had put on her makeup hastily and I could see the line where the base coat met the pale flesh of her throat.

"Mom, please," I repeated as my father, seeing my hesitation, approached, his arms still outstretched, his old yacht-patterned boxers flapping in the breeze. He came so close I could see the tears streaming down his face, soaking his chest, forming rivulets of pain that cut like tracks across his chest, his torso, down to his groin.

He came within ten feet of the car, and it was then that I felt hung for some eternal, vertiginous moment, as if over a cliff, looking down. The picture is fixed in my memory like a freeze-frame in a movie: my left foot on the brake, my right on the accelerator, my hands trembling as he moved within a foot of the car. At that moment, with him drawing nearer and my mother so far away, I could have reestablished our old bond as easily as winking.

"Megan, butternut, cinnamon buns . . ." He approached the driver's side, winking through his tears, his arms outstretched.

I could have let myself fall down into that pit; I could have sunk back into the pernicious and lethal communion of our love as easily as I had once before, long ago, when I sank into my daddy's lap, his arms wrapped around me like a seat belt, as we drove his great big Chrysler New Yorker down the gentle slope of our street.

Our eyes met and my hands shook. I felt a sudden terror at the weakness our contact produced. I turned to my mother again. She looked beautiful, she looked pathetic, she looked as if she didn't know where she was, couldn't figure out where she was going.

"Mom?"

She turned to me and something strong and deep surged up within me. I pressed the accelerator.

Backing onto the street, I saw my father standing at the edge of the driveway, withered then to half his normal size. He was sobbing so deeply that he looked as if he'd been wounded, crying so heavily— collapsed in on himself—that it looked as if someone had thrown something at him—a knife, a stone, a bullet.

Once past him, I moved slowly up the street I knew so well, the street that led at one end to the dump, at the other end to his office, and I didn't look back. I put my hand over the mirror as if to stop him from coming any closer, I put my hand over the mirror so that I couldn't look back, I could only go forward.

I did not look back.

My mother and I are driving toward Vassar, away from my father, who, for all we know, is still positioned at the end of the driveway. My mother is saying that we are the luckiest people in the world and I say yes, we are. Her voice is like music when she says that we have escaped, and I say, yes, completely. For the rest of our drive, we continue like this: she begins sentences and I finish them, our voices weaving in and out of the other's almost like lovers'.

Reaching through the distance, her eyes open wide and she says, "We are going to make it."

"And there's nothing between us."

"Together." She smiles.

I love her in the deepest cells of my being when she says that. Her breath perfumes the air in our car, making me woozy and faint.

"Mom?" I turn to her sitting beside me.

She turns her ravaged face toward me and the vision breaks. She does not seem to recognize me; she looks as if she thinks I am speaking too loudly. "Mom," I repeat, but my voice trails off as I realize she is not really listening, that she doesn't quite know who I am. Wanting, for some reason, to spare her the pain of recognition, I turn back to the road, away from her face. There are traffic cones there, very bright, positioned like little orange sentries doing what

they can to keep me and the woman beside me from hurtling ourselves into the wooden meridian that divides the northbound from
the southbound lanes of traffic. They stand between the woman and
the girl and the oncoming traffic, they will not let the two women,
this mother and daughter, abandon themselves to that unrestrained
zone.

"We don't need him," I wanted to say. He is making us sink,
taking us down.

"They'll probably go and muck up this road too," she says, shutting her eyes, closing it out.

She says they'll probably go and muck up this road too and I did
not give in to temptation, I did not turn the steering wheel off to the
right or the left, I did not smash the car into the orange and red trees
that glow in the twilight by the side of the road.

The road narrows to one lane. Turning back to the uncharted
darkness before us, she says, "Please watch where you're going. We
don't want to have an accident."

Emptying my books, my clothes, my fantasies onto the vast,
insurmountable steps of the dormitory, she lifts things clumsily, not
sure what to do, what to say. Standing there in the pinkish glow of
the halogen light, she looks pathetic and shriveled, she looks as if she
were saying that it wasn't her fault, that she hadn't asked for any of it,
that she had done the very best that she could.

Then a crash, unendurable, as a porcelain lamp, wrapped loosely
in blankets, slips from her hands and shatters on the asphalt. She
turns her distraught face to me as a child would.

"We can fix it," I say, picking up pieces.

"Silly," she mutters. "Clumsy," she says, shaking her head mis-
erably.

"It's no big deal, Mom; don't worry about it," I say, jamming the
fragments into her hands.

"I should have known better. I should never have done it."

Still shaking her head, she puts down the pieces and reaches for the keys, which I drop into her palm. Then she says she's sure he'll be out by the time she gets back; she's worried about him, she adds, she thinks he might be getting worse, he might be drinking more, she reminds me that he does have his good characteristics.

I watch as the hand folds around the keys, the tight-fisted fingers excluding me, as her voice, dull and hollow, seems to be moving away, coming at me from a distance of hundreds of miles.

She backs down the drive and I watch as her figure gets smaller and smaller, watch as she disappears into the darkness and the road becomes just a blank hole, filled with a vast emptiness it seems nothing could fill.

In my room, I move toward my bed and slide open the window. Framed as it is by a lavender and white sill, the air, the darkness, looks like a great open mouth. If I were to fall asleep with my bed pushed against that open window, I could easily tumble into the darkness, into a place or space in which I imagined I might finally find peace.

It was then that I swallowed a handful of Valium, downed it with a pint of Jack Daniels left over from the last dorm party. Then I stripped and lay down on the bed.

The sheets, cool with night air, make my skin feel damp and cold. I let the cold wetness wash over me, enjoying as it chills me the sensation of releasing, of surrendering to the cold, to the nothing, the no-feeling. There was no weight and no pressure, no bottom and no end, just an unrestrained zone that engulfed me, an ocean of space in which I felt finally restored.

The stained toilet bowl spun like the bottle of Jack Daniels on the cold bathroom floor. I pressed my cheek into the decades of grime crusted in the dusty floor tiles, then I hauled myself up, again, to the edge of the bowl as my body pumped out the poison, insisting on life. I heaved again, expelling little yellow suns that surfaced in the detritus of my being, refusing to let me sink down.

Then, far away and just for a second, I saw, somewhere on the other side of an ocean, a thatch-roofed cottage.

There was smoke coming out of the chimney.

There were only fragments of the wreck in my dream—the shattered ribs of the hull, the mast cracked in two, the waterlogged instruments sinking like stones. As the unfamiliar waters filled our lungs, we thought we'd drown, but then we remembered our ancient gills and the water was no longer an enemy. We swam together effortlessly, she and I, her movement repeated by mine, mine then repeated by hers, as our bodies grew long and sleek in the water and our hands became webbed, our legs and arms strong as otters'.

We joined with others and we all moved together, all those who had survived, one giant, glistening serpent, a growing, glowing cohesion gliding in a strange and powerful trance of movement. We swam in the warm belly of the sea, a tongue of light from above leading us on, compelling us to surface, refusing to let us sink down.

PART FIVE

"Mom, you said you always knew we were close."

"Thick as thieves. You had the same sense of humor."

It is a volatile spring day, with sheets of rain changing in seconds to beautiful blankets of sunshine. It is the eve of my twenty-ninth birthday, and we are inside, sitting at her kitchen table, drinking tea. The quiet orderliness of things—the regular patterns on the iced cookies, the repeated border of daisies on the new Lenox, the pretty way my grandmother's sterling sugar tongs hang from the handle of the Wedgwood sugar bowl—reassures us both.

"And you've said that you knew he was always nicer when I was around."

"Yes. *Anybody* could see that," she exclaimed, as if protesting against an unjust allegation of myopia that had yet to be proven.

"Anybody? Just what do you mean by 'anybody'?"

"I just mean that you were always with him."

"Not *always.*"

"It seemed that way."

"He paid attention to me."

"You didn't want to do things with me," she said, steadying her lips.

"You rejected me."

"I thought you liked him best. You even walked like him. Be-sides," she shot back, "you were very self-sufficient. You didn't like to be helped."

"I didn't like to be helped?"

"That's what I said."

"But how can a three-year-old not like to be helped?"

"I don't know, but that's how you were."

"I was a child; I went where I could get attention and love."

"I would have loved you."

I paused for a moment. "Well then, how come you didn't love me? How come you didn't help me?"

"You were a very vindictive child."

"Mother! How can a three- or four-year-old be vindictive?"

"Easy. Lots of them are."

"But what would have made *me* vindictive?"

"I told you: you were always with him."

"But why did you think he was vindictive?"

"Because he was. Underneath it all, he was unhappy, a sad sack. I thought I could make him happy."

"Did you want to make him happy?"

"I was his wife."

"But did you want to make him happy?"

"I was his wife." Then, after staring through the kitchen window as though hoping to find something outside that might explain everything, she said, as directly as perhaps she ever had, "Don't you understand me? I was married to him. I was his wife."

"Don't you understand, dear," Shep said in the fastidious British accent he had adopted, as he filled out my application to Vassar, "the sticker will look soigné, shall we say, on the back of the car." Besides, he reminded me with his grunts, his groans, his swollen joints, and his disfigured fingers, as I filled out the application to Reed, Oregon's college for the seriously alienated and my first choice, the Old Kipper would surely sink without me.

The first day we drove to Poughkeepsie, the morning mist had vanished, bright sun dazzled my eyes, and the Hudson Valley air moving gently off the Catskills was clear and fresh. When the guard shut the iron gate behind my father's car (which he had waxed and polished in anticipation, I suppose, of its new sticker), we entered an unreal sanctuary surrounded by stone fences and huge pine trees. This was an extraordinary place, beyond the grip of time. Here were the daughters of foreign textile merchants and investment bankers, some with diplomatic connections and others holding upper echelon positions in Washington. There were Armstrongs and Weyerhausers and Ingersolls, girls who thought it nothing that Jackie Kennedy and Jane Fonda, Edna St. Vincent Millay and Elizabeth Bishop and Mary McCarthy had gone here. There were children with funny names like Biffy and Lindbergh and Drayton, children with numbers after their names, whose fathers were, like mine pretended to be, casually wealthy. It was clearly, they said with their languorous postures, their elegantly rumpled clothes, their disdainful gestures, a wealth that came without strain or fight, almost as if it were their genetic due. These were children who smoked Gallois or Marlboros languorously, always languorously, blowing smoke in soft streams from their thin, clearly defined lips or, as did the Francophiles, through their noses and mouths, simultaneously forming elaborate and graceful curves of ash gray that dissipated languorously into the air. It was there where I learned that anything—cars, lineages, accents—could be put on a scale where this was better than that; where one's genetic predisposition to high spirits compelled one to forget about the war, forget about individual suffering, forget about pain, as if these were but mild embarrassments, too trivial really to interfere with the daily conduct of living. It was a place from which most emerged, their faith that all they wanted would be granted expediently and with all good grace, even more firmly entrenched than when they had entered.

On that first day, my father held my shoulders, looking as if he would like to pin my hips to the dark, icy wall of the hall, a tear in his eye. As usual, my mother stood to the side, holding the corridor door for him, waiting but not watching until finally he had released me.

As my parents turned and walked away, I watched as the series of dark wooden doors of the dormitory corridor multiplied, in my consciousness, their distance from me; then, as the gate shut them out, I could see the gatekeeper's sure hand drop the strike into the latch.

I remember little that is specific about those four years; it's almost as if that time were somehow pleated up, one year upon the next, leaving but a trace, a single fold. For four years, I felt as if I existed outside or just slightly to the side of an enormous fishbowl, unable to touch all this glittering, unsullied existence, but remaining always fascinated by the flashing colors within. I lived convinced that I would wake up some morning and find that this clean air, these brilliant teachers, and all the interesting books had vanished and that I would be back in my parents' house, back in a place where there were no borders, no limits, no locks. Sitting in classes was like sitting in a dream. Everything was new and marvelous, but somehow not real and therefore not to be trusted. I felt in a state of continual surprise: for the first time in my life, I had no one else to look after, no one to coddle, no one else's burdens to bear. I lived in perpetual fear that something ghastly would happen to me whenever I was doing something I enjoyed instead of servicing someone else. It all seemed so odd, and even incredible at times, the most incredible aspect being the distance between my father and me protected by a towering gate and a Yale lock.

It was from this perspective that I experienced college: the more wonderful or joyous the scene, the more unreal it seemed. I went about somewhat vacantly those four years, the pine trees and locked gate forming a boundary between me and hell, with hell being the only thing that seemed, ultimately, real. I felt certain that none of these girls had experienced what I had; it was as if the gold hoops they wore in their ears, the pinkies they raised at four o'clock tea, the "bloodies" they consumed at brunch, the way their mouths held vowels as if they were jewels with rough edges—all this served somehow as a talisman, some kind of magical amulet, forfending, like a cross before the devil, even the potential for engagement in sordid affairs.

"I don't know if one would want to call his behavior sordid," Kyle said as we walked toward the apartment he and Deborah had rented just after they announced their engagement six months before.

It is 1973, a week or so before he is to marry Deborah Rosenzweig, a woman who had a penchant for precise calculations and, therefore, my brother. They will be married in the woods by a former nun, now a Unitarian minister, and then, as stipulated in their marriage contract, both will smash a glass hard against a rock. The reception to which both families are invited will be held in the arboretum on campus.

Deborah, as usual, has taken care of everything, hoping to ensure that this "happy little shindig" will run as smoothly as the stars, her only concern being Shep's "inimitable form." But she needn't have worried about that, for Shep arrived, true to form, ten hours before guests were due. He pulled up, honking the horn of an emerald green Lincoln Continental with a white vinyl roof and white leather upholstery—his present to the happy couple. The swank automobile, although somewhat incongruous with Deborah and Kyle's down-home style, was festooned with pink and white ribbons, an assortment of tin cans and garters, and a hand-painted sign, taped to the back window, that read JUST HUNG. Twirling a half-empty bottle of Dom Pérignon as if it were a lariat, he tumbled up the stairs to their apartment dressed in a groom's traditional costume: gray slacks, a wide cummerbund, an understated tuxedo shirt, a cravat secured with a "diamond," a black swallow-tailed cutaway coat, a felt top hat, and spats (the other half of the bottle had been consumed, he explained, along the Pennsylvania Turnpike, in an effort to entertain some lonesome young hitchhiker). The rest of the case of "D.P." was in the trunk. Throughout the trial, it never was made quite clear whether this car (and/or the champagne) were also part of the scandal cache. At the time, we didn't even wonder.

I had been called out a few days early to help with the arrangements and that morning was sent by Deborah to retrieve Kyle from his cell in the library. On his second attempt, Kyle was admitted to every college to which he and my mother had applied. "They just weren't ready for you the first time," my mother cooed, clapping her hands as she read the letter announcing his admittance to Oberlin, her first choice. "That's God's country," she told him in reference to the blighted agricultural wastelands of the Midwest.

There were no future ambassadors at Oberlin, no aspiring heads of state or Nobel Prize winners, no budding secretaries of defense or CEOs or real estate moguls; these were not the petty and well-mannered sons of good old boys you might find at Harvard or Yale; rather they were sober and diligent boys who were committed to changing the world, boys who wore straggly beards and jeans that sagged in the crotch, boys who, being ranked second best instead of just different, studied so hard that by sophomore year, their loose flesh hung from their arms, their torsos in soft, sad heaps like ice cream moving slowly down the sides of a cone. The girls, like Deborah, suffered somewhat from a kind of guilelessness; they were easygoing and gullible creatures, intelligible and unequivocal women who arrived imagining themselves responsible and left, like Deborah, not demanding much of themselves, since the future was hardly dependent on their own efforts. Kyle was, after only three years, graduating with honors and would enter Princeton's Ph.D. program in the fall.

I found my brother in his dingy, windowless carrel in the penumbral basement of the college library, where he had been since 6:00 A.M. Because of his study habits, he was known as St. Jerome; I never found out whether the reproduction of the Dürer engraving of the saint that hung on the door was placed there as a joke or for inspiration.

After hearing his perfunctory response, I let my initial question drop, and we walked across the quad in silence. It was a gray day and I couldn't tell if my brother was weighed down by his ponderous thoughts or whether it was something else.

"You know," he said suddenly, as if answering a question, "she has an admirer."

"She?"

"Deborah. My wife. My wife-to-be."

"I see," I said.

"He thinks she's like the earth, and the moon," he added.

"And?" I asked, not sure how to continue.

"And probably the stars as well, although that he hasn't said; that's something I've just now made up."

I turned to him confused.

"He calls her 'little.' Little Deborah."

"She's not so little," I commented, thinking of Deborah's long, slender face and figure.

"No. But he calls her that nonetheless."

We walked a moment more in silence.

"Well?" I asked.

"He watches her, in the weight room, from the bleachers."

"Really?"

"Yes. I've seen them dance together. That's when he started calling her 'little.' "

"How do you know all this? I mean the 'little' business, the moon business?"

"She's told me."

"Of course she has," I added uncertainly.

We continued on, in silence, heads down, hands behind our backs.

"He wants to go to bed with her."

"Oh dear."

"Yes."

"She's flattered, I suppose," I said finally.

"I suppose," he repeated, monotonously. "I wouldn't know. I haven't really asked."

"You're going to ask?"

"It's really none of my business."

I pondered for a moment. Perhaps he was only pulling my leg.

"Are you serious?"

"Dead," he answered without hesitation.

"You're concerned?"

"Concerned? No. What gives you that impression?" Then, perhaps softening a little, he added, "I don't think I would really call it 'concerned.' It's really more like . . ."

"Like?"

"She wants to know what to do," he said abruptly.

"About . . . ?"

"About him."

"Of course," I said, feeling slightly idiotic. "But just what is it that concerns her?"

"I wouldn't say she's concerned. No," he said, shifting the weight of his backpack. "She's not concerned."

"I'm not at all sure I follow."

"She wants me to tell her whether or not to sleep with him," he added impatiently, as if I were being deliberately, offensively obtuse.

Feeling the picture at last clarified, I said simply, "But she's marrying you."

"But don't you see?" he asked, still irritated. "That's just the thing. She's not married to me. Not yet, that is."

"But she will be married to you in a number of days."

"But she's not married to me now. She can still do what she wants."

"You've discussed this?"

"It's only right."

"Who says?"

"I says."

"You mean right as in—"

"As in every way. She has the right to do what she wants. She'll see him this afternoon."

"To sleep together!"

"To decide. And, I suppose, to play basketball. They like basket-ball."

"You've told her your feelings?"

"I have no feelings about the matter."

"You have no feelings about the matter?"

"No. I mean, yes; I have no feelings, just as I said. Aren't you paying attention to me?" Then, adjusting his tone, he added, "She has the complete freedom to do what she likes. There has been no legal commitment made. It's up to her to decide."

We turned left on Maple Street; his apartment was in sight. Turning his stolid face up to me as if I had asked a question, he said, "I've spoken to him."

"And?"

He was silent for a moment. "He's all right." Then, as if he were holding something back, he added, "An engineer."

"Oh, I see. Did you know him before?"

"He makes stupid jokes," he said, ignoring my question. "It's a habit with engineers." Then, after a pause, he said, "He's told me he has nothing but the highest possible respect for me. He just also happens to like my wife—my wife-to-be, that is."

"Does she want to?"

"She says I've slept with more people than she has." He readjusted his pack again, this time slinging it over one shoulder.

I was both fascinated and pained watching my brother that late morning, watching his sclerotic intelligence at grips with itself. Would anything ever provoke him? Seeing his eyes protected by blankness, I couldn't help feeling sorry for him and asked again, "Does she want to?"

"I don't know," he said, seeming truly puzzled. "You'll have to ask her. He says he thinks I'm a lucky man."

"Are you sure that she'll meet him?"

"Why are you asking me questions that I cannot possibly answer?" Then, as if it had been me and not him who had brought up the whole thing, he said, "If the answers are so important to you, why don't you just ask her?"

I tried a different tack. "What do you want her to do?"

"She told me if I didn't want her to go, that would put a stop to it."

"But you didn't say that?"

"I didn't say that."

"Have you told her you'd be hurt if she went?"

"How do you know that I would be?" he asked the same way a child does when faced with an adult who knows better than it does. "I'd have to wait and see what she did."

"What will you do if it happens?"

"Why bother thinking about things like that now? There's no sense thinking about things before they happen."

We were at the apartment and we climbed silently up the single flight of stairs to the floor he and Deborah rented. Then, as if he felt his thoughts had been left incomplete, he added as he pushed open the door, "Actually, Megan, I've never really much believed in anything that happens to me."

A shaft of light fell upon us as we stepped in the door.

"Howdy," Deborah called from the front room, where she was arranging a small potted cactus among the picture frames and polished stones displayed on top of the piano.

"No doubt from him," Kyle said, it seemed, both wanting and not wanting Deborah to hear.

"You're not jealous?" she asked coyly. Passing by on her way into the kitchen, she tousled his limp hair the way she might a child's.

Kyle dropped into a chair and reached for the stereo. With the push of a button, the apartment was filled with the sound of the Grateful Dead trucking so loudly that not only the window panes but the entire floor rattled with the beat. This had been Kyle's habit for as long as I could remember: hating silence, he always turned the stereo on as soon as he entered his room.

"Well?" Deborah shouted, still smiling sweetly as she returned from the kitchen with a watering can.

"Should I be?" he hollered as she passed by and continued out of sight.

Turning back, she said, winking at me, "I would think—"

"What would you think?" he demanded, turning his face away from her. As I watched him sitting there, inert in his chair, while Deborah, ignoring this outburst, continued to the front room, I wondered how I would ever be able to describe my brother to a stranger. He neither tapped nor chewed his fingers, nor raked his hands through his hair, nor pulled at stray threads in the upholstery; he just sat there blankly, his face gaunt, not moving an inch. This memory of him sitting in incorruptible, chaste silence got lost among the refuse heaped in my memory until shortly after his marriage, when Deborah reported that he had regular nightmares in which he became lost forever in some smothering, black hell.

Returning, Deborah sat on the arm of his chair and, pulling his head to her breast, said, "What if I met him?"

"What if you did?" he asked dispassionately, without moving his head away. "You tell me. What if you did?"

"No," Deborah said as if he were a child who hadn't understood. "I want to know what *you* would think, what you would feel." She ran her fingers through his hair, pulling it back from his forehead.

"It's a decision you'll have to make, Deborah. I have no right, no authority by which to dictate your behavior. You are free to decide."

"But just tell me you'd be a little bit jealous," she said, cuffing him once under the chin.

"How do I know what I'd feel?" he demanded, pushing her away and reaching for the volume control on the stereo. "You ask me questions that I cannot reasonably answer."

And this was just the moment Deborah was waiting for. She never admired Kyle as much or found him as irresistible as when he was being adamantly intellectual with her, when he put her in her place, so to speak, by refusing to engage on her level. As I watched, she seemed nearly to swoon, his intellectual dispassion making her feel woozy and, in some irresistible way, insubstantial. It was the exhibition of his unyielding intellect that moved her most and made her deliriously happy that she had, as she once confided to me, "snared" him. At these moments she feels almost as if she would like someone to pinch her to see if she is really, in fact, awake.

"I know it matters to him," she said, smiling brightly at me. Then, chucking him under the chin again, she added, "You may not think it matters, but I know it does." Then, rising, kissing him on the top of the head, she said, "I'll make lunch."

Her skirt—a full-cut, unrefurbished 1940s model with three-inch blue and red and orange polka dots—swished back and forth, making a hushed, sexy sound as she padded confidently into the kitchen. Watching her go, I could tell that, despite her devotion to her husband-to-be and to their domestic well-being, she would always be experienced by others as, in some way, self-centered and controlling, offering, unremittingly, a kind of gentle and loving care unto death. Here she was acting as his intermediary, helping him negotiate the path between the abstract and the real, controlling the flow of substances between his flesh and the world. When lunch was served, she didn't eat with us but rather worked around us, polishing cabinets, rubbing at stains in the Formica, sponging the oven top, eliminating disorder, getting rid of dirt, halting decay: all part of a benign frenzy of activity perpetuating the simple happy present. I was certain that she had no real intention of sleeping with her nameless suitor but instead simply hoped to provoke my brother, to tease him into an expression of that dispassionate intellect that so thrilled her with its tenacity, its obduracy.

When lunch was over and Kyle and I were sitting in the living room, she appeared from the bathroom in her wedding gown. "What do you think?" she asked, twisting the gown, adjusting her figure in the hall mirror. Standing there, framed by the ornate gilt border of the mirror subtly illuminated by the filtered afternoon light, she became for us a kind of portrait in white, contained and framed, her beauty immobilized, for a second, as if behind glass.

I don't think my brother said anything; he just smiled as she approached. He rose and I watched them embrace and then Kyle turned so that his back was against her breasts. Appearing infinitely relieved, he moved back and forth there, melting into her love as he used to with my mother, feeling his muscles go slack and the tension run out of him. With his eyes shut, he looked as if he had just found something he thought he had lost, some exchange that would provide some of the early magic of childhood and give him, in some way he couldn't describe, a sense of oneness with the world.

He rubbed his back once more against her breasts. "I couldn't bear it," he said suddenly, lowering his head away as if ashamed of himself.

I picked up my jacket. As I headed for the stairs, I heard their bedroom door shut quietly behind me.

"Of course, no one would deny that he was always his own worst enemy." My mother pushed the plate of cookies in my direction.

My mother had been struggling during the recent days with a new theorem: if, as she continually reminds us, he is a "good" alcoholic but society sends him to jail, then he is a bad man. And if he is a bad man, then what might he be—or have been—capable of?

Our exchange that night was, as usual, made awkward by years of misunderstandings, ignorance, and pain. By working together, I hoped we could make our way toward some light.

After settling her cup in its saucer, she declared, "And I had decided long ago that if there wasn't anything to be done about it, I didn't do it."

I let this drop, hoping to make some headway in another area.

"Mom, you once told me I had trouble sleeping, ever since I was an infant."

"You were just like King Henry the Eighth—so afraid of your dreams that you refused to go to sleep."

I pondered this for a minute before, noting my silence, she added, "But if someone were to ask me, I'd tell them that you were basically a happy baby."

"But didn't that make you think?"

"Think what?"

"Think about why I might not be able to sleep, about him and me?"

"Well," she said, ducking, "it wouldn't be fair to say that I didn't think about you. That's just not right. I thought about you night and day. Any mother does. Besides, everybody has a bad dream now and then."

"But how could you have thought that I was a happy baby if by age two or three, I couldn't sleep and was having nightmares almost every night?"

"Was it really that early?"

"You're the one who told me."

"I do remember you were always hearing things."

"Things? What kind of things?"

"I had never heard of a child hearing things like that." Then, after a pause, "You had such a good imagination; it's the one thing your teachers always praised."

"You've also said that I was afraid to go to bed. Was that because of the things I was hearing?"

"Are you sure that I was the one who said that?" she asked, draining the rest of her cup. "I'm sure that's not what I said. That may be what you heard—"

"I'm sure that *is* what you said."

"Well, that's not what I meant then."

"Well, just what did you mean then?"

She paused for a moment, suddenly looking much older than her fifty-eight years. Then, turning to look directly at me, her eyes keenly accusing, she demanded, "What could I have done? I had no skills. I had two children."

"What did you want me to do? What could I have done?" she repeated. "Move us into a cold-water flat in Fort Lee?"

"There was not a thing one could do," Shep declared as we strapped the weights to his legs. He had begun having odd, elaborately choreographed "accidents." First there was the "fall" down the basement stairs after he had tripped, he said, on his laces. "I should never have given up the penny loafers my mother sent me to Choate with," he remarked, reknotting the ascot he thought most perfectly accompanied his new accent and history. And then, within days of his release from his "ball and chain," he was laid up again, having positioned himself before a car careering through the middle of the parking lot at the dump, his head turned down, he explained, as he groped blindly for his keys. And then there was the time he decided to change the left rear tire of his car at three in the morning on the northbound ramp leading to the Henry Hudson Parkway from 125th Street. He couldn't understand, he'd said, couldn't figure out how the other driver hadn't seen him as he leaned over to insert the jack under the fender.

And each time, as if he were a plant we had given up all hope of reemerging, Shep sprang back from the black and fertile depths of his soul as prolific and hardy as before, stunning us with his indomitable energy and force, with his sheer, unearthly resilience.

If I shut my eyes, I can still see his delicate body splayed over the surface of the stiff sheets that came with the hospital bed rented for home use, his thin ribs arranged as if they were wooden beams articulating the structure of a small cathedral within him. I can still hear him baying at the night like a wolf that had been wounded—a long, feral keen that permeated the house, the walls of my room, my heart, until at his command, I agreed to place two round tablets, like consecrated wafers, on his tongue, the fingers of my free hand holding his mouth open the way he had years before, when helping us feed hard-cooked eggs to chickadees tossed too early from the nest. I see him, hear him whimpering like a child, begging my mother and me to relieve him of the weight that hung over the steel end of the bed, to relieve him of the burdens that were making him feel as if he had been just dropped into a turbulent dark sea, his hands tied behind him with a belt or a rope.

Seeing him there, strapped like a raving beast to his cage, I wonder: did he think I'd never find a way to tell on the gypsies? Did he think I'd always come save him?

Did he think I would never find a way of forgiving myself?

It was while Shep was in the hospital, after a minor accident, during the summer of 1978 that the scandal broke. According to *The Wall Street Journal*, my father was charged with accepting more than $850,000 in bribes and cash kickbacks from a broadcast concern in Memphis. According to Premier Products, their ad director's shenanigans cost the company millions of dollars in damages. My father, the report noted, was and would remain, unremarkably, unavailable for comment.

As if he were the manifestation of some kind of unspeakable moral delinquency to which the ad world had never before been exposed, Premier Products stripped Shep's office of its accoutrements within twenty-four hours of the article's appearance. They took away his mile-long desk and his secretaries, his credit cards and his yellow legal pads, his fancy pen-and-pencil sets, his TVs and his account sheets, even his office clocks, and announced their intention to vilify him and, most important, to get every penny back, plus treble damages.

At home, his well-tailored suits hung in his closets like exotic if now worthless pelts. His shiny ties and shoes lay in neat rows like soldiers who, having just been relieved of twenty-five years of duty, knew nothing but to stand there waiting for orders. On his dresser lay, gaping like an old person's mouth, his attaché case showing all the bare places that had once been filled. Next to it, half-empty bottles of Maalox and Talwin and Valium and codeine, there were drops and salves and syrups and capsules, lozenges and tonics and stimulants and palliatives, ointments and liniments, sedatives and analgesics, enemas and emetics, expectorants and antiseptics—all things Shep had perhaps hoped might ease the way for him, all things returned by Princess Cecilia just before she too was retired.

After my mother and I unloaded the debris of my father's career, we stared speechless for a moment as if before a temple or tomb. Then we shut the door to his room behind us, the gesture both sacred and final. We held our breath then, for a second or two, before my mother, looking puzzled, walked across the hall to her room. Stopping at her door, she turned back abruptly.

"Well, I guess it just goes to show that you can't make a silk purse out of a sow's ear," she said.

"You know, he promised me a Silver Cloud for our twenty-fifth anniversary," my mother confided one night while we were rearranging, for the fourth time, the furniture in her new condominium. We stopped for a moment to brew a new kind of tea: rose hips with oranges, and the piquant perfume filled the kitchen.

"A Silver Cloud?"

"Yes. You know, I had always wanted one."

"No. I didn't know." I paused for a minute, refilling my cup. "You didn't really expect one, did you?"

"He promised me."

"Even if he promised you, Mother, they're expensive cars. How could he have known when you first met that he would have ever made enough money to buy one?"

"Then he shouldn't have promised. He should never have said such a thing."

"But, Mother, if he'd said he'd buy you the moon and the stars, would you have believed that too?"

"I might have."

I had been working in my new garden on a recent spring morning, raking up young carrot tops, trying to teach myself to have faith, to not be afraid of things that grow spontaneously, gratuitously, right before my very eyes, when my mother called announcing what we were told was the last of Shep's accidents.

"He's delirious and he wants to see you, now, in the hospital," she said, her voice drifting down.

The dark brick and glass building was cold and stinking, so filled with the smell of death and antiseptics that I wanted to pass out right there in the elevator and be forever free of all the cold and stinking death that surrounded me, my father, my father and me.

Without saying a word, a nurse directed me, as if she knew who I was, through the maze of glass doors, green countertops, and computer stations and then into the room where they'd been attempting to revive my father. The first thing I saw was my picture—larger than life—I was dressed as a gypsy for Halloween around the time I was five.

"He wanted it," the nurse explained as she watched me take in the heap of gauze and tubes on the bed. It was nearly unrecognizable except for the cracked lips that held a respirator tube and the nearly shut greenish brown eyes—the eyes that I'd loved so deeply—located somewhere within craters of gauze and tape.

"I'm sure he'd like you to take his hand."

"Can you hear me, Dad? Dad?"

"I'm sure he can hear you, dear," the nurse said as she checked the lethargic peaks on the EKG screen. "He may be undone, but he's definitely not deaf," she added, pronouncing it "deef," as she shut the door quietly behind her.

"Shep?"

He moved his lips slightly and I felt my heart surge. I lifted his hand and his eyes opened. As I felt his fingers nest weakly within mine, my heart swelled with an appalling rush of love and recognition. I held there for a moment looking at our hands, our fingers tangled together, afraid to look at his eyes, knowing that I wanted to say something, that I had to say something, when, irresistibly drawn to his face, I saw the Cheshire Cat grin appear for a second and then vanish.

Seeing me blush, Shep winked, and it was then that I found myself bearing down on him in a way I never had. The vehemence of my tone surprised me almost as much as my words.

"Do you have any idea how much I long to kill you, Shep?" I said, bending his fingers back out of mine. "Do you know how tempting it is, how hard it is for me to resist turning the switch on this thing and cutting you off from everything—anything that might sustain you?"

I reached for the switch on the respirator. I tightened my thumb and forefinger around the knob; I rubbed my palm over its oily smoothness the way Shep used to rub his over the swell of the shiny oak newel post in the green and brown hallway. Still squeezing the switch, I lowered my face to within a few inches of his.

"But you don't think about that, do you, Shep? You just lie there, howling, baying up to the moon, making sure that nobody lets you die from neglect, that we don't simply forget you. That would be the worst thing, wouldn't it, Shep? To die simply forgotten, swollen but empty, a small, shrunken man with delicate skin, your pockets full of nothing anyone else would want."

Shep's eyes hardened and then they began flicking back and forth. I thrilled at my power over him, my power just then to reduce him so completely. All I had to do was turn the knob.

Hearing Shep whimper, I lifted his hand and lowered myself even nearer to him. Our faces were so close I could see the gold spokes that radiated out from the center of his eyes.

"Did you think we'd never try to stop you? Didn't you think I'd ever get my revenge?"

I flung his hand on his chest.

"If so, dear pater, you failed."

I walked along Passaic Avenue when I left the hospital, toward town, away from my parents' house. There was something strange in the air that afternoon: shot through with a mysterious brilliance, it seemed, like an intimation of something to come, to presage a new or different event. As I turned right onto River Edge, I felt not so much as if I were walking, but rather surfacing and I was concentrating on that sensation when suddenly I saw it, there in the distance, the once brand–new Chrysler New Yorker with the windows that shut at the touch of a button and the antenna that hid in the trunk, crumpled into a heap on the service station lot. I moved a step closer and saw radiating lines forming a magnificent pattern across one side of the windshield and blood stains splattered across the upholstery and floor.

It was then that the first gush came, a great wave of bile spewing forth from my mouth and onto the trunk of my father's banged-up Chrysler New Yorker. I struggled to pull myself away from that wreck of a car, when I felt another seizure, and I cursed that car and my father as all that was unacceptable gushed out again, leaving me limp, hanging onto the fender. As if I were a child and had just become aware that my punishment had been unjust, I kicked the car where I had vomited on it, kicked it as another surge came, leaving my mouth tasting bitter and foul.

Let him be dead, I heard myself say. Let this last fiery crash through the windshield, this magnificent headlong collision be his swan song, the final mark he will make on me.

I don't know how long I stood there, heaving up the detritus of my father and me. All I know is that it took me hours to get back to my parents' house that afternoon, not because I was lost, but because there suddenly seemed infinite ways of mapping this new territory, of charting the land before me. I stood for a long time near that wreck of a car in the center of town, dizzy and bewildered, not uncomfortable, but simply elated and a little confused.

When I returned I bathed in water scented with flowers. I rubbed my body first with a harsh, stinging loofah, and then with a pure-smelling oil, an aloe oil meant to heal. I kneaded my neck, my shoulders, my wrists, and then I kneaded my toes and my ankles and my shins, allowing myself to feel the dead flesh come back to life.

I lifted the fat natural sea sponge and let the bubbly rivers run down. I felt the water cascading over my breasts, across my firm belly, down to my groin.

"Doesn't that feel like silk? Doesn't it just feel like silk?"

Eight days after he entered the hospital, twenty-four hours after he was supposed to die, Shep, walking only slightly unsteadily, limping, it seemed, somewhat histrionically, reentered our lives like something from a horror movie that refused to die. "I hate wheelchairs, matey," he said, winking at me as he resumed his position at the head of the table.

While Kyle, who had shown up for the first time in years ("Distance," he assured me, "makes the heart grow no fonder"), frantically called airlines in order to ensure his immediate release, our mother, feeling momentarily relocated, propelled herself throughout the house as if she were a refractory appliance stuck on "ON," her arms filled with cleaning polishes and furniture waxes. She was making things even, making things pretty—balancing a bud vase and a picture frame here, rearranging some throw pillows there, straightening the magazines on the coffee table so that they formed tidy piles. The pots and pans perpetually drying on the counter rack were put away, the sheets and towels in all the bathrooms were replaced, and the wastebaskets were emptied into one large trash bag, which she dragged happily behind her as if it contained all the dirt of the world. "They say he has the constitution of a bull moose," she boasted as she passed by en route to Shep's room, a dust cloth in one hand, lemon Pledge in the other. "And she," Kyle quipped quietly as he stuffed the last pair of socks into his duffel bag, "has all the resilience and tenacity of a trained circus pooch."

When Shep arrived, she stood at arm's length from him, her hands on his waist, his resting on her shoulders, and she stared up at him eagerly, looking for all the world as if he—this banged-up, profligate specter—were the augur of a new age, a new dawn before them. "I got everything ready," she announced, her voice vibrant and cheerful. "I put those nice blue and brown sheets you like so much on your bed, and there's a little bell on your night table if you want to call me for anything, and I got another remote control for the TV; I thought just in case one dropped off the side of the bed, you'd have another one right there and ready. And I cleaned up your bathroom, and we got rid of that coffee can you'd put back under the sink," she added, winking knowingly. "And did you notice the tulips outside?" she asked, not pausing to switch gears. "They're beginning to bloom, just for your arrival. That's precipitous."

Gazing deeply into Shep's grinning eyes, she stuffed her words between them, desperately offering them to him as a kind of gift, a picture of domestic harmony and bliss that she hoped he would find, as she did, utterly irresistible. "I know now," she continued, eager to cash in on her decades-old investment, "it just takes some alcoholics longer than others, that's all. But when a man comes so close to death, I know things have to change, I know something has to give. I

knew A.A. was right: sooner or later you all have to hit bottom."
Then, seemingly propelled by a force larger than herself, she beamed
at him again and, as if she hadn't already said enough, added, "In a
way, this accident was really a blessing in disguise. I know you're going
to get better now, dear; I know it's all going to work out."

She kept it up, apparently without effort; it seemed there wasn't a
thing that could stop her. She *had* married a good man, she was
saying with her outburst; it hadn't all been a failure; they could be
born again. She continued to fill his silence with proclamations of his
essential decency, his fundamental strength, his desire—she knew it
was there—to finally be the kind of man, the husband he had it in
him to be.

Shep had only to nod and to smile to make it all right. He
wouldn't have had to promise her anything—the most casual appearance of accepting would have been enough at that moment to quiet
my mother. But instead he kept silent, bearing down on her from
above, the Cheshire Cat grin broad on his face. And the more he
remained silent, the faster her words seemed to come, desperate, as
she was, to keep her version of things before him, before he could do
anything, say anything to erode it.

Then suddenly his lips seemed to part—he would tell her what
she needed to hear. She positively glowed, feeling certain that Shep
was about to say the words that would make her give way, the words
that would allow her, finally, to surrender the way she longed to into
his arms. She watched his lips, intensely waiting for them to move;
she listened and waited as one on a deserted island awaits the distant
drone of a motor indicating that she would indeed be saved. But
when his lips didn't open, she began moving her eyes faster and faster,
back over his face from his eyes to his lips to his eyes, and then
desperately back to his lips, seeking from him the words that would
allow her to recover her hope, to redeem what she felt she'd been
promised; she stood before him seeking anything but degradation,
but she knew not what.

But the words didn't come. Instead Shep only grinned and, pushing her away as if she were a child whose enthusiasm it was his responsibility to check, laughed tolerantly and asked, "Did you mean 'precipitous' back there, dear, or were you after 'propitious'?"

With that, my mother seemed to hit bottom. She shuddered, and then the cold chill of Shep's reality permeated her body, making her go rigid again. He chuckled again and that made her bend her head back. She bent her head back not so much to avoid seeing, but more as if she were appealing for an end to what she did see, appealing to a place she thought might finally grant, without a moment's more doubt, that she had indeed had enough—it was perhaps the closest my mother ever came to a scream. They stood there resisting each other, until finally my father, chuckling as if he had just heard a good joke, lifted his nose and, laughing, said, "It smells awfully good in here, matey. What's for dinner?"

"So you say that by the time Shep came home from the hospital, you had already decided to divorce him?"

"I had already decided to divorce him if, that is, he lived, which he did." After taking a sip of her tea, she continued, "Well, that's not quite right. I had already investigated divorcing him."

"Without having made a decision?"

"Without having made a decision. But then, I trapped a mouse."

"You trapped a mouse?"

"Four, actually."

"Four mice."

"Yes. And that decided it."

"That decided it?"

"Yes, that decided it. Is there anything else that you wanted to know?"

. . .

Some months later, my mother and I found ourselves driving to Newark Airport in her new Honda Civic to pick up Kyle and Deborah and Aaron, who were "surprising" my mother by taking her out to dinner for her sixtieth birthday.

When, a month ago, Kyle called and told me of his plans for her birthday, he said, "It's been some time since I offered my pint of blood." He also told me, as he had our mother, that he was soon to be offered a position at Yale. "I suppose," he added dully, "it will be a dual celebration."

We had been driving without speaking for over half an hour, my mother gripping the still shiny steering wheel as if she didn't quite believe that she could control this potentially recalcitrant machine.

I looked at her hands, which suddenly seemed old, webbed with tangled veins that knotted and clumped, and I wanted to touch those hands, the hands that once bathed me, to lay my two hands over each of hers and make them receive mine, if only for a moment.

Doesn't it feel like silk to you, Mother? Does anything still feel like silk to you?

Perhaps in response to my gaze, she removed the hand nearest me and tucked it under her thigh.

I searched her face. There were new creases along her nose, some between her eyes, and others, deeper, in places I'd thought would always be smooth. Defying her own rules, she had put her makeup on flagrantly and had drawn high reds next to flaming oranges, forming a blotchy pattern of vibrant unnatural color across her cheeks.

We drove, most of the time, in silence. It was only when we stopped in line at the tollgate that she turned to me. "You know, I feel good enough about myself right now to think that I could have done something in the world. I could have been something."

Looking into her unwavering eyes, I didn't know if I wanted to scream or to cry. Then the car behind us honked and a flicker of embarrassment passed over her face. She shifted the gears and I was saved. "I don't mean anything . . . anybody famous or anything," she said, stepping on the gas. "I just mean I could have done something useful in the world."

A moment later, as we sped down the airport ramp, my mother said she felt tiddly, the way she does after drinking too much champagne. We moved quickly, the high pitch of her emotions seeming to make the car move even faster. As we turned off at the parking area almost before the road would allow, she seemed in an odd way relieved. "This is what we've been waiting for," she announced, nearly yanking the parking brake out of its socket.

At the end of the Northwest terminal, my mother, her hands gripping the velveteen rope, stared down the rippled tunnel of the mobile corridor just as Kyle's plane was being announced. When Kyle finally came into sight, his stern mouth sealed as it had been for thirty-one years, his eyes dead color behind his thick glasses, she looked as majestic as she ever had. Seeing him walk toward her, she seemed barely able to control herself and beamed out at him as if he were an idol, a shining divinity with whom she had never imagined herself sharing time and space.

With some emotion greater than pleasure, she pulled him from the ramp and held him—her son—while Deborah and Aaron, who had appeared from behind, stood aside, waiting until she released him. Only after kissing her on the cheek was he set free, and then he turned away from her, his body held rigidly, his mouth still sealed.

For a moment, his sheer physical proximity was enough for my mother, and the erasure of their distance allowed her, for a moment, finally, to relax.

After exchanging cursory greetings with Deborah and Aaron, she turned on Kyle and demanded, "Did you hear?"

"I don't know. Did I, Deb?"

"Don't tease," Deborah answered as she reached for Aaron, lifting him before her as she might a shield. "You'll have to tell her sooner or later."

"You got it, then, didn't you?" our mother pleaded.

"We're going to be late, Mother, if we don't get a move on. We still have to collect our bags and then, as I remember, it takes at least half an hour to get to the restaurant," Kyle demurred as he led us through the crowd toward the baggage claim.

We drove quickly away from Newark with Kyle and our mother in front, Aaron between Deborah and me in the back. As she gabbled on, Kyle sat beside her weary, inarticulate, somber. Despite his successes, his first years at his new job had been strenuous, and although he had received assurance of tenure after only one semester, he had continued to work with his typical meticulousness, and his hair had turned almost entirely white. For a time, his few letters from the West were filled with indignation: after being appointed temporary Chair, his department was presented with a bogus award for excellence. When it was revealed, only after Kyle had publicly accepted the honor, that the ousted Chair had forged the award to embarrass my brother, Kyle, claiming he wasn't resentful, wrote only of his shock upon discovering, "the deviousness of which people are capable." In the three years he had been gone, I received only one other brief note, in which he, without emotion, confided that two years' worth of notes for his study of Durkheim had been lost; he had, as a result, begun again, a weary Sisyphus unable to find within him a way of refusing the gods who pressed him on. When we arrived at the restaurant, he pitched himself into a chair and asked that a double bourbon be brought, neat and in a hurry.

"All right," our mother chided, "now you must tell me. I've waited long enough. You got it?"

"I got it," Kyle answered indifferently.

"That is good news," she said, glowing like a signal light.

"What did you get, Daddy?" Aaron, perched on two telephone books, moved his head ceaselessly, seeking things out that might keep his unflagging energies amused. During the past year, he had grown to be a lanky but slight boy, even for five, and his curly blond hair had yet to show signs of turning dark. He was a congenial, cheerful child, except for the occasional moment when, without apparent premeditation, he held an adult with a thoughtful and pitiless stare.

"I was offered a different job, son."

"Not just 'a job,' " our mother rang out, "but a position as head of the Department of Philosophy at Yale University in New Haven, Connecticut." These words sailed from her mouth, borne aloft by the immensity of her emotion.

"Not head, Mother," Kyle said without her hearing. "Just an assistant professor."

"I'm very proud of him," Deborah inserted, her pretty smile spreading across her face like an invitation my mother had only to take up.

"*You* are!" our mother exclaimed. She glowed out again, silently, directing her energy toward Kyle, confident of her part in this, my brother's latest triumph, as Deborah, noting her satisfaction, turned her back on them as if they were part of a scene she wished not to witness.

"Well," she said when the silence began to weigh, "We've done it, haven't we? Just three years after graduate school. I always knew. . . ."

Kyle turned, stopping her, his face struck by her choice of pronouns, and then, changing his mind, lifted his glass.

We carried through our entrées, Kyle studiously avoiding conversation about himself, despite our mother's unflinching perseverance. Above the apparent mirth at the other end of the table, Deborah attempted to describe the latest workshop she had participated in— ultraorgasmic sexuality—designed to demonstrate how elements of Tao, Karezza, and other Oriental orgasmic practices could extend sexual rapture, even with your husband, while Aaron marched around the table, as Kyle used to do, swiping a small morsel from each person's plate as he passed. Since I had last seen him, Aaron, who had always appeared undernourished despite his parents' care, had developed an insatiable appetite; he ate as he moved and moved as he ate without ever putting on weight. "And then one from you and one from you," he chirped giddily.

It was when dessert arrived that our mother, still bursting, asked, "So when will you move?"

"Hmmm?" Kyle muttered, apparently hoping to forestall her attempts at staking him down.

"It will be wonderful to have you in the East again, close by. It will make us a family once more."

"A family?"

"All of us, all together. With you in command of the Philosophy department at Yale." She spoke as if the words alone—devoid of their meaning—held some special, even mystical significance. She shone out at him, having been relieved, at least momentarily, of her lifelong sense of disqualification, her own unfitness. As she leaned back, the muscles in her neck relaxed as she allowed herself at that moment to imagine that what she feared had been irretrievably lost had been, in the end, restored.

"We're not moving," Kyle blurted out as Deborah, perhaps wanting to assure my mother's attention, arrested Aaron and held him at arm's length.

"Owww! Mom-mmm! What are you tryin' to do to me?"

"Not moving?" Our mother faltered, letting her fork drop with a clink against the edge of the pink and green Limoges. She stared at him as if he were mad.

"No, we're not moving because I'm not taking it."

"You must be joking."

"I don't see anyone laughing," Kyle retorted.

"Just what are you driving at?" she demanded, looking suddenly lost.

"You heard me correctly. I'm not taking the job. I'm giving it up."

With this, she turned to Deborah, apparently hoping his wife could help find her direction.

"He's not taking it," Deborah repeated in response to my mother's stunned features.

"I wish you'd be serious with me," our mother begged. "After all, I am your mother."

"That's why we're telling you first," Kyle said, perhaps vaguely aware, perhaps not, of his own brutality, his desire to avenge things he couldn't begin to articulate, even to himself.

"I'm not going to believe this," she announced, her voice slightly tainted with fear. "This is a once-in-a-lifetime opportunity. You should be proud to take it. It would mean so much, in terms of the family." She chided him the way she might a small boy who, without thinking, had reneged on his obligations.

Hearing this, Kyle bent forward and kissed her on the cheek. Then he pulled back and, for the first time since he had arrived, looked directly into her eyes. "Happy birthday, Mother."

"Happy birthday, Nanny," Aaron chimed in.

"How do you expect me to take this?" She spat the words before her as if they were grape pits.

"Any way you wish," he answered, slumping back into the chair. His voice had become flat, even more monotonous than usual.

"You're all mixed up. You're not thinking clearly," she said feverishly. "You've not thought it through. What kind of a reputation will you have if you turn this one down? Who in the academic community will ever befriend you again?"

"Maybe no one," he answered curtly, having given over any pretense of docility or patience.

"I'll be your friend, Daddy," Aaron offered as he stretched his little arms around his father's neck. And then for a minute, their talk stopped while Kyle, for the first time I could remember, allowed himself to accept, without a moment's hesitation, solace from another person. For a few seconds, something was shared between them, between my brother and his son—something ineffable and exclusive, that resisted, by its awesomeness, any attempt at intrusion. But then our mother, unable to contain herself, barged forward: "Think of your family."

"Deborah wants to stay in the West."

"It's true. I really do prefer it out there," she offered, intending, it seemed, to console. "We'll always come visit."

"That's not what I mean!" our mother boomed. "I mean this family. The one you've just left here. What are we to do?" Then she pleaded, "Don't you see what I'm saying? Can't you understand me?"

"It must disappoint you so, Mother, having a son who so fails your expectations." Saying this, his eyes pinched together at the corners as if the words stung more than he had known to expect.

"It will be all right, Evelyn," Deborah said, squeezing her hand.

"Don't cry, Nanny," Aaron said, returning to his march and scooping up a fingerful of chocolate mousse from her compote. "It's your birthday!"

"Without this . . ." she stumbled, her words collapsing in on themselves.

Despite the still vital envy that made my mouth taste bad, I couldn't help feeling sorry for her at that moment. Somehow, for some moments, Kyle's announcement seemed to cut her off from all possibility of redemption; as if a door had just slammed shut against her, she sat there, her lips trembling, her eyes fighting back tears. As if she would like to be elsewhere, somewhere where things wouldn't matter or at least wouldn't matter so much, she leaned her head back and rolled it against the cool wall behind her.

Seeing her response, Kyle sat back in his chair, seeming both amused and moved in some way by her display, his power, perhaps just at that moment made conscious, to reduce her so completely.

Finally pulling herself forward one last time, she demanded, "You assume, I suppose, that doing this—rejecting this offer—will make you happy?"

"Happy?" Kyle asked, regaining ground. "That's an impossible question to answer. I suppose my answer would depend on what we mean by happy. I mean, if by happy you mean—"

"Oh, to hell with it," our mother whispered, throwing her napkin down.

Refusing to be put under by this, Kyle announced, "OK—everybody ready to go back and open presents?"

"Presents? Are there any for me?" Aaron asked.

"Might be, son. We'll have to go back to Nanny's house and have a look."

Lifting the boy before him as he might a trophy, he looked back to make sure we were all with him.

"Come on, Nanny," Aaron called, reaching back for her hand but missing it by a foot. "It's time to open your presents."

"But, Mother, the guy said I had an ulcer. Even Kyle remembers this."

My mother and I found ourselves trekking, once again, through the tangled brush of our memories.

"What I believe he said was that you had all the symptoms of an ulcer."

"So what's the difference?"

"The difference is that he didn't think you had one."

"And you . . ."

"Didn't think anything could be bothering you that much. After all, you were only twelve."

"Why didn't you tell him what was going on?"

"I didn't know what was going on," she repeated adamantly.

"No, I mean about the alcoholism and stuff."

"Well, he already knew about that."

"He already knew about that?"

"Yes. He was the one treating your father."

"He was the one treating my father?" I pounced on this as if it were a gold coin or a bread crumb.

"Yes, an internist, highly recommended by Dr. Stanton. He was affiliated with Columbia Presbyterian."

"And this is the guy who said it was impossible for a girl of twelve to have an ulcer?"

"The same one."

"Didn't that make you think?"

"Think what?"

"Think about that connection. That he might have been—"

"Protecting someone?"

"Yes, protecting 'someone.' "

"Well, I suppose that's a possibility, but I had never heard of a doctor doing that."

"You had never heard of a doctor doing that?"

"That's what I said. At least, they're not supposed to do that sort of thing."

"Therefore they couldn't?"

"Well, they're not supposed to."

"So they couldn't?" I insisted again, ready to give it all up.

"Should I have despaired?" she shot back. "Would that have satisfied you? If I had just given up? Decided to let it all go to hell?" Then, thwarting me entirely, she hissed, "I loved you. I love you now. I did what I could.

"You were *my* daughter too, you know."

"I haven't the foggiest notion what they're talking about," Shep said in a letter addressed to all of us that he had, in the style of other notorious petitioners, tacked to my mother's door in the middle of the night. The letter was written on creamy, one hundred percent cotton from Cartier's. My father's name, raised and engraved in ornate Palace Script, filled the top quarter of the page; he then listed his "address" (a suite number at the Plaza) and a telephone number (which we later discovered was the laundry room's). He was eager, he assured us, to return to advertising, but until that time, he had a few favors to ask. First, as the local "constabulary" had "absconded" with his car, he would be renting an Alfa to take him to "Club Allenwood." Would my mother be kind enough to pay that bill and his Paul Stuart bill

("I'll be needing a few things for my holiday") directly so that we might maintain our good name. Second, he asked if we'd be good enough to write the judge telling him what a good, loving father he had been, in the hope of dissuading him from any untenable ideas he might have about lengthy incarcerations. We were encouraged to emphasize that he had, as he wrote, "suffered considerably" because of his alcoholism.

As far as I know, only Kyle wrote, detailing, in a twenty-page brief, his feelings about the criminal justice system, what he considered to be our father's basic innocuousness, and his doubts about the rehabilitative function of prisons. It didn't help. Shep was found guilty of racketeering, wire fraud, mail fraud, tax evasion, and breach of fiduciary duties and sentenced to a year and a half in prison. Naturally, he conned his way into a sentence half the original length.

(Only later did Kyle wish he could have rescinded his letter to the judge, when, a month after Shep had been jailed, he received a notice from a New Jersey bank reminding him that the mortgage payment on his co-op in Englewood Cliffs was ten days late. As the story goes, it was just after he said, "We don't have a co-op in Englewood Cliffs," that Deborah slammed the door to their bedroom, decisively. When Kyle finally untangled the plot ["I can't believe the old guy did that . . .], he felt he could do nothing but fly east to meet with our father in jail. Kyle tells me that when he told Shep that what he had done—forging ownership—was ethically dubious, to say nothing of wrong, our father shrugged his shoulders, smiled, and, chucking him under the chin, said, "Sorry about that, matey. Never thought a little thing like that would bother you.")

In the few letters we received while he was in jail, signed only with his ten-digit ID, Shep complained about the plumbing fixtures that banged through the night, the rough bedsheets that irritated his sensitive skin, and especially about the loose morals of his "somewhat prurient fellow guests of the state." "You wouldn't believe," he once wrote, "what some of these men have done."

Three months after he entered Club Allenwood, *Advertising Age* reported that Shep was considered a "model prisoner" and had pulled duty as a clerk typist for the facility's public affairs department. George Klimt, the facility superintendent, described Shep as "a real class act," "a civilized guy" who "seems to get along with everyone." His "good behavior" earned him parole three months before his sentence was up.

He was released six months ago, and last week, on the eve of my thirtieth birthday, I received a photograph of him taken somewhere on a desert highway, just outside Tucson, Arizona. He drives constantly, traveling alone, from one part of the country to the next, fancying himself the next William Least Heat Moon. No one knows where he gets his money from, no one knows where to write him.

In the photo, he is laced with jewelry—shining copper bracelets, flamboyant Navaho chains, leather boleros strung with huge chunks of turquoise. On his fingers, two star sapphires set in silver and, on the pinkie of the left, a questionable diamond. His white shoes appear to be made of cheap patent leather, which I'm sure Shep finds swank; there is a brass-colored buckle on each side. They match his belt and complement, in an odd way, the royal blue golf slacks, the clinging red-blue-and-orange-striped shirt, and the green and gold ascot. He is standing with one foot on the fender of a champagne and gold Cadillac, circa 1970. The Oklahoma license plate, which is just barely discernible, reads OLDKPR. He is smiling irresistibly, his eyes sparkling, laughing at himself and the world. Like a man who has just pulled off the biggest hoax the world has ever seen and knows he is going to get away with everything, he looks the picture of content-ment, the picture of insouciance. Here is a man who leads and will continue to lead a happy and well-to-do life, he is saying with his smile; here is a man who will pull off—absolutely—whatever he so desires. There is not a scar to be seen from his accidents or from his few months in prison anywhere on his body; Kyle tells me he drives as many as thirty thousand miles a year.

On the back he has written, "Water's great. Wish you were here. Your cher amour, Pierre." For him, nothing has changed; nothing has happened.

I hold that picture close and see the man who would drive for miles all over the state just to track down a new kind of ice cream I wanted to try, the man who taught me to appreciate the lost art of the dump, the man whom I would watch rub his palm around and around the top of the newel post excessively, intemperately, just for the sheer pleasure of feeling the polish under his hand. I hold that picture close, I turn it to the light and see the man whose excesses regularly fractured other people's lives, the man whose exorbitance almost killed me, the man who adored me, the man who nearly destroyed me.

I look at that picture again, that photo of happy, insouciant Pierre, that photo of crazy, inscrutable Pierre. I have not forgotten how I loved him. And I know that I do not forgive him. I will never forgive him.

I will dance on his grave.

"It all happened so long ago—how can you even be sure it really happened?" Kyle smiled at me, indulgently, as if I were a small child or perhaps some poor, deranged thing he felt compelled, by his own inner sense of decency and largesse, to humor for a moment. He had flown to New York for a two-day philosophy conference called "The Concept of Subjectification" and asked me to meet him for lunch. I hadn't yet decided how or if I should respond to his question.

Pulling the door open with one hand and playfully squeezing my arm with the other, he chided me, smiling, as if we were on opposite sides of a fence and he were trying to win me over to his. "Are you going to hold on to this thing forever?"

Unlike the last time I'd seen him, he seemed in remarkably good spirits, having just boasted of Shep's recent decision to take an apartment in the university town within a mile of his home. Sitting confidently in that deli, he looked almost exhilarated, as if he had, in some miraculous way, been rejuvenated by this dubious gesture of Shep's. He only wishes that I could reconnect with Shep: "Underneath it all, he's really not such a bad guy. You don't know what you're missing."

(What Kyle didn't tell me, but Deborah did, was that until Shep's "return to advertising," he had taken it upon himself to keep up with Shep's varied and capricious wants and needs: ivory-capped walking sticks, sets of silk ascots, pigskin gloves, and, of course, boxes and boxes of Pears soap to help protect his sensitive skin.)

Perhaps in response to my silence, when we sat, he proffered, still smiling, "Your life has always been different from mine, Meggie, kind of zigzaggy." He laughed at his own colloquialism as he ran his forefinger back and forth along invisible diagonals in the air. "You know me: I'm on the straight and narrow, only making express stops between nursery school and tenure." He laughed again, extending his arms before him, palms forward, as if he were afraid the pink Formica-topped table separating us were not a sufficient divider.

"My life hasn't been so zigzaggy, Kyle," I said, sounding more like a child than an adult who, having been spanked, turns around red-faced and shouts, "That didn't hurt!"

Kyle smiled generously, intending to placate. He then quickly recounted the details of his academic career, successfully reducing it to a series of uninterrupted continuities manufactured in the hope of restoring to himself some sense of personal integrity. Watching the synchronic assemblage of his life unfold before my eyes, the salt and pepper shakers, the sugar packets, and strips of napkin marking off discrete eras and forming, no matter how insubstantially, a clear line between us, I realized that I would never, no matter how I tried, fit into his "normal" avenues of interpretation; that I would always be, to him, kind of "zigzaggy." As he spoke, arranging his time line, filling in gaps, his happiness infused his voice with an irrefutable confidence.

When he was done, the napkin holder, the largest item on the table, marking his present position at the end of the line, I asked, "Do you ever regret not taking the Yale job, Kyle?"

"Of course not—why should I?" he snarled, propelled by something in my question back into his seemingly instinctual reserve. He took a large bite of hamburger and stared at me, a nonstaring stare that wavered somewhere between blankness and obstinate, defiant immunity.

Then he added, "I don't regret anything except, of course, contact with Mother."

"What do you mean?"

"I mean she makes my skin crawl."

"Pardon me?"

"You heard me."

"What has she done?"

"She exists. Isn't that enough?"

"I don't think she's that bad."

"That's funny coming from you, Megan."

"I don't think she ever intentionally hurt anyone; I mean—not like Shep."

"Shep's a defenseless old man, scapegoated by his company, divorced by his wife, abandoned by his daughter. How can you blame him for anything? He was sick—still is—he has a disease; half the time, he didn't even know what he was doing."

He carried on for a few minutes, giving me a great deal of information about Shep, his psychology, his "diseases," his small triumphs, and his enormous struggles. Developing this profile, he seemed almost giddy and his eyes were wide open. Kyle knew Shep, he was saying with his details, his anecdotes, better than any of us, better than any of us ever could.

"Somebody has to take care of him. Mother," he added snidely, "has no excuses."

"Yes, but Mother"—I heard my voice rise urgently—"is, well, if not innocent—"

"You calling her innocent! That's a good one."

"You know, Kyle, it's hard to communicate human wrong—male wrong—to Mom. Her mind is sealed to it; it keeps her from comprehending the things that have been done to her, and to her complicity. Wouldn't you call that sort of a naiveté?"

I wanted Kyle to confirm my tentative conclusion, but before I could find words, he had thrown his napkin down in disgust. Grabbing the check from the edge of the table, he said, his words so clearly enunciated they might have been cut with a knife, "You want to know what I think, Meggie? I think—" Truncating his thoughts, he then spat out, "I wait for news of her death."

Standing, I looked at my small, unsmiling brother, who, after adjusting his glasses, focused on the wall behind me. Blinking, he then turned to the cashier and I grabbed his arm.

"Kyle, can't you—won't you—admit, just once, for me, that Shep was awful to me? That he hurt me?"

I realized only after I spoke that my question had the air of a condition about it, and I wondered if Kyle had perceived it that way. He seemed, by the way he stared beyond me, pulling on his mustache, to need to gain time and I realized this as a drawback in him, a final, horrible confirmation of some failing that was thrust uncompromisingly before me, when, after altering his expression, he remarked congenially, pathetically, "You know, I've got to deliver this paper in ten minutes."

Outside, we pulled our jacket collars tight against the late March wind curling around the sides of the skyscrapers and hurried toward the Sheraton at the end of the block.

"You don't have to walk me."

"I know," I said as I began following, jogging one step behind and a little to the left of him, just as I had when we were in grade school and I would race along behind him, struggling to keep up as he shot toward school, his heart throbbing, his lips pulled tightly over his teeth, always fearing that my mother might discover that he had been late.

At the entrance to the hotel, panting, he threw his stiff arms around me and a shudder passed from his body to mine. Then he pushed me back and we held each other at arm's length.

"You really ought to come west again," he said. "Save your pennies and come out. It'd be real nice to have you out again. We'd have a good time, goof around a little. Last time," he added, "we didn't even get into the mountains."

After he dropped his arms, I smiled and said, "I guess I'll think about it, I guess there's always a possibility that I'll come out."

With that, he turned and I watched as he moved, really almost trotted, toward the tinted glass doors of the lobby. Knowing this was an end of some kind, fearing whatever it was I was about to feel, I positioned myself to smile once more; I raised my hand to wave.

He didn't look back.

I was driving south on the Taconic en route one recent Saturday to my mother's condominium in New Jersey for our first dinner alone since the divorce. It was a prematurely warm spring day, one that bore an intimation of a long summer before us, and the light drizzle that had been falling steadily since dawn made the late afternoon colors look richer, almost like something from a dream—the green hills looked as soft as giant velvet cushions. The magnolias and dogwoods were not yet in bloom, but the small, round blossoms that swelled the ends of branches spoke of a promise of unfolding to come.

I had stayed in my garden for some time on that morning, consulting all of its barely apparent growth as if it were a talisman, something that could bring me good fortune and protect me on the trip ahead. As I walked, I was aware of a strange sense of connection with all living things, all the things that had survived the harsh winter and were ready to rise again. I didn't want to be anybody but who I was at that moment, and felt, perhaps for the first time in my life, that the swelling around me—that burgeoning life, that fertile soil, the boundless infinity above me—was, for me, enough.

I had moved upstate, away from the city, and now live thirty miles from Poughkeepsie, one hundred and thirty from Fifty-seventh Street in Manhattan. The place I live, like most other rural areas in this part of the country, is one where it gets cold in the winter and hot in the summer, where the few neighboring homes are occupied by farmers and laborers and a couple of artists. I'm employed by the local library; most of my time is spent helping others reconstruct their pasts; I help them retrieve records of their histories. On weekends, I work in my garden. This morning the peas were up and I think I saw, like slender stalks of new grass, a few thin filaments of spinach.

But in terms of my location, none of that seems an accurate description—the words sound hollow and have little resonance. It might be more accurate to say that I inhabit some interstitial place, a space between no longer and not yet. It's a place I've yet to fully arrive at, a place I've not yet left.

Driving along that road I knew so well but which still surprised me with its unexpected twists and curves, I can see my mother waiting for me at the end of the drive leading into the condo community. Standing there alone, her eyes focused beyond the world around her, she feels as if there has never been a better time or place to be alive, that there is no life better than her own. Happy and complacent, she exists without sorrow, without any childhood memory of fire, in a limitless space that pain can't possibly permeate. Looking at her there, I know that all is possible; we will say what we mean to say, we will understand, and we will forgive.

Returning my gaze to the road, I saw, in the distance, the regular matte-finished condos, the sad, gray place where my mother lives. Through the dull yellow haze of pollution, they appear almost flat, the poor sameness of tone making them seem part of a stage set for some surrealist play about the quality of contemporary life. Like most condo communities in the area, this one was distinguished by its immaculate uniformity. Each gray door matched the next, each Palladian window was balanced on either side by picture unit flankers, even the pansies, poking their heads out of stout terra-cotta urns, were all the same color—sunshine yellow—and all had been placed on the left side, not the right side, of each stoop.

On the other side of the road, beige and white bungalow-style houses, each with its well-manicured square of green, its asphalt driveway, its Chrysler New Yorker or new Dodge Caravan in the driveway or tucked into the open garage. The cheerful hydrangeas were still there, hugging walkways and lot corners, along with the carefully trimmed rhododendrons, azaleas, forsythia, wisteria. Everything looked peaceful, ordinary, quiescent. There was even a girl playing with her father—he was holding her buttocks, helping her shimmy up the trunk of a tree. Pausing at a light, I remember thinking how difficult it was to imagine anything unpleasant here, anything out of order. Even the girl was laughing, making herself silly over some secret her father had just whispered into her ear.

As I turned into the community boulevard, I felt her pulling me toward her. There was no place more perfect, more beautiful on earth, no place that filled me with such hope than this flat gray place.

I will smile, I told myself as I checked my face in the mirror. I will risk erasing this tension that kept us apart.

Positioning my smile, I looked toward her condo and it was then that I saw her, at the door, not smiling, not waving, just staring out at me from behind the screen door, her face frozen as if she had just seen Cassandra come up the drive. Standing there behind the mesh, garishly illuminated by the fluorescent light coming from the kitchen behind her and the dense twilight in front, she did not look like a goddess, but instead looked somehow frightened and uncertain, more like my real mother.

"Hi there," I called as I approached, fixing my smile. She was not wearing lavender gingham but was instead concealed in a baggy blue and white sweat suit.

"Welcome," she called back, the word wobbling from her mouth, refusing to stand on its own. With unaccountable energy, she pushed open the screen door; it flew from her arm, rebounded, and slammed again shut. She blushed and we both laughed uneasily as she struggled to free the latch that had inadvertently locked shut.

She looked older than when I had last seen her. With her head turned down, I could tell that she had tinted her hair silver; through the screen mesh and the filtered light of the dark sky it looked slightly blue, like early morning sky through a dense fog. And she looked somehow shrunken. Her once buoyant breasts lay flat across her chest and her shoulders looked not caved in but certainly narrower. Staring down at her as she struggled to release the lock, I wondered if she had always been that small. Even her head, despite the blue halo, looked wizened.

"Well, here I am," I announced idiotically as she held the door ajar. She still didn't speak but stared at me in a strange way, biting her lip. And perhaps it was that look, perhaps not, that made me run out again, away from her eyes, the unstated requests that served as a desperate reminder of my own, glaringly exposed by the light of the kitchen.

"The dessert," I hollered behind me. "I forgot the dessert," I said, not caring if she heard, just glad that I had, for a moment, escaped.

"I'm so happy to see you," she said when I returned as she brushed one hand across her left eye. Could she have been wiping away a tear, I wondered, as she surprised me by reaching out to embrace me. Was she trying to say with her tentative smile, her apparently patient eyes, that we might be able to try again? I wasn't sure, and as I stooped to her height, my jaw locked shut and my well-rehearsed smile slid from my face.

Feeling her arms stretch as far as they could around me, I caved in a little as if to protect our dessert, and then I pulled back.

"Mom, the tart," I scolded, the irritation I was able to bring up defending me from any emotion that might be aroused by her touch.

"Ooooh! Raspberry tart, my favorite! You can put it right here," she said, clearing a block of *Weight Watchers* magazines from the counter.

I searched her eyes for some indication of how to read her response. Raspberry tart was not her favorite; chocolate mousse was. Turning away from her, my cheeks flushed with embarrassment, I wondered if I would ever be able to give her what she wanted, what she needed from me.

"Did you have any trouble finding the place?" she asked, turning her attention to the roast she had pulled from the oven.

Why was she asking me that? I had been there before. Was it possible that she didn't remember our visits? I turned to face her. Bent over that way, she suddenly seemed immensely old, well beyond her sixty-some years. Something about her posture reminded me of a crone from a fairy tale I wasn't sure whether to trust or to fear. I'm not sure why I didn't challenge her, I don't know why I just said, "No, no, thank you for asking." Searching her face, half hidden in shadow, I repeated, "No, it was no trouble at all," as I began pacing up and down the length of the kitchen.

"I cut an article out for you. It's there on the sideboard."

"Oh?" I asked, both pleased and distressed that she had bothered to do something for me. I found the folded pages in the dining room.

"It's about someone like you, and her mother," she said, following me into the room. "Well, really about the whole family."

"The whole family?"

"Yes, can you imagine?"

"Mom, you remember the time you said your father was worse than a Gestapo agent?"

"Is that something I really said?" she asked, giggling.

"Don't you remember, Mom? You said he was not a very nice man."

"Sounds more like something you might say."

"Don't you remember? You said you thought he might have—"

"Could you give me the month? Where were we?"

"Oh, Mom," I begged, my voice sinking down.

"Look, Megan, if the article's not of interest to you, you're welcome to do with it what you will," she snapped, as she marched back into the kitchen.

Following her back, I saw that it was only 5:30; I had been there just half an hour, yet it already felt like an impossibly long time. Would we ever be able to forgive each other? Would there ever be enough time for us to sort through, to weigh, to try to start over?

In the kitchen again, I turned my gaze away from her floppy jowls, the loose flesh of her upper arms, her crooked legs, one up and one down, and I noticed that she had already arranged her breakfast things: a Wedgwood tea cup with a packet of Sanka was placed by the stove, two slices of Arnold thin-slice were in the toaster oven, a glass to the right of the plate stood waiting for juice, and a pretty pink napkin was folded neatly and tucked under the edge of the plate. Now that it was, as she claimed, all over, and her life was no longer controlled by chaos, my mother rejoiced in her ability to make as much of her life as she could imperturbable. Like a testament to her own fortitude and endurance, the breakfast dishes shone out at us unimperiled, waiting to greet her with their stability in the morning.

Perhaps it was the sight of that still life, perhaps it was something else that made me try again. "Mother, last night, my cat gave birth," I offered, the words unsteady on my lips. "Five kittens. Five," I repeated somewhat stupidly, not knowing what words to use to describe the warmth, the promise I had perceived in those new, just-born things, just knowing urgently that I needed to say that.

"Really?" she asked, smiling as if she had, in some way that surprised me, understood what I wanted to say.

"That's good," she said firmly, nodding her head. "That's good, isn't it?" she repeated. "That's very good."

And then, for the first time since I had arrived, our eyes met and something finally allowed our jaws to relax. What was that power held between us, shared by both of us, just at that moment, that enabled us both to smile?

I was the one to break that time. Turning away from her eyes, her lovely powder blue eyes that I felt follow me as I paced, I paused and wedged myself at the far end of the room, away from the oven, between the wall telephone covered with dozens of emergency numbers (including, I noted, my father's last laundry room number), and the refrigerator papered with photos of Kyle and Deborah at their wedding, Kyle and Aaron at the playground, Kyle and his colleagues outside a Gothic, ivy-covered building in Princeton, Kyle and Deborah and Aaron looking a little like young Kennedys on the beach in their windbreakers, their hair blowing in the wind, their small sailing skiff moored behind them. There was also one of me, a passport photo, my mother's favorite, looking a little blighted and dazed, looking like my mother, en route to Vassar. As she stirred the gravy, I studied my forlorn, dispirited face on the refrigerator, engulfed, as it was, by Kyle's, and wondered: had she once had hopes for me too?

"You know, when you were a baby, just a little, little baby," she emphasized, her voice curling up on itself, "when I came into your room to say good night, after your father had put you to bed, your smile used to light up the room. You used to beam out at me like there was no tomorrow." As if searching for words, she paused for a minute, her mouth open. Then, perhaps feeling that she had already gone too far, she turned and lifted the baster.

As I watched her wash the warm brown juices over the roast, I tried to imagine what her face must have looked like when she would come into my room on those nights. Had she smiled, content with her feelings—with her feelings for me? Or, having a premonition of what was to come, had she only stared back silently, unable or unwilling to find words?

"We can eat whenever you're ready," she announced, precluding, perhaps not intentionally, any response from me. "Why don't you help yourself to a drink? I think I've got almost anything you might want."

The day I had helped my mother move in, she had taken me by the arm and we had hopped, like children, over the rolls of carpet still to be laid. "Wait till you see," she had said as she pulled open the door to the closet, exposing dozens of alphabetized bottles and cans and jars. There were whiskeys and ryes and cognacs and brandies and gin and vodka and rum, beers and wines and cordials and stouts, sour mixes and seltzers, bottles of grenadine and lime juice, soft drinks and tonics—more liquor than my temperate mother could consume in a lifetime. But they hadn't been purchased to drink—that was perhaps furthest from her mind. Rather she had wanted them simply as they would remain intact and inviolate, yielding, finally, to her control. We had stared at those bottles for some moments, our arms crossed, admiring their as yet unbroken seals.

I hadn't had a drink then, but that night, I reached for the Tanqueray and called out, "Mind if I open the gin? It looks like it hasn't been touched."

"No, of course not, dear; that's what it's there for."

"Can I get you one?" I asked as I entered the kitchen.

"No, thanks, a spritzer is fine with me," she called out, unaware that I stood directly behind her. "There's tonic in the refrigerator."

"I'm right here, Mom," I said putting my hand on her shoulder. My stomach heaved as I felt the warmth of her body passing from her flesh to mine.

And that's when she winced. Twisting her head around, she looked first at my hand and then at my face. As she pulled away, I jammed my hand into my pocket, searching her eyes, still hoping I might find what it was that I wanted to say, what I needed her to know, within her own eyes.

"Maybe I could set the table or something," I offered, perhaps as an apology.

"You could set the table—" she paused, unsuccessfully trying to modulate her tone of voice—"or you can just sit down and relax. I leave it to you to decide." Then, clearing her throat, she called out, "We ought to use the good silver." Swinging me back from my caution, she added that it wasn't every day that she got such a distinguished visitor.

It was then that I noticed a new paperback on the hall table: *Observation: Your Key to Success.* "What's this?" I asked, waving it from the dining room.

"Oh, just something I picked up at the store the other day. I thought—" Then, her back to me, she added, "You know, I never really was very observant."

Was that offered as an apology? Or perhaps it was only an excuse? It was impossible for me to tell and, as yet, just as impossible for me to ask. While she brought in our plates, I put the book on top of a stack of *Good Housekeeping* magazines, its cover down. Returning again with the gravy, she paused before a small opening in the dining room curtains. Yanking the cord back, she smiled and said, "It looks like it's going to be sunny tomorrow."

"Yes, I guess," I answered tentatively. "You're right," I tried again, my voice unsteady.

For a few moments after we sat down, we didn't speak. Out of the corner of my eye, I watched her cut her meat into small portions and then she chewed twenty times, the loose flesh of her cheeks moving in and out, not so much to enhance digestion but rather to experience the full pleasure of the movement of chewing, the delicate flavors, the growing satisfaction in her mouth, her stomach. This was perhaps my mother's most intimate pleasure, the pleasure of eating, the pleasure of feeling, at last, filled up. As she swallowed her food, I could see her whole body begin to relax, I saw the muscles begin to go slack in her shoulders, her neck, her jaw. And then, as if to further enhance her pleasure, at least momentarily, by shutting all the rest out, she closed her eyes and sighed.

Watching her mouth begin to move again, her firm lips relaxed around strong, efficient white teeth, I felt as if I could have wept. Would whatever I wanted to say ever become clear? Would I ever be able to figure out what I wanted her to know from all that there was left to say?

Having taken the edge off her hunger, she put her fork to the side and asked, "Did you see the tape of Kyle? Sometimes he reminds me of John-John Kennedy."

I had seen the tape Deborah had sent of my brother stumping in Seattle for the last Democratic presidential nominee. He was talking about the environment, talking about jobs, talking about the homeless. Watching him on tape, self-possessed and so full of promise, it was possible to believe that anything could happen, that our words, joined with his, could create anything we wanted, everything we had ever hoped for. Wealth would be distributed equally, people without homes would be sheltered, drug addicts would be rehabilitated, and the children contaminated by waste from the Hanford nuclear plant would rinse the radiation off their bodies and run through fields of flowers again.

"Yes, I saw it, Mother," I said, turning my head away from her urgent eyes, which served, at that moment, as reflections of my own. I began twisting and folding the edge of my napkin, the same pink linen cloth she had pleated when, as a child, she had sat mutely suffering some interminable hope that she might be able to win the attention she longed for. She started up again, but then, after only a word or two, she broke off. Looking at me in a funny way, her mouth twitching at the corners, she said, "We forgot the toast."

"The toast?"

"I wanted to toast you," she announced again, embarrassed, it seemed, at having to repeat herself but nonetheless patting the top of my hand.

Feeling her warm, throbbing palm press down on my hand, I turned my hot face toward the window, away from the seductive pressure of her touch, and concentrated on the wet panes, the shimmering oil puddles in the parking lot, the moon just barely visible rising over the tops of the trees to the east. Would my mother's prediction come true, I wondered—would it be sunny tomorrow?

Blinking back tears that had arrived unexpectedly, I turned back to her and our eyes met. We held there for a minute, silently, our faces so near that I could feel her breath washing coolly over my cheeks and lips. She smiled, patiently waiting to see if I would speak, the tension aroused with my arrival apparently tucked away, at least for a moment.

"The toast," she urged again, lifting her glass when I remained silent.

I paused then for what seemed an eternity before reaching for my glass. And then my mouth began to form sound before I knew what was going to come out.

"Mother, once I tried to kill myself."

Her eyes froze and she lifted her hand from mine.

Seeing her retreat, I felt as if I couldn't stop. "It was so bleak, Mother, I couldn't stand it. But I woke up, Mother. I survived. I'm alive, Mom. And you're alive. We survived. We survived, Mom. We're alive," I said, my voice rising as I lifted my glass to meet hers.

She gazed at me, her eyes so remote that for a moment, I wondered whether or not she had heard me. Was it really too late for us?

"Mom?"

"Yes?"

Our eyes met as our glasses fell together, giving off a deep-toned sound that rose vibrantly in the air.

"We're alive, Mom," I urged, reaching for her hand. "We're alive. We made it."

I cupped my hot young hand over her cold bony fingers. She allowed me to take them tentatively, neither wholly accepting, nor wholly refusing.